TERMINAL

TERMINAL

JOHN LEIFER

For information about this title or to order other books and/or
electronic media, contact the publisher:

Earhart Press
P.O. Box 6131, Overland Park, Kansas 66206
www.earhartpress.com

ISBNs:
978-0-9995655-2-0 (print)
978-0-9995655-3-7 (ebook)

Printed in the United States of America

Library of Congress Control Number: 2018903489

MAJOR CHARACTERS

Ahmed Al Hameed: Al Hameed is the protégé of Ibrahim Almasi al-Bakr, the leader of the United Islamic State (UIS).

Ibrahim Almasi al-Bakr: Al-Bakr is the founder and leader of the United Islamic State, an organization committed to establishing a holy Caliphate ruled by Sharia law.

Commander John Hart: Physician, Navy Seal, and CIA operative, John Hart officially works for the Defense Advanced Research Projects Agency (DARPA).

Sayed Tamari: A young CIA recruit fresh out of graduate school at the University of Indiana, Sayed grew up in Pakistan where he attended a Saudi-funded madrassa.

Beibut Valikhanov: A bio-weapons expert responsible for developing a highly lethal form of genetically modified smallpox virus, Valikhanov is a Muslim Kazakh by birth.

Elizabeth Wilkins, M.D.: Dr. Wilkins is a senior scientist for the CDC's Biosafety Level IV laboratory.

Other Characters

Tariq Abu al Khayr: A UIS jihadist who accompanies Sayed Tamari to a training camp for terrorists, Tariq is one of the four Islamists who attack the United States.

Ahmed al-Shishani, Kameel Imad al-Din: Two jihadists responsible for transporting a bioweapon, and two of four responsible for the attack on the U.S.

General Mike Anderson: Chairman of the Joint Chiefs of Staff

Fuad Areem: Operates a Detroit-based safe-house for the United Islamic State

Taras Azamat: A childhood friend of Beibut Valikhanov's, Taras still lives in their hometown of Almaty, Kazakhstan. He has ties with al-Bakr.

Basheera: A Syrian immigrant who befriends Sayed at the University of Indiana

Dr. Anatoly Belikov: A former senior ranking official with the Soviet bio-warfare program, Belikov defected to the U.S. in the 1990s.

Joe Blevins: Secretary of the Department of Homeland Security

Carl Chandler: Assistant Secretary, Department of Defense

Jonathan Conner: President of the United States

Council: A group of tribal leaders who coalesced to form the United Islamic State under the leadership of Ibrahim Almasi al-Bakr

Sue Goodman: Deputy Director of the National Geospatial Intelligence Agency at Fort Belvoir, Virginia

Mr. Habib and Mr. Saleh: Pseudonyms for Valikhanov and Al Hameed while they are in London

Sam Hardesty: Iraq war veteran and father responsible for "Sam's Uprising."

Arnold Haroldson: Director of TSA

James, Seth, and Andrew: CIA para-military operatives assigned to protect Wilkins, Hart, and Scanlon

Marvin Kahn: Deputy Director of Operations for the Central Intelligence Agency

Colonel Alexy Kurtova: The Russian head of security for VECTOR, the bio-warfare lab where Beibut worked

Aaron Littleson: National Security Advisor

General Malik: The most senior ranking officer in the Pakistani Army with strong ties to ISI

President Mughabi: President of Pakistan

Babur Qaisrani: A member of the University of Missouri faculty and part-time jihadist

Sarah Qaisrani: The wife of Babur, aka Rachel Carson Patel

Omar Qazan: An agent with the InterServices Intelligence (ISI), Pakistan's equivalent of the CIA

Scott Rowland: Assistant Secretary for the Department of Homeland Security

Thomas Scanlon, M.D.: Head of the Prophecy (Pathogen Defeat) program at DARPA

Carl Taylor: Sheriff's Deputy of Boone County, Missouri

Bill Tilson: Sheriff of Boone County, Missouri

Mohammed Umami: A London-based arms dealer whose clients include CIA and UIS

Irina Valikhanov: The wife of Beibut Valikhanov

Omar Warum: A covert CIA agent responsible for infiltrating Middle Eastern terrorist organizations

CHAPTER ONE

George Mason University

DR. ELIZABETH WILKINS FINISHED her presentation with a sober warning: A molecularly engineered bio-weapon could create an unstoppable pandemic—analogous to the 1918 flu epidemic that had infected more than a quarter of the U.S. population and had claimed between 20 and 50 million lives around the globe. She paused before continuing.

"Ladies and Gentlemen, the knowledge required to produce such weapons is no longer the province of a handful of laboratories. It has proliferated and now is within reach of rogue nations as well as most terrorist organizations. And, unlike nuclear weapons that require massive infrastructure, a bio weapons laboratory can be constructed anywhere in a matter of months."

Wilkins was not some ivory tower academician theorizing about potential threats. As the head of the CDC's Bio-safety Level IV laboratory, her knowledge was experiential. She spent most of her days in a spacesuit, not the stylish red dress she was wearing on this occasion. Such total body protection was essential when dealing with category IV pathogens, such as Ebola, Crimean-Congo Fever, and Lassa virus.

Wilkins brought up a final image . . . one of Aladdin: "The genie is definitely out of the bottle and is not going back in. That's why we must persevere in our biocontainment efforts. Thank you for your time and attention."

A warm round of applause followed, providing Wilkins with the time needed to collect her notes before surrendering the stage to John Hart, the event's final speaker.

Hart acknowledged Wilkins with a tip of his head and a smile. At six foot four, the former Navy SEAL towered over most women, but not the five-foot-ten scientist. He waited for Wilkins to step off the stage before extending his hand to her in introduction.

"I know who you are, Commander. Your reputation procedes you," Wilkins said with a firm grasp of his hand.

Wilkins sized up Hart's lean, hard body. It formed an inverted pyramid with a small waist giving rise to massive shoulders. Hart's neck measured more than twenty inches in circumference and led to a strong, handsome face with intense brown eyes. A clear product of his military training, she thought.

But as tough as he looked, it was not his physical condition that was most intimidating. It was Hart's reputation for having a formidable intellect. One did not argue with Hart unless they wanted to be proven wrong.

Without betraying her thoughts, Wilkins took a seat in the front row.

Conrad Lieben, the head of George Mason University's Biodefense Program, approached from Stage Right. Lieben tapped the microphone, summoning the attention of the two hundred counter-terrorism specialists assembled for the conference on bio-preparedness.

"We've been graced by an outstanding group of pre-senters today." He clapped his hands, eliciting a polite round of applause.

"You are in for a treat," he said, turning towards Hart. "Before I relinquish command to our final speaker, allow me to share a mere snippet of his long list of accomplishments.

"Upon graduating from Carnegie-Mellon University with a degree in nuclear engineering, Commander Hart joined the Navy, where he was assigned to an Ohio-class submarine.

"After being submerged for three years, Hart was ready to be top-side and applied to the Navy's Sea, Air, and Land Forces. Not only did he pass the rigorous physical screening test, the commander set a record in the 500-meter swim—one that still holds today."

Lieben continued: "Our speaker spent six years working black-ops in far corners of the world before returning to graduate school to pursue a Master's in molecular biology.

"The commander graduated from Georgetown with high honors and then matriculated to Johns Hopkins, where he earned his medical degree. He completed Fellowship training at the United States Army Research Institute of Infectious Diseases and then became a valued member of our intelligence community. Today, he serves as part of the counter-terrorism team dedicated to addressing bio-defense threats against our nation. Please welcome Commander John Hart."

Hart stepped up to the podium and scanned the crowd, making eye contact with a dozen people before speaking.

"I think that's what they call *spin,* Ladies and Gentlemen, though I appreciate Mr. Lieben's kind words. But we're not here to talk about my eclectic background. We're here to discuss a deadly serious matter—the proliferation of weapons of mass destruction, specifically living weapons. You just heard a powerful speech from Dr. Wilkins outlining how advancements in molecular biology allow scientists to improve upon nature's ability to kill. Smallpox was horrific in its original incarnation. Genetically modified smallpox represents an almost unfathomable nightmare."

Looking directly at Liz Wilkins, he continued: "Dr. Wilkins is correct: We cannot put the genie back in the bottle, but we can try to ferret out who might utilize such a weapon and stop them."

Hart spent the balance of his presentation outlining a hierarchy of threats, holding the rapt attention of his audience. At the top of his list was the United Islamic State, which Hart described as "a reconstituted, rebranded, and infinitely more deadly version of Al Qaeda."

"As you know, the United Islamic State is committed to the creation of a Holy Caliphate governed by Sharia Law. Its leader, Ibrahim Almasi al-Bakr, has called for the wholesale destruction of the West . . . a purging of our decadent and blasphemous lifestyle. I can promise you that al-Bakr will use every tool at his disposal to realize this vision, including bio-weapons."

Glancing at his watch, Hart realized he was out of time.

"I promised Mr. Lieben that I would have you out of here on time. Let me stop and take a few questions, and then we'll call it a day."

A Marine captain was the first to stand and address Hart: "As you well know, Commander, discharging a bio-weapon is not like firing an artillery shell. There's a high level of unpredictability regarding the spread of the disease. If an enemy combatant releases an infectious bio-agent, what prevents him from eventually falling victim to the disease?"

"In the event of a global pandemic, nothing would prevent the perpetrators from being exposed to their own weapon. A sophisticated adversary would presumably understand this fact and, unless suicidal, work to develop some form of immunization against the pathogen."

As the captain sat down, a heavy-set woman in jeans and a t-shirt stood. "Commander, you referred to bio-weapons as 'the poor man's atomic bomb.' You and Dr. Wilkins have convinced me that the knowledge and material to produce such a bomb have proliferated throughout the world. So my question is: What can be done to eliminate the threat . . . remove it from the radar screen?"

"There is nothing that can be done to eliminate the threat. Our only option is to reduce it by bolstering our intelligence-gathering capabilities and improve our ability to intervene at a moment's notice."

The blunt assessment tumbled out of his mouth before Hart could soften his response.

"That's a pretty dire prognosis, Commander."

"Yes, it is, Ma'am. I'd be candy-coating the truth to tell you otherwise."

CHAPTER TWO

*Near the Pakistani border
with Afghanistan*

AHMED AL HAMEED WAS TALL AND PALE—his ghostly pallor the result of a small error in a single gene. That mistake of nature, an indelible defect, impacted far more than just the pigment of his skin. In many ways, it defined him. He would always stand out, always be at risk for ridicule—a lesson he had learned at a very young age. But now, thanks to the intervention of one man, he stood on the edge of greatness.

Al Hameed stared in awe as the last rays of daylight illuminated snow-capped mountains stretching high into the ether. It had taken four relentless days of travel to reach the Bajaur tribal region of Pakistan—a few kilometers shy of the Afghan border.

Clouds were beginning to roll in, and with them a cold, damp wind that chilled him to the bone.

At 14,000 feet, the weather here could turn in an instant, bringing a quick death to anyone caught on a high mountain pass. Equally dangerous but more fickle were the region's shifting political alliances. Yesterday's ally became today's enemy. It took tremendous acumen to survive in this harsh, ever-changing environment, which was why his mentor, al-Bakr, had chosen it as his refuge.

Al Hameed was flanked on either side by men carrying Kalishnakovs. They had met him upon his arrival in Karachi and had not left his side since. They would ensure his safe delivery to al-Bakr, the man whom they were sworn to protect.

As dusk turned to darkness, the wind's vigor grew in intensity, robbing Al Hameed of sensation in his fingers and toes. He thought about the long chain of events that had led up to this moment, and how the will of Allah had delivered him to al-Bakr. And he prayed that the wait would soon be over.

Ahmed Al Hameed had been born at Al Mashfa Hospital in Jeddah, Saudi Arabia—at the time, the finest facility in the region. Yet even the most skilled specialists could not change the reality of Ahmed's birth. When the gynecologist handed the crying baby to his mother, she recoiled. Her baby was stark white, with fine, grayish/silver hair covering the crown of his head.

Over time, his strange appearance would be linked to a condition and given a name—Griscelli Syndrome. It separated him from the homogenous, dark-skinned community of Jeddah. The embarrassment of his condition affected his parents, who found themselves ostracized by friends who had normal children. Others did not want to be reminded that, but by the hand of God, their child might have been so cursed.

Ahmed's father, Azra, believed that his son's only hope for a normal life was to move to America. There, among many whites, he would blend in. The time to move was now, before he became aware of his differences.

Azra understood that the family would be trading one set of challenges for another. America represented decadence and godlessness, but he believed there must be islands of virtue populated by Muslims.

The family settled in Dearborn, a suburb of Detroit. Dearborn had experienced a tremendous influx of Sunni Muslims from Lebanon in the early part of the twentieth century—most motivated to relocate by well paying jobs at the Ford Motor Company. In the ensuing decades, the Muslim community continued to expand, with immigrants arriving from a diverse array of Middle Eastern countries. Even so, Azra soon realized that the difficulties they sought to avoid had followed them to their new home.

As he was growing up, virtually all of Ahmed's playmates were Muslim. Dark-skinned, they took note of Ahmed's distinctive appearance. At first, they asked gentle questions that reflected their innocence. As they matured, however, their acceptance was replaced by harsh judgments and then rejection. Each jeer and taunt that Ahmed endured left its mark on the evolving psyche of a vulnerable young boy.

But with the onset of puberty, something changed. Rather than wither under the scathing eyes of his classmates, Ahmed seemed imbued with a new sense of power and purpose. It followed an epiphany—a dream in which he realized that he had been marked by God and chosen to lead rather than follow. His parents had long told him so, but it was the word of God that made him believe it.

His classmates noticed the change immediately. He no longer looked down at the ground. Instead, he looked through them. It was chilling. Rather than continue to belittle him, most of the boys had the good sense to back off. All but one.

Omar was the largest boy in the sixth grade and proud to be its bully. He was also a Shia whose parents had emigrated from Iran. That made him a sworn enemy of Sunni Muslims, including Ahmed. Omar had long been Ahmed's nemesis, and he was not about to capitulate to this *spook*, as he called Ahmed. By bringing him down, Omar knew he would further solidify his hold over his classmates.

So he followed Ahmed home from school one day, all the while launching a relentless barrage of insults as he trailed a few feet behind. Five or six boys lined up behind Omar, egging him on to violence. It was a public stoning of sorts, where sharp and weighted words, rather than rocks, sought to hit their mark.

When he finally reached his home, Ahmed turned and took three steps towards Omar. His eyes were unflinching. With his classmates as witnesses, Ahmed beat Omar senseless. Even after he went down, Ahmed pummeled the boy's face with his fist. Finally, covered with Omar's blood, he stood and glared at his classmates, who took off running.

His mother burst out of the house screaming at Ahmed and ordering him into the house. Omar gathered enough strength to stumble away.

"Go upstairs now, and draw a bath. I want every bit of blood removed from my sight!"

"No, it stays. I will wash it off when I am ready!" he said defiantly.

Ahmed did not bathe for three days—showing up for school with dark, caked blood covering his hands and arms. It was a message delivered with resonating clarity to his classmates and his teachers.

This was Ahmed's coming out party: Emerging from a chrysalis of shame, Ahmed Al Hameed stepped out of the shadow of fear . . . emboldened and ready to take on any challenger.

Al Hameed relinquished the ghosts of his past—suddenly alert to movement nearby. A man was emerging from behind massive boulders tucked close to the foot of the mountain. Even in the dim glow of a waxing crescent moon, Al Hameed recognized the silhouetted figure.

Ibrahim Almasi al-Bakr was small in stature, his head covered with a white kufi and his face framed by round wire-rimmed glasses. The feared al-Bakr, whose name was synonymous with radical Islamic terrorism, looked far more like a teacher than a terrorist. And, indeed, mu'allim—teacher—was how Al Hameed addressed him.

When the men were within arm's reach, Al Hameed stopped, folded his hands, and bowed: "As-salaam'alaykum."

"Wa 'alaykum salaam," Al Hameed responded. With nearly a foot difference in the men's height, Al Hameed had to bend low to kiss each of al-Bakr's cheeks.

"There is much to talk about. I hope you have slept, for we will see the rising of the sun before our conversation ends," al-Bakr said. "Come, let us get out of this cold."

"Indeed, Mu'allim."

Their relationship had begun years before when Al Hameed was in high school. At the time, al-Bakr was a guest imam at his family's mosque.

A physician by training, al-Bakr spoke of the return of al-Futuhat al-Islamiya—the Islamic Conquests. As a pure Islamist, he believed in a Caliphate ruled by a prince who united Muslims across the globe. It would be a grand Islamic state governed by Sharia law—a captivating vision for a young man such as Al Hameed, in search of an identity.

Al-Bakr was also a gifted recruiter who identified the best and brightest talent to propel his movement forward. Al Hameed remembered the pride he had felt when he was introduced to al-Bakr as someone worthy of his mentorship. If he had harbored any doubts about pursuing jihad, it had been erased on that fateful day.

When Al Hameed was ready for college, it was al-Bakr who steered him towards Jamaa Islamiya—a jihadist group with chapters on many college campuses that would ensure his talents were put to optimal use. He also directed his protégé towards an interesting field of study—molecular biology. It would be an essential stepping stone on Al Hameed's journey to become the deliverer of destruction to the infidels.

As they walked beyond the boulders, a vertical fissure measuring no more than eighteen inches in width appeared in the massive rock. Al Hameed wondered if it resulted from the timeless, undulating seasons of stifling heat and bitter cold, or if it had been chiseled by men.

He watched al-Bakr slip between the sharp edges and disappear into the crevice. Then, with far more deliberate movement, Al Hameed followed, emerging in a massive chamber.

Al-Bakr gestured with a wide motion of his arm: "This sanctuary has been here for thousands of years and undoubtedly harbored hundreds of souls seeking refuge from their enemies. As you can see, it extends far into the mountain. Though it narrows, it never really ends. It just leads to other tunnels. One has to be careful not to get lost in the maze."

Near the center of the chamber, Al Hameed saw a small fire, its smoke drifting upwards to a hole piercing the cave's ceiling. Resting atop the fire was a cast iron pot from which a potent and familiar aroma arose.

"Chicken biryani?" Al Hameed asked in disbelief.

"It is your favorite, is it not?" al-Bakr questioned, although he knew the answer.

"You are very kind, Teacher."

"I have been accused of many things, Ahmed, but kindness is rarely among them. Come sit, and let us enjoy each other's company while we discuss the issues that have brought us together."

An outcropping of rock formed a natural bench close to the fire. It had been worn smooth, as though polished day and night by a legion of invisible hands. Shallow depressions in the stone revealed where countless warriors had once sat.

After studying his guest, al-Bakr spoke: "Why do you not celebrate this occasion? What weighs so heavily on your heart that it dampens the joy of this moment?"

"I am grateful to be with you, my teacher. But you are right. There is something that I carry with me . . . something that consumes me."

"Part of that is simply your disposition."

"And part of it is not, my teacher."

"Then speak of it now," al-Bakr commanded.

Al Hameed's body stiffened. His chin rose, and a brief flush of color passed across his face as he locked eyes with al-Bakr.

"My soul cries out for vengeance. It drinks from an ever-deepening pool of vitriol, fed by an utter contempt for America. I lie awake at night while shouts of *Death to America,* shouts that you helped inspire, reverberate in my ears. And I wonder, my teacher, when will we move beyond rhetoric?"

Without a second's pause, al-Bakr responded: "Do you call 9/11 rhetoric? And what of our attacks on other American cities? Do the families of those we have slain think our swords consist of mere words? No!" al-Bakr shouted, jumping to his feet. "Our message has been communicated not by words but by planes, by bombs, and by the barrels of AK-47s. Ahmed, do you not see? We have been faithful to the word of God, as expressed in the Quran: 'When ye meet the Unbelievers, strike off their heads!'"

Al Hameed studied the piercing eyes of his teacher before lowering his gaze. "Forgive me. I have spoken in haste."

Al-Bakr took in a deep breath, then let out a long sigh, expelling the anger that had possessed him. His body, moments ago tense as if ready to strike, was now relaxed as he settled back onto the bench.

The storm had passed, at least for the moment.

"Ahmed, rather than focus on what we have failed to accomplish, why not see the glory in our successes?"

"Because I believe with all of my heart in your great vision—a vision that demands global jihad, not the mere skirmishes that we indulge in today." Al Hameed's voice rose, imbued with emotion.

"Your passion must be tempered and your patience cultivated, Ahmed."

"How can I be patient while our people continue to suffer the degradation brought on by a godless, imperialistic regime? When will the deaths we have inflicted number in the millions, not thousands? When will Sharia become the governing law of all lands? And when, my teacher, will we finally have the Caliphate of which you have long preached?"

"Jihad is not won in a single event, but over hundreds of years," al-Bakr reminded him. "The final battle may not be something we witness, but, if Allah wills it, our children's children will one day live under the flag of the United Islamic State. That is what we are fighting for with every skirmish and every life taken."

Insistent, Al Hameed responded: "But is it not our moral duty to use every tool at our disposal to defeat the Great Satan? Why would we unnecessarily prolong that which we hold to be inevitable?"

"How long, Ahmed, does it take for the cliffs along a coast to be eroded by the slow pounding of the waves? Do they not eventually yield to the incessant surf? Are we not like those waves—hitting hundreds of shorelines around the world, and each year eroding more and more of the bedrock?"

"Now you sound more like a Sufi than a Salafist. You may have your slow, rhythmic waves, my teacher. I would prefer a tsunami. That is what I am calling for."

"We have attempted such a strategy in the past. Have you forgotten, Ahmed? We spent years working on your so-called *tsunami*—building access to radioactive material for a dirty bomb. Had Jose Padilla not been arrested in Chicago, we might have transformed the so-called *Miracle Mile* into an uninhabitable wasteland."

"It was a good plan!" Al Hameed interjected.

"Yes, but it failed. Not because it was a poor plan, but because we allowed our arrogance and impatience to impel us blindly forward. We were not methodical, Ahmed. We could have accomplished far more terror through a rash of suicide bombings in Times Square. We don't need mass destruction. We need mass hysteria and the resulting financial destruction."

"Teacher, you have invested in my education. You guided me towards the field of molecular biology, which I trust you did not pick at random. So rather than speak in metaphors of small waves versus tsunamis, let us discuss what you have long planned for me."

"First, tell me of your schooling," al-Bakr responded.

"I have completed the coursework for my doctorate and passed the preliminary examinations. The research for my dissertation will begin shortly. I have learned a great deal at the University of Michigan, my teacher."

With his eyes lowered as if in prayer, al-Bakr nodded his head. "For this I am grateful."

"But how am I to use it? I have learned of biological weapons so lethal that they make a dirty bomb appear no more threatening than a child's cap-gun! Weapons capable of ushering in an apocalyptic pandemic! Yet these weapons remain mere theory." Al Hameed paused to study al-Bakr's reaction before continuing.

"I believe we have the ability to prove these theories—to create such a weapon, though it will take time and a level of resources that we have heretofore been unwilling to commit." He added, "If you wish to see a return on your investment in my education, then allow me to pursue such a weapon."

Al-Bakr smiled. "I had faith that you would reach this point."

"But what of all your talk about 'eroding shorelines over centuries' and my need for patience?" Al Hameed was incredulous.

"I have never wavered in my determination to bring the West to its knees, to establish a Caliphate across the globe, and to restore God's law over his people," al-Bakr said quietly. "You do need to learn patience, Ahmed. As for the other, I had to test your conviction. You have faced many trials in your life, but none like the one you are about to embark upon."

He placed his right hand on Al Hameed's shoulder. "When you leave tomorrow, you will be on the path to greatness. This is the realization of Allah's plans for you. You will usher in the rebirth of the Islamic state, and your name will be remembered throughout history as the great-est of warriors, our redeemer. You must never look back, Ahmed." Pausing momentarily to let Al Hameed bask in this vision of glory, al-Bakr continued. "There is a missing piece to our plan—someone whom we must recruit."

"To whom are you referring, Mu'allim?"

"A Kazakh who is working for Russia. If you wish to have your tsunami, you will need this man's help."

"Did this man approach you?" Al Hameed was momentarily confused.

"He did not approach me . . . he does not yet know of our plans. But trust that he will join us," al-Bakr assured him. "His name is Beibut Valikhanov. Remember that name. Once he is on board, I will send word. Together, you and Valikhanov will forge the great sword with which to slay the infidels. But you must be patient; this will not happen overnight."

Although he was left-handed, al-Bakr picked up his fork with his right hand, emulating the Prophet: "Now, let us enjoy a meal together before you must depart."

CHAPTER THREE

Ann Arbor, Michigan

THE DAYS FOLLOWING AL HAMEED'S RETURN to Ann Arbor passed laboriously as he returned to the routine life of a graduate student. His research involved novel methods for identifying breakthrough antibiotics based upon molecular models. The prevalence of multi-drug-resistant pathogens imbued such research with more than academic value—it was a way to save lives.

That was the message he kept hearing from members of his dissertation committee. His most ardent supporter was Joshua Goldman, a Nobel Laureate who had been one of the pioneering figures in molecular biology. But to Al Hameed, Goldman was foremost a Jew.

He didn't need Goldman to validate his research. He wanted to ensure that his toils would save only Muslim lives . . . not those of apostates, Jews, or infidels.

Each day, he moved closer to accruing the information needed to complete his dissertation. It was hard to accept the tedium of academia when he knew he was destined for greatness. A degree, even a lofty Ph.D., was merely a slip of paper. Armageddon, the great apocalyptic event that he would usher in, would forever change the fate of mankind and return the world to the true law of God, Sharia.

Weeks gave way to months as he awaited word from his teacher. His meeting with al-Bakr began to seem more like a distant memory than a stepping stone on the path to global jihad.

Al Hameed was deep in prayer at the Masjid Al-Falah mosque when a message finally arrived. The mosque was a low-lying brick structure that had originally served as an elementary school. It stood midway between Max's Delicatessen and St. Mark Apostle Catholic Church . . . a few blocks from Al Hameed's rented home on Lawrence Street. For Al Hameed, the mosque was an oasis in the vast desert of infidels.

As he was finishing Morning Prayer, a man in an ankle-length, white thaub approached.

With his attention still riveted on God, Al Hameed rose to his feet, reciting: "Sam'i Allahu liman hamidah, Rabbana wa lakal hamd (God hears those who call upon Him; Our Lord, praise be to You)." Only then did he turn toward the man.

"He is awaiting you," the man said in a hushed tone, gesturing for Al Hameed to follow.

He didn't need an escort, but Al Hameed respected the protocols established to protect the inner sanctum of the mosque.

A flight of stairs led to a sparsely lit and seldom used corridor. It was lined with classrooms that had sat empty for half a century. Like a giant time capsule, it contained miniature desks and chairs sized to fit their first and second grade occupants. They remained neatly aligned in rows. Yellow No. 2 pencils waited to be embraced by tiny hands.

Al Hameed could almost hear the loud clang of a vibrating bell announcing the end of class and imagine a swarm of children bolting from their desks and flooding through the doors. But, for now, there was only silence. He prayed that the silence would one day be replaced by the disciplined tone of young students reciting the Quran in a madrassa.

When they reached the final classroom, his escort pulled out a key and unlocked the door.

"I will leave you now. The door will lock behind you."

Hands raised and pressed together as in prayer, Al Hameed bowed ever so slightly and thanked the man.

Stepping inside, he chose not to turn on the fluorescent lights. Guided by the pale aura of a green, oval nightlight, Al Hameed navigated past rows of desks and stopped in front of a wide bookshelf anchored against the far wall.

The bookshelf held an assortment of children's books from the 1950s and '60s, their once brightly colored covers now faded into subtle pastels. He picked up a ragged copy of *The Cat in the Hat* and smiled cynically before tossing it back.

Then, placing his right hand atop the shelf, he gave it a swift tug. It shuddered momentarily before pivoting on its hinges and releasing its grip on the wall. As it swung outward, a room opened before Al Hameed.

Glowing with the warm radiance of candlelight, the room was bare except for a handful of prayer rugs covering the green linoleum floor. Sitting in its center was the mosque's imam.

As Al Hameed stepped forward, the imam rose to greet him. Grasping Al Hameed's hand firmly, he said, "Assalamu Alikum."

"Assalamu Alikum Wa Rahmatulah Wa Barakatuh (peace, mercy, and blessings be upon you from Allah)."

"Your teacher has asked that I convey a message to you."

After so many months without word from his mentor, Al Hameed had begun to wonder if al-Bakr had lost his appetite for killing on such a massive scale. Three thousand people in the heart of Manhattan was a far cry from the millions who would succumb to a global pandemic.

The imam continued. "He has arranged a meeting for you in Faisalabad. In three days you are to meet a Sunni from Kazakhstan. The man's name is Beibut Valikhanov. I believe you have heard his name before?"

"Yes. Months ago." Al Hameed's terse response telegraphed his frustration.

"Patience, Ahmed! If you truly follow our great leader, respect his wisdom, as well as his timing."

The imam did not wait for a response. Registering his disdain with a quick shake of his head, he handed Al Hameed a sealed manila envelope. "From our friend."

Al Hameed rose, tucked the envelope under his kurta, and bid him an obligatory farewell.

Freed of the irritating cleric, Al Hameed's mind shifted to the package. He couldn't wait to get home and tear into it.

He exited the mosque onto Jefferson Street. Every muscle in his body yearned to sprint the few blocks to his home, but he knew better. The last thing he needed was to attract attention. So he walked slowly, counting his steps, until he reached the door of a small brick house with black and white trim. Once inside, he bolted the door and pulled the drapes. Then, with a long wooden match, he ignited kindling in the fireplace.

He waited until the logs began to crackle and hiss before pulling a chair close to the fire. He removed the envelope from his kurta and ran his finger along the raised edges of the crimson signet. It was forged from hot wax and had been sealed in a cave thousands of miles away. His heart was pounding as he broke al-Bakr's seal and extracted the contents.

A photograph of a heavy-set man with a broad nose and wide lips lay atop a thick wedge of papers. The man's oval eyes were framed by jet black hair parted on the right and combed back. He was wearing a Russian military uniform and appeared to be in his mid-forties. Al Hameed could discern the insignia of some type of medical corps but nothing more. He set the photo aside and focused on a bound report.

The cover page was printed on CIA letterhead.

CLASSIFIED: TOP SECRET
Dossier on Beibut Valikhanov, M.D.
A Critical Asset in
Soviet and Post-Soviet Bio-Warfare Initiatives
Lead Analyst: Katrina Yurshova

Al Hameed wondered how Ms. Yurshova would react if she knew that her analytic work was informing the United Islamic State. Perhaps he should send her a thank you note, he thought with a smirk.

It had become far easier to procure such documents following 9/11, a time when the Agency virtually doubled in size overnight. The CIA's demand for warm bodies, fueled by a fervor to speed retribution for Al Qaeda's attack, overshadowed the need for ultra-tight vetting. This momentary lapse in security provided UIS with opportunities to place highly productive operatives in sensitive positions. That silent network, buried deep within the CIA, was now being exploited to full advantage.

Al Hameed turned the cover page, and began to read.

HISTORICAL CONTEXT:

Shortly after signing the 1972 Convention on Biological Weapons, which banned all production of offensive biological weapons, the Soviet Union embarked on a massive, covert bio-warfare program. Integral to the success of that effort was the recruitment of highly skilled and motivated scientists and physicians.

FAMILY OF ORIGIN:

Valikhanov was born in 1960 in Almaty, Kazakhstan, to parents of modest means. His father, Suiundik Valikhanov, farmed a meager piece of land and maintained a small herd of goats. He died in 2014. Valikhanov was alienated from him at the time. He maintains a close relationship with his mother, Raushan, who continues to reside in Almaty. Valikhanov has two brothers and two sisters, all of whom reside proximate to Almaty.

MARITAL STATUS:

Valikhanov married Irina Servanich in 1985. They have no children.

EDUCATION & TRAINING:

After completing his medical degree, Valikhanov matriculated to Krasnoyarsk State Medical Academy. In 1981, Valikhanov was assigned to a bio-warfare manufacturing facility in Kirov.

Valikhanov's work was the continuation of a covert program known as Enzyme. It was the outgrowth of Soviet leadership's conviction that bio-warfare agents needed to be an essential component of their strategic arsenal. That conviction led to the arming of Soviet ICBMs with massive payloads of anthrax capable of annihilating population centers, while preserving important infrastructure.

The ambitious goals associated with Enzyme became the responsibility of a newly created division of the Army's 15th Directorate—the Biopreparat. It served as the nerve center for a growing network of research, manufacturing, testing, and armament facilities.

DISTINGUISHING SKILLS OR ACHIEVEMENTS:

Valikhanov was recognized twice with medals of commendation for his development of genetically modified pathogens, specifically tularemia and Q fever.

POST-SOVIET CAREER DEVELOPMENT:

Valikhanov survived the demise of the Soviet Union and found that his talents were still much in demand by Russia. In 1996, he was transferred to VECTOR (The State Research Center of Virology and Biotechnology)— the Russian equivalent of USAMRIID—located in Novosibirsk Oblast south of the West Siberian Plain.

Here he worked under the supervision of Col. Anatoly Belikov, leading a team of research scientists focused on weaponizing smallpox. During this time, he played an important role in furthering VECTOR's exploration of genetically engineered chimera pox viruses.

KEY ACCOMPLISHMENTS:

The Soviet military has long been interested in smallpox. After it had been deemed "eradicated" in 1979, protective vaccination all but ceased. As a result, there were large, unprotected populations that could easily fall victim to an unnatural release of the disease. For military planners, this represented a tremendous opportunity to prey upon vulnerable targets.

The military was concerned, however, with a thirty percent average mortality rate for smallpox, viewing it as insufficient for a weapon of war. They aspired to be armed with an agent possessing far greater lethality. So Belikov's team refocused its efforts on a rare, hemorrhagic variant of the disease with mortality rates exceeding ninety percent.

Valikhanov led the team's efforts in selectively modifying its genome. Through subtle manipulations, Valikhanov transformed the virus into one unrecognizable by the immune system. In the process, he rendered it impervious to all existing vaccines.

It was a stunning scientific accomplishment, but not one for which Valikhanov would be recognized. Rather, Moscow credited one of his superiors, Yergeny Bucherov. Though Bucherov possessed none of Valikhanov's brilliance, he was ruthlessly ambitious and dexterous in manipulating the truth. He took credit for his subordinate's work. As a result, Bucherov received the Lenin Award.

PSYCHOLOGICAL EVALUATION:

Valikhanov is most at home in the laboratory, where his interaction with colleagues can be kept to a minimum. When forced to interact, he appears obsessive and emotionally unavailable. Co-workers suggest that he has little tolerance for the foibles of others.

He appears to feel no compunction regarding his role in the development of tools for mass destruction and appears to take pride in the fact that he is a master at developing ever more virulent weapons. Interestingly, he also devotes considerable time to developing effective counter-measures, including enhanced vaccines.

Valikhanov is known to be profoundly claustrophobic.

Outside of his marriage, he is reported to have two close relationships: one with his mother, the other with a childhood friend in Kazakhstan. There are unsubstantiated reports that Valikhanov's wife left him shortly before he vanished.

CURRENT STATUS:

Towards the end of his tenure, Valikhanov was purportedly in charge of testing the genetically modified smallpox virus in an airborne release on Vozrozhdeniye Island in the Aral Sea. Though monkeys were normally used for testing, the Kremlin demanded more reliable results.

According to eye-witness accounts, fifteen enemies of the state were chained to posts as bomblets dispersed the aerosolized virus in close proximity. All but one of the prisoners died within nine days.

A short time later, Valikhanov disappeared—a fact that Russia denies to this day. Two weeks after his disappearance, Yergeny Bucherov became symptomatic with an unknown disease. He was placed in an isolation unit at VECTOR. He died seventeen days later from the ravages of Marburg, an almost universally fatal hemorrhagic disease. It should be noted that while Bucherov's research never involved Marburg, Valikhanov worked extensively with this Category A pathogen.

As Al Hameed finished reading the dossier, he tossed it, along with the photo and envelope, into the fire. The only thing he retained was an airplane ticket to Pakistan.

CHAPTER FOUR

*Novosibirsk Oblast south of the
Western Siberian Plain*

IRINA VALIKHANOV DESPISED THE HARSH COLD of the Siberian winters almost as much as she despised her husband.

She sat at the small, round table, mindlessly rotating a short glass tumbler between her thumb and index finger. Stretching out her left hand, she felt the edge of Beibut's dinner plate. Not a touch of warmth remained. His dinner was a single mass of congealed gravy, cold roast, and soggy vegetables. She lifted the glass of vodka to her lips and drained the remaining drops. There had been a time in their marriage when she would have cried at this moment, but that time had long ago passed.

Irina pushed back from the dinner table and tried to stand on wobbly legs. Listing to the right, she walked towards the kitchen where a half-empty bottle of Skirmantas sat, cap off, on the counter. As she started to pour, she heard the handle of the door turning. It opened slowly. Beibut entered, his head held low. It was 9:30 PM.

"Where the hell have you been?" Irina blurted out, slurring the words that she hoped would strike him like a slap.

In a muffled tone he answered her "At the lab, where I always am."

He turned and pushed the door closed, hoping to keep Irina's shrill words from being heard by their neighbors.

"You and your goddamn lab! I am so sick and tired of it. You are married to your lab!" she shouted in her opening salvo.

The barrage continued. "You slink in late at night, long after decent husbands have been home for hours. Like a fool, I watch as the dinner I cooked for you turns cold, just like your heart, Beibut. You don't give a damn about me!"

Beibut remained silent.

"Talk to me, you bastard," she seethed. But he said nothing.

"Пошел на хуй!" she shouted in a final flurry of anger—"Fuck you."

Beibut remained detached as though he was not a part of the conversation. That was what hurt Irina the most. She would have been grateful for his anger. It might indicate that a spark of life remained in their relationship. But who was she kidding? His apathy was too profound.

Early in their relationship, she had accepted Beibut's difficult nature as a concession to their marriage, convincing herself that there had to be real emotion beneath his detachment. She prayed that the impenetrable wall guarding his soul would crumble over time, and she would become privy to the riches of his inner life.

But after nearly twenty years of marriage, she could no longer deceive herself. If there was a key to unlocking

Beibut's vulnerability and, with it, some deep-seated source of love and warmth, she did not possess it. She had tried. God knows how hard she had tried to be a dutiful wife, often aided by a bottle of vodka. But now the vodka only increased her desperation.

Her friends told her to be grateful that Beibut did not beat her, as was the case with other Muslim husbands, whose wives were viewed as mere chattel. Irina, a secular Muslim, had never understood why women permitted such abuse.

But there were other forms of abuse, including neglect. Her tolerance was exhausted. She wanted a life—a real life far removed from the secret laboratories of Siberia. She craved friends whose husbands had normal jobs—not like Beibut, a laborer in the field of destruction.

The next morning, Beibut escaped the turbulent house just as the morning sun was rising. It would be hours before the effects of the alcohol would leave Irina's system, and he was in no mood to be harangued by a hung-over wife.

By the time he arrived at work, all thoughts of Irina had been purged from his consciousness. His solitary focus was on the lab and the painstaking job of genetically engineering a new microbe. He walked past his colleagues without acknowledgement, as was his habit. Not even a slight bob of the head in recognition. Parking himself in a secluded office, he remained, with scant interruption, until night. At 9:52 PM, Beibut left the lab, arriving home shortly after 10 PM. It was a familiar routine.

But this night would prove to be different.

As he entered the house, there was no acerbic greeting. No greeting at all. Only silence.

"Irina, I am home," he announced in a monotone.

There was no reply.

"Irina!" he called out, his voice tinged with annoyance, not knowing where his adversary was lurking.

Beibut began surveying the house. It was not only Irina that was missing. He began to notice voids—empty spaces that had once held his wife's most treasured objects. Gone was the faded photograph of her parents on their wedding day. Gone . . . the antique cobalt-blue plate of her grandmother's. Gone . . . the decorative pillow embroidered on the occasion of their wedding, wishing them a long and happy life. It was as if Irina had erased every trace of their twenty-year marriage.

He started to call out again, but he knew there would be only silence in response.

Though surprised, Valikhanov was emotionally untouched by the loss. It had been a marriage long dead. In many ways, it was a weight off his shoulders. Unshackled from Irina, he could finally spend as much time at the lab as he wished. But the relief of being unfettered was short-lived.

He knew that people did not come and go from Novosibirsk Oblast as they pleased. It was remote and inhospitable, with temperatures in the winter plunging to -40 Celsius. More importantly, Novosibirsk was a critical element in Russian biodefense. No one entered or exited the city without the knowledge and supervision of the Main Intelligence Directorate of the Ministry of Defense.

Valikhanov did not go directly to the lab the next morning, but rather to the office of Colonel Alexy Kurtova, the man responsible for security at VECTOR. Walking past Kurtova's assistant without breaking stride, Valikhanov barged into the office. A surprised Kurtova looked up from the papers he had been reading.

"Good morning, Beibut." He paused to size up the man staring at him before continuing. "Do you normally barge into the office of a superior officer without invitation?"

"Tell me where Irina is. I don't really give a damn about her, but I want to know who gave the GRU permission to interfere in my marriage!"

"Calm down, my friend, or you may find yourself in a very undesirable position," Kurtova cautioned him.

"Пошел на хуй!" came the swift response from Valikhanov.

"How dare you speak to me that way!" Kurtova slammed his fist against the desk. Before he could utter another word, Valikhanov was in his face.

"Don't even think about threatening me, Colonel. We both know that she left this god-forsaken city with your blessing. More importantly, you know that my value to VECTOR is a thousand times that of a colonel responsible for security. Now I am going to ask you one more time. Where is Irina?"

"She has returned to her family," Kurtova said, slumping into his chair. "Beibut, your wife has pled her case to me on many occasions. And though you will choose not to believe it, I defended you for a long time. Finally, I knew that if I didn't let her go, she would leave this life in a more dramatic and permanent fashion."

Beibut laughed. "Are you implying that Irina, my wife who drowns herself in vodka every day, would have the courage to take her own life?"

"Yes, and it was not only my opinion, but that of others to whom she turned."

"Others? How many people know the intimate details of my marriage?"

"What does it matter, Beibut? Your wife has left. From what I can determine, you probably feel a degree of relief. So let it be. Return to your lab and the brilliant work you do for VECTOR, and we will forget that this little incident ever took place."

Beibut raised his chin and looked down at Kurtova, assessing the merits of what this despicable man had just said. Perhaps it was best to play along . . . at least until a clear plan emerged in his mind.

"You are right, Colonel. You have my apologies. I have much work to do. I trust you will excuse me," he said with mock decorum.

"No apology necessary, Captain. Go now, and do what God has gifted you to do . . . for Mother Russia."

Beibut saluted and walked out the door. With every step, he began planning his own exodus. It would take three months before he was ready to act. They would be months filled with increasing alienation and isolation.

Though the fate of the marriage was of little consequence to Beibut, the colonel's actions stoked a resentment long smoldering within him. That resentment had been kindled many years earlier when Russia cozied up to the West during the era of Perestroika.

Thanks to Gorbachev, a once clearly illuminated enemy—an enemy who Beibut prayed would one day experience the full brunt of the Soviet biological warfare program—was fading from sight. Democracy was no longer despised by compatriots, but embraced by opportunists eager to be beneficiaries of the country's growing wealth.

Beibut wanted no part of it. He hated the decadence of the West. He wondered what his life's work would mean in a world no longer divided by good and evil—in which a thriving Soviet empire had capitulated to a debauched, imperialistic regime that was now spreading its values across the Baltic States like a metastasizing cancer.

The Soviet Empire had been his True North . . . a compass setting upon which he could always rely. But Russia seemed to lack the same moral compass. He was now living in a country that had deprived him of recognition for his scientific accomplishments, aided and abetted his wife in her efforts to leave him, and abdicated its responsibility for the destruction of the West. His world was becoming unhinged, and Irina's abandonment was simply the final straw.

As his faith in Russia withered, he had turned increasingly to his Islamic faith in search of salvation. Whereas before he had prayed infrequently, Beibut now prayed five times a day and devoted hours to studying the Quran, Hadiths, and other holy books.

With each passing day, the words of the Islamists rang truer. Perhaps the Soviet Empire was not meant to succeed, nor Russia. Perhaps the great empire meant to rule the world would come in the form of a restored Ottoman empire—a new, global Caliphate.

He knew it was time for him to leave, but where was he to go?

A few weeks later, an email from an old friend answered that question. Valikhanov planned a trip home to Kazakhstan. He would take a few weeks, spend time honoring his mother and catching up with his friend, Taras Azamat. He prayed that, in the process, Allah would mercifully show him the way forward.

CHAPTER FIVE

Almaty, Kazakhstan

BEIBUT'S LAST VISIT TO KAZAKHSTAN had been on the occasion of his father's death—an event he viewed with the ambiguity of a son who had never won his father's approval. Though Suiundik Valikhanov had known little of the true nature of Beibut's work, he nonetheless felt obliged to disparage it.

Beibut understood that his father's rantings were those of a man who had lived too long and accomplished too little. Despite how his father had treated him, Beibut craved his father's praise. No one else could fill that need. But now it was too late.

These were the thoughts that resurfaced as Beibut prepared to return home.

His mind eventually turned to his mother, Raushan, and how lonely she must be following his father's death. Though their marriage had seemed emotionally distant from the outside, Beibut knew they had once been close. Perhaps familiar was a better word—the familiarity that comes with five decades spent learning to tolerate one another.

Beibut had two brothers and two sisters, but they were caught up in their own struggles and failed to see the joylessness in their mother's heart. Their lives consisted of days spent toiling at menial jobs only to return home to the demands of tired spouses and needy children.

Amidst the darkness, however, there was one thing Beibut could count on to bring light into his life—the unconditional love of his mother. Her eldest son had always occupied a special place in her heart. What his father had failed to give him, Raushan delivered in abundance. Holding on to these memories, he filled out the requisite paperwork to secure a one-week leave to visit Almaty. The request for leave was granted without question, and he left a few days later.

Beibut arrived in Kazhakstan only to discover that his mother was far frailer than he had anticipated. How long might she live, he wondered, fearing that her passing might be imminent. Despite her physical infirmities, Raushan's mind remained astoundingly sharp. Beibut knew that she was the source of whatever genes underlay his genius, though his mother's lack of education prevented the gift of such an intellect to be fully realized. He wondered what this remarkable woman might have accomplished if she had been given the opportunity.

But such was not their Muslim tradition. Women did not need an education. Their job was in the home honoring their husband and family. Suiundik had ensured that his wife understood this dictum, just as he had made certain that she never appeared in public without a niqab covering her face.

"Beibut, I am relieved to have you home, if for only a week."

"I am sorry that it has been so long. I have no excuse, only regrets," the son said.

"Your father's death was hard on you. I know this, and understand why. He was a good man, but his heart could be like stone. He admired you more than you can ever imagine, but he could not admit it even to himself, for it made him aware of his failings," his mother said, attempting to ameliorate the pain her son carried in his heart.

"Father is gone, and with his passing, a great many ghosts may finally be vanquished. I'm grateful for the love I felt within our home—a love that you always bestowed upon me, my brothers, and sisters. It is you I honor with my return."

"Tell me of your work, Beibut," his mother instructed. "Are you appreciated for what you bring? And what of Irina? I've not heard from her in months."

Though their conversation had just begun, his mother had already unearthed the two issues that now consumed much of Beibut's waking moments.

"What I am about to share with you stays in this room. You must not tell anyone—not my brothers, my sisters, not anyone."

Raushan nodded in agreement.

"Irina is gone. She has left me, and it is for the better. The marriage died many years ago. She is an apostate and will endure the torment of the most intense blazing fire," he said, quoting the Quran. Beibut waited for an acknowledgment before continuing.

His mother nodded without making eye contact with her son.

"As for my co-workers, that is a far more complicated matter. Though I love my work, my contributions seem to go unrecognized.

"And finally, my dear mother, I worry about our once great empire. It has been replaced by a collection of nations loosely aligned with Russia. The Russian people, who were once so disciplined, have fallen victim to greed, profiteering, and decadence. I have little faith in Russia . . . my only faith now is in my family, and in Allah."

"Allah Akbar," the Islamist's refrain, rose slowly from Valikhanov's lips—not as a defiant shout, but as if seeking his mother's permission to utter the words.

"What are you saying?" she asked in a voice laced with fear. "Why do you come to my home and speak these words to me?"

Undeterred by his mother's reaction, Beibut responded: "Because Allah is our deliverer, and we must be prepared to embrace great change."

"I'll have none of that, Beibut . . . not while you are under my roof. Your beliefs are your own, but respect my desire to live and end my life in peace . . . not listening to you preach words of hatred."

Beibut sought to put a quick end to the disagreement. "So be it, my mother. Let us not spend another moment in opposition. Our time together is far too precious."

Raushan realized how much her son had changed during his two-year absence. His radical faith, now a far cry from the beliefs she had sought to inculcate in him as a child, would serve as his guiding light. She wondered what lay ahead for Beibut and prayed that Allah would instill a sense of purpose and meaning in his life that was driven by generosity, not barbarity or hatred.

CHAPTER SIX

Almaty, Kazakhstan

BEIBUT ROSE WITH THE SUN and spent the morning helping around the house. Nothing was said of the prior day's conversation. He completed numerous chores that were once the duty of his father but had been neglected since his death. Grateful to have been of some service to his mother, he left to visit his childhood friend, Taras.

Beyond his mother, Taras Azamat was the only constant in Beibut's life. Though their paths had diverged many years ago, they remained faithfully in touch. Taras had become an Islamic scholar and lecturer at Al-Farabi Kazakh National University. The bond uniting the men was built upon their history and a mutual passion for discussing their Islamic beliefs.

Taras' heavily bearded face broke into a broad smile as he welcomed his dear friend. "Beibut, I am so happy that you have come to visit your mother. I'm sure she feels honored, as do I, by your presence."

"My dear friend, it is I who feel blessed. So tell me, I'm eager to hear about your family, your work, whatever it is that you wish to share," Beibut said with a warmth reserved for precious few.

"So much to tell! Miriam has gone to the market, and you remember how much Miriam loves the market. We have several hours to talk. Sit, sit." Taras gestured to the most comfortable chair in his Spartan living room.

He paused. "I did not wish to say too much in my email, only enough to elicit your attention. I trust that it is not merely your eyes that gaze upon such correspondence."

Beibut almost chuckled at the thought of uncensored communications. In his friend's presence, Beibut experienced a lightheartedness that he had not felt in years.

"Taras, your discretion is appreciated and warranted. So what is it that you really do wish to discuss? Radical elements at the university? Women wearing skirts in public? The public persona of Putin?"

"Actually, Beibut, it is a matter of great importance." The message was reinforced by the serious look on Taras' face.

Beibut raised an eyebrow.

"I am sorry to steal the joy from our reunion. Perhaps we should save any serious talk for another time," Taras suggested.

"No, please, let us talk now. You said we would have a few uninterrupted hours. Let us use them well," Beibut encouraged his friend.

"Beibut, a very powerful man requests your help. He is a soldier of Islam, and he commands a growing army. He seeks to create a unified Islamic state—a Caliphate."

Beibut studied his friend closely before speaking, contemplating the significance of what he had just heard.

"You speak of Ibrahim Almasi al-Bakr?" Beibut questioned, awaiting confirmation, though it could be no one else.

Taras nodded.

"How is it, Taras, that you have become acquainted with al-Bakr? And what is it that al-Bakr could seek from this humble Kazakh?"

"My work at the university has put me in touch with many people, Beibut, just as has your work in Russia. I was introduced to al-Bakr long before there was a United Islamic State. Early on, I looked upon his ambitions with suspicion, but he has proven to be a true believer with absolute fidelity to his faith. He has earned my sworn allegiance."

"But you've never discussed this relationship with me before?"

"Even among the closest of friends, there remain secrets. I would never deceive you, Beibut. But neither would I impose upon you the burden of keeping an unsolicited confidence regarding my work and affiliations."

"Until now," Beibut corrected him.

"Yes, until now. You are humble, Beibut, considering the contributions you have made to Russia. But you are also powerful—in possession of great knowledge, as well as great weapons."

"What is al-Bakr asking of me?"

"He wants you to bring your knowledge to the aid of those fighting to honor God's words—holy warriors of Islam."

"Taras, I see a battle being waged by young martyrs armed with AK-47s and a zeal for killing infidels. What role does my knowledge play in this holy war?"

Taras stood, momentarily ignoring the question.

"First let me bring you a cup of hot tea."

The brief interruption allowed both men to compose their thoughts. After raising their cups in a toast, Taras continued, "Al-Bakr wants you to help build a bio-weapons facility in Pakistan. You would have every resource you need at your disposal. He asks that you bring samples of your work and the digital manuals that detail the process used to weaponize each pathogen."

"What do you know of this work, Taras? Is it written of in the Quran?" A tinge of sarcasm crept into his voice. "Why have you become al-Bakr's emissary?"

"I have learned much through Jamaa Islamiya. I know that we are to rule the earth, and Sharia law is to govern it. I know that al-Bakr is the visionary leader that we have long awaited. And I know that you are the premier scientist who can provide a weapon that, Allah willing, will usher in Armageddon. So I ask you, what have I failed to understand that is relevant, Beibut?"

Valikhanov fell silent. Taras was illuminating a new path forward for Beibut, a path that had been indiscernible while he was in Russia. This could be his ticket out.

"There are thousands of vials of material, but it will not be easy to pilfer them without running the risk of being discovered," Beibut cautioned.

"Al-Bakr anticipated your response and said that if you are able to bring only one vial, make certain it is the hemorrhagic smallpox virus that has been the focus of your work."

"How could he know that?" Valikhanov demanded.

"Beibut, you are my friend—family, really. It doesn't matter where or how al-Bakr collects his information. I, too, have been astonished by the things he knows. It's best to simply do as he says, if you are in agreement. If not, I will tell him that, as well."

"Tell him this: We were once a part of a unified state—much of it Islamic. That state no longer exists, and my loyalty now belongs to God. Tell al-Bakr that I will await his instructions."

"He hoped you would respond in this way. Meet me tomorrow following evening prayer. I will have word for you then."

The next day, after completing evening prayer, Valikhanov exited the mosque and began walking towards Taras' home. He had gone only a few blocks when his friend appeared at his side.

"Let us walk together," Taras suggested, engaging Beibut in small talk about the weather until they were safely ensconced in his house.

"Ah, now, Beibut, we can finally speak freely."

"What word do you bring from al-Bakr?" Valikhanov asked eagerly.

"He will arrange for your safe transportation to Pakistan. You will leave from here in exactly thirty days. You will be escorted to your new home by men in whom al-Bakr has complete trust."

"How long is the trip?"

"It depends upon the weather and road conditions. Do not bring any identification. Beibut Valikhanov will, for all purposes, simply disappear."

"And what am I to tell my superiors? How do I travel from vector to Almaty without detection?"

"You will travel freely, having told your superiors that your mother has fallen gravely ill. They will understand your need to return home immediately."

"And when they check on her?"

"Your mother will have been admitted to the Private Clinic in Almaty, where a physician will take excellent care of her. He, too, is a member of Jamaa Islamiya, and a man whom I would trust with my life."

Taras paused long enough to ensure that his words were reassuring to Beibut. "Your mother's chart will indicate that she is dying of heart failure. You will visit her once before departing. Do not be surprised or concerned if she appears heavily sedated."

"Does she know of this plan?"

"No, I would never be so presumptuous, Beibut. It is your job to tell her and acquire her cooperation."

"I may spare her some of the details. I will explain that it is the only way I can gain safe passage from Russia to a new life. Thirty days, then. I will return home . . . visit my mother briefly . . . and be ready to leave for Pakistan."

As he left, Valikhanov began to think about a parting gift for Yergeny Bucherov.

CHAPTER SEVEN

Novosibirsk Oblast, Siberia

ONCE BACK IN HIS LABORATORY, Beibut was relieved at the ease with which he was able to steal viral samples. Yet as a Russian military officer and chief scientist, he was appalled at VECTOR's lax security. He wondered how often the laboratory had been pilfered and if there were seed cultures proliferating in the clandestine facilities of rogue nations.

Stealing viruses had proven easy. But that would not be the case with the digital instruction manuals accompanying the cultures. These were the recipes for transforming a minute culture into a viable bio-weapon . . . and they were essential to Beibut's future work. VECTOR utilized software that logged each time a digital file was copied. He could only hope that the discovery of duplicated files would not come until he, too, had disappeared.

Beibut was grateful when he received confirmation that his leave had been approved. No one had questioned his need to be at his mother's bedside, nor whether the two weeks he had requested was appropriate.

On his final day in the laboratory, he paid a visit to his colleague, Yergeny Bucherov. It had been several years since Bucherov stole the stage from Valikhanov by taking credit for Beibut's breathtaking scientific breakthroughs.

"Yergeny, I trust you've heard that my mother is gravely ill."

"Yes, Beibut, I am so sorry." Bucherov struggled to sound sincere.

Nodding in acknowledgment, Beibut explained, "I must return to Almaty. I will be gone for two weeks, maybe more. I have a favor to ask of you, and I hope it is not an imposition."

"And what might that be?"

"I need someone to monitor my research while I am away."

Bucherov's lust for recognition overrode his wariness of a colleague whom he had intellectually swindled. After scanning Beibut's face for any hint of deceit, he took the bait. For Bucherov, it would provide unhindered access to all of Valikhanov's data. Perhaps there would be another Medal of Lenin in his future.

"It would be an honor, Beibut. Go, and let your only concern be your mother."

"Thank you. That's one less burden for me to carry with me to Kazakhstan. May we drink a toast to you, for your help and friendship?" he asked, revealing two glasses of vodka held discreetly behind his back.

Alcohol was abhorrent to Valikhanov, but he knew that, under Sharia law, the principle of *taqiyya* allowed such behavior in efforts to deceive the infidels.

"And all this time, Beibut, I thought you were such a devoted Muslim."

"I only drink with true friends, and only on rare occasions," Beibut responded. "And you, my friend, are you not Muslim?"

"I was born a Muslim, a fact which I cannot change. But I can choose to live my life as I please," Bucherov responded, as he reached for the glass Beibut held out to him. He belted it down in a single gulp.

Beibut smiled. He wanted to remember this moment. Millions of particles of the Marburg virus were now flooding Bucherov's gut and would soon be entering his bloodstream. The vodka would kill many of them, but it only took a handful of viral particles to bring on a fulminating infection. He was looking at a dead man. It was just a matter of time.

Bucherov would become symptomatic in about a week. After two weeks, he would likely experience a short-lived "reprieve" before the virus roared back to life and engulfed every inch of his body. It would be a particularly hideous death, with his internal organs liquefying and blood streaming from every orifice of his body. A fitting tribute, Beibut thought, to an apostate, and to the winner of the Order of Lenin.

"You will, of course, make sure that my research notes are carefully guarded," Beibut toyed with his victim.

"Of course. No one will lay an eye on them except me."

"Thank you, Yergeny. May God smile upon you until my return."

"And upon you, my friend."

After bidding his colleague adieu, Beibut returned home. He walked silently through each room of the house he had once shared with Irina. The silence evoked a powerful cascade of memories. They were the final scenes of his old life playing out. A new life awaited him.

He picked up the small bag that he had placed by the front door, stepped outside, and pulled the door shut behind him. He locked it for the last time.

And then Beibut Valikhanov vanished.

CHAPTER EIGHT

Almaty, Kazakhstan to Faisalabad, Pakistan

RAUSHAN WAS A WILLING CONSPIRATOR in Beibut's exodus from Russia. Despite her misgivings about his apparent conversion to radical Islam, she felt compelled to support him. It was the only way now to assuage her guilt—decades-old guilt—for her failure to protect Beibut from her husband's emotional cruelty.

Though sedated, she was coherent enough to give Beibut the tearful embrace of a mother who knowingly hugs her son for the last time. She would once again be alone, this time until she died—although Taras had promised Beibut he would serve as a surrogate son. Raushan bestowed her blessing upon Beibut, and then, turning her head away, told him it was time for her to sleep.

As he exited her room, he could hear the muffled sobs that his mother fought to silence. He wanted to go back, to console her, but he couldn't. Better to leave now than extend the agony of parting.

Early the next morning, four war-hardened men loaded Valikhanov into the back of an aging Toyota Tacoma pickup.

The trip from Kazakhstan to Pakistan would be slow and arduous. Their route took them south from Almaty through the far eastern tip of Uzbekistan, then diagonally through Tajikistan. They entered Pakistan near the Turikho River.

The mountainous terrain of northern Pakistan made travel by truck all but impossible, requiring a hand-off of sorts. As the pickup came to a stop on a high desert plateau, a wave of panic gripped Valikhanov. He realized he was about to be loaded onto a STOL (short take-off and landing) plane for the final leg of the journey. He knew from experience that the tight cabin would feel like a coffin. His chest tightened, and he struggled for breath as he forced himself to climb into the fuselage of the Antonov AN-14 Pchelka, a Russian plane built before his birth.

The runway was little more than a dirt trail running a quarter-mile through the high desert pass. In the cockpit was a man who looked far more like a goat herder than a pilot. He jabbed his finger incessantly at Valikhanov's unclasped seat beat until Beibut fastened it.

As the pilot throttled up the sputtering engines, Beibut thought this might be his last flight. If so, he prayed he would enter paradise and enjoy its many pleasures.

The plane lurched forward, momentarily dislodging Beibut from his obsessive worries. Its twin 300 HP engines struggled to create sufficient lift to free it from the earth's hold. Within seconds, the craft was airborne. Still sputtering, it climbed upwards to an altitude of 16,000 feet, near the limit of the plane's ceiling. Unaccustomed to the thin air, Beibut felt a sudden dizziness that was exacerbated by the claustrophobic cabin. He closed his eyes and began to recite verses from the Quran.

Despite his misgivings, the plane made it through the valley and across several mountain passes without incident. Beibut watched the seconds, then minutes tick by slowly on his watch. Two hours later, the plane began to descend. After a brief refueling, the pilot continued on a southeastern heading and eventually landed at Faisalabad airport. Exhausted and filthy from days of travel, yet thanking God that he had arrived safely, Beibut sprang from the plane the moment its props were secure.

A small welcoming committee was on hand, courtesy of al-Bakr. They would show him to his new home.

The modest bay-and-gable house on Qauid E Azam Street was surrounded by floral trees that served as a privacy fence. The group entered by the front door and walked through the entry hall before turning right into the kitchen, where Beibut was startled by the sight of a slight-looking man with round glasses. The man was sipping a cup of coffee, a newspaper in hand.

"What is this world coming to . . . all these random acts of terror," the man murmured mockingly, gesturing to the newspaper headline declaring a state of emergency in Paris.

Although they had never met, Beibut recognized the man in front of him. "Al-Bakr!" he exclaimed, surprised not only by the man's presence, but by his casual demeanor.

Al-Bakr rose, shook his hand, and kissed each cheek. "Welcome, my dear friend. We owe you a debt of gratitude for what you have done, and for what you will do in the months and years to come."

"What I do, I do in the name of Allah."

"As do we all," al-Bakr nodded. "Correct me if I am wrong, Beibut, but I understand that you have only recently devoted yourself to Allah."

"For many years, I allowed my work to be my faith, but that has changed," Valikhanov responded.

"And what causes a man, late in life, to embrace such a transformation?"

"When one loses faith in his worldly attachments, only God remains. I hope you do not fault me for the blinders I once wore. Today, I see the world as it is, as Allah would have us see it," Beibut said, lowering his head in a gesture of reverence.

"Yes, I know of your disappointments in Russia. And although I am sorry for whatever suffering you endured, I am grateful that you have turned to Allah. Islam will benefit from your wealth of knowledge."

Throughout his questioning, al-Bakr had not broken eye contact for more than a second. He continued: "We will spend today together, and then I must leave. You will not see me again for a very long time, and there is much to discuss. So forgive the brevity of our introduction, but our sacred mission demands it."

He started his briefing. "We selected this city, much as we selected you, because it provides exactly what we require to complete our bio-weapons facility. You will find ready access to rail and air transportation, with daily flights to Karachi. My point is that the equipment you need can be delivered to your door."

"With a population of three million people, you should have few problems recruiting the necessary staff. Skilled workers can be found within the chemical and dye industries, and medical personnel are in relative abundance thanks to numerous health care facilities. They will, of course, have to be carefully vetted by your security team. We will also ensure that you are connected to local groups that may be of service.

"It is important that you recognize that we are here as the guests of ISI and will operate under their protection." Al-Bakr raised his hands to emphasize the point.

Valikhanov had heard a great deal about the ISI, Pakistan's third-world version of the KGB. They had supported the Taliban, then Al Qaeda, and now UIS, all the while maintaining a façade of cooperation with the United States. More importantly, they had proven invaluable to Jamaat Al Fuqura, despite the Pakistani president's ban on the jihadist organization.

"How can you trust them?" he pressed al-Bakr.

"How can we not?" came the instantaneous response. "Most importantly, when the moment is right, you will meet with my protégé, Ahmed Al Hameed. Do as he tells you, for he speaks for me. Know that you can trust him—always."

CHAPTER NINE

CIA Heaquarters

JUDGING BY THE GRIM FACES STARING BACK at him from around the table, Hart knew that bad news was sure to follow. His intuition was confirmed by CIA Deputy Director of Operations, Marvin Kahn, moments after Hart was seated.

"Commander, we received a communique from our operative in Novosibirsk Oblast late last night."

"VECTOR?"

"Yes. It appears that Beibut Valikhanov has gone missing."

Hart shook his head in disbelief. "How does a chief scientist disappear from a totally secure military installation?"

"I wish I had a cogent answer for you," Kahn responded. "What we do know is that certain materials are also missing—including a vial of smallpox and the digital instruction manual on how to replicate the virus on a large scale." Kahn paused to let his words sink in. "I'm afraid the problem gets worse, Commander."

"How is that possible, Sir?"

"The smallpox virus was genetically engineered to increase its utility as a weapon of mass destruction. Our operative said it has a ninety percent mortality rate."

"Who's looking for Valikhanov?" Hart cut to the chase.

"Besides the FSB and Russian military?"

"On our side, Sir."

"He's our top priority, Commander."

"What else do we know about him? I'm talking about recent intelligence," Hart asked.

Kahn shoved a folder across the table. "Here's an updated dossier. As you know, Valikhanov is Muslim. Once more secular than observant, it appears that he's found religion and with it, a zeal for expressing his love for Allah."

"Did something trigger his recent conversion?"

"His wife left him a couple of months ago, though a break-up had been brewing for years. Irina Valikhanov was interviewed by FSB and cleared of any complicity in her husband's disappearance."

"What about other family?" Hart asked.

"Valikhanov is Kazhak. He has a mother and four siblings in Almaty."

Hart stood up abruptly.

"Where do you think you are going, Commander?"

"Almaty, Sir."

"Sit down, Commander. We've got agents poised to meet with the family, but I doubt it will yield anything of value. My guess is that Almaty was a jumping off point for a new life . . . I just don't know the final destination nor who booked his travel."

"All the more reason I need to go to Almaty, Sir."

"He could be anywhere, Commander. Until Valikhanov surfaces, you are staying right here."

Six hundred fifty miles southwest of Washington, three people sat cloistered in the inner sanctum of the CDC. The meeting did not appear on anyone's schedule . . . certainly not Liz Wilkins'. She had been summoned by Julie Venard, the Centers' Director, in response to an urgent request by the CIA.

A stern-looking man sat across from the two women. He placed a thin leather briefcase on the table, extracted a thick folder, and removed a photograph.

"Do you recognize this man?" he asked, his attention focused on Wilkins.

"Beibut Valikhanov. I've never met him, but I heard him speak last year at a conference."

"And what was he speaking on, Doctor?"

"The need to safeguard against the proliferation of bio-weapons."

"How ironic," the man replied with a flat affect. "From apocalyptic prophet to proliferator."

"What are you talking about?" Julie Vernard asked, annoyed by the cryptic manner in which the man responded.

"Dr. Valikhanov has disappeared, and with him a culture of genetically modified smallpox."

Wilkins raised a hand to cover her open mouth, a look of shock on her face.

"My purpose is not to alarm you, Dr. Wilkins."

"What is your purpose, Mr. Thompson?"

"To see if you can render any insights into what Valikhanov might have been working on and whether claims of a ninety percent mortality rate associated with this virus are achievable."

"Valikhanov is an expert in the genetic modification of human pathogens. You know VECTOR's mission better than I. As for the enhanced mortality, it is achievable in theory."

"What does that mean, *in theory*, Dr. Wilkins?"

"That means that every time you mess with the genetic code of a bacterium or virus, there are unexpected consequences. You may increase lethality but weaken the organism in the process. Like all things, for every action there is a reaction."

"So you are suggesting that we have little to worry about . . . that this super-bug may be short-lived."

"That's not what I said. Valikhanov is masterful at his art. If anyone is going to unlock the code of the variola virus and identify which genes to alter to yield a novel pandemic virus, it would be Beibut Valikhanov."

CHAPTER TEN

Faisalabad, Pakistan

THE MONTHS PASSED QUICKLY as Valikhanov found himself absorbed in the frenetic push to meet al-Bakr's construction deadlines. He had been given a year to construct a scaled-down version of VECTOR—complete with laboratories, testing facilities, and production capabilities.

Beyond the challenges of bricks and mortar, three critical tasks awaited Valikhanov's attention. First, he needed to recruit a small, but exceptional staff of molecular biologists and recombinant chemists to supply the intellectual horsepower required to nurture the seed culture pilfered from VECTOR into a full-fledged bio-weapon. Just as importantly, this group would have the formidable task of developing a novel vaccine for the genetically altered virus.

Next came the manufacturing process. Not only would there need to be sufficient quantities of the bio-weapon, but millions of doses of vaccine would have to be prepared for worldwide distribution to those individuals deemed worthy of surviving Armageddon.

The final challenge was to construct an engineering group responsible for developing effective methods for dispersing the weaponized pathogen. This group would bear responsibility for safety and security.

All operations, with the exception of human testing, were housed in a single location—the site of a former food factory. The factory was essentially hidden in plain sight. Neighbors were relieved to have a new owner take over the long-abandoned property. There was no hint that a state-of-the-art BSL-4 lab housing genetically modified pathogens lay buried deep within the facility.

Human trials required a different setting, however—services more aligned with the needs of a hospital than a manufacturing plant. It was neatly concealed in the sub-basement of a gray, concrete building designed to keep its horrific secrets far from prying eyes.

A large red sign was the only splash of color against the monotone façade of the building. It read Population Health Services, which had become known as PHS to the community. The building was adjacent to Faisalabad General Hospital, giving its staff access to essential health care services and, most importantly, to the morgue.

The construction was completed on time, and the facilities deemed fully functional. Beibut sat in his office contemplating the long journey to this point. He laughed, realizing that it was Irina he had to thank for his good fortune. Had it not been for her abandonment, he might still be trudging through the thick snow each day on the way to VECTOR, working for a government in which he no longer believed.

His concentration was broken by a sharp rap on the door. His assistant ushered in a young man who appeared to be in his early twenties. Valikhanov greeted him, "As-salāmu ʿalaykum."

Covering his heart with his hand, the man responded, "Waʿalaykumu s-salām. I have been asked to give you a message: The man you have awaited will visit in three days."

CHAPTER ELEVEN

Washington, DC
CDC Headquarters, Atlanta, Georgia

LIZ WAS SURPRISED when an invitation to the annual dinner meeting of Business Executives for National Security arrived in the mail. The event, held at the Ritz Pentagon City, brought together senior ranking national security officials with the key executives from the nation's largest corporations, many of whom benefited from sizeable contracts with the Department of Defense.

There had been no indication of her benefactor . . . only a table designation. As she circled the table looking for a place-card bearing her name, a man stepped forward and pulled back her chair.

"I believe you are seated here, Ma'am," Commander Hart told her with a smile.

Caught off guard, Liz was momentarily speechless.

"Thank you, Commander, and thank you for including me in this special event?" She said it as a question awaiting confirmation.

"No thanks necessary, Ma'am. I thought you might enjoy the guest speaker."

Joshua Goldman was scheduled to speak. His topic: *How Advancements in Molecular Biological Could Lead to a Biological Arms Race.*

While she was grateful for the opportunity to hear Goldman, Liz wasn't sure how she felt about being Hart's date. She wasn't one to be attracted to military types. Although she made an effort to be polite, she remained reserved—not chilly, but far from inviting.

Over the course of the evening, aided by three glasses of chardonnay, her cool demeanor began to warm. Before the end of the night, Hart invited her to dinner on her next visit to Washington. She accepted without hesitation.

The next morning, after catching a 5:30 AM flight back to Atlanta, Wilkins was changing into the cumbersome spacesuit required to work in the Biolevel IV lab. As she was finishing, her closest friend, Dr. Karen Johnson, joined her in the airlock.

"Well, aren't we the bubbly one," Karen commented on the smile that seemed permanently affixed to Wilkins' face. "So who is it this time?" she asked, knowing her friend's penchant for short-lived episodes of infatuation.

"He's a SEAL, Karen."

"No, Liz. You don't do SEALs or guys in Special Forces . . . or anyone in Black Ops. We both know better," she advised.

"I was initially turned off by the guy, and you're right about how I feel about military types. At least, that's what I thought at first glance. But this guy is far more than just a rock-hard body. He's scary smart."

"If you'd prefer an intellectually challenged, middle-aged guy with a paunch, I can set you up with my ex," Karen offered.

"Very funny, Karen. No, I just don't want to get involved with someone whose idea of a good time is playing army or shouting *oorah*. But I did tell him I'd have dinner with him when I return to DC."

"It seems like you're really into this guy, but I'll bet a little voice in your head keeps telling you to stay away," Karen ventured. "What did you say his name was?"

"John Hart. Commander John Hart."

Karen Johnson giggled.

"What's so funny, Karen?"

"My God, Liz. Don't you know who he is?"

"I've heard him speak at meetings, but I don't know much about him . . . outside of his role in counter-intelligence."

"I met John during my tour of duty at USAMRIID. From what I could tell, he works for Marvin Kahn at the CIA. Maybe you'll find out more over dinner."

"Yes, I will," Liz said, "On my next visit to Washington."

CHAPTER TWELVE

Faisalabad, Pakistan

THOUGH MODEST EVEN BY PAKISTANI STANDARDS, Valikhanov's home on Qauid E Azam Street was anything but ordinary. An ISI safe house, it had harbored a Who's Who of Islamic terrorists and political dissidents—all of whom bartered something of unique value in exchange for their host's protection. But no one to date had offered the value brought by its latest inhabitant, Beibut Valikhanov.

All the more reason why security was of paramount concern. Nothing could jeopardize the mission nor risk compromising this invaluable asset, a point reinforced by Omar Qazan, Valikhanov's ISI contact. Qazan appeared at the front door the evening following the messenger's arrival.

"Please, come in," Beibut beckoned to Qazan, who was already halfway across the threshold.

With the door closed, Qazan brought a finger up to his lips to ensure silence, then pulled a small pad of paper and pen from his pocket. He wrote, "Do not speak until I tell you."

Qazan was a short, muscular man with a jagged scar running halfway across his throat. Beibut wondered what had happened to whomever had inflicted that wound but failed to complete the job.

Qazan led Valikhanov to a closet inside the bedroom. Opening the closet door, he pulled up a one-meter by two-meter square of carpet, uncovering a yellowed linoleum floor. The faint outline of a seam could be seen against the patterned tile. Qazan extracted a folding knife and gently guided its point until it made contact with one corner of the square. Carefully lifting the tile, he revealed a trapdoor. He grabbed a metal ring folded flush against its top and lifted. Valikhanov stared downward into a narrow, black abyss.

Almost immediately, Beibut was overcome with a suffocating sense of anxiety. He quickly backed away from the hole and its impenetrable blackness.

Qazan grabbed Beibut's arm with one hand and pulled him towards the darkness. Feeling Beibut's resistance, he slowly tightened his grip until Beibut's fingers grew numb.

Beibut was in the throes of a full-fledged panic attack. If he entered the abyss, he feared he would die of a heart attack. If he failed to move forward, he was sure to incur the wrath of Qazan, who was mystified by his inexplicable disobedience. Beibut took a reluctant half-step forward. As he did, the posts of a ladder became visible beneath the ledge of the trapdoor.

Valikhanov grasped the posts of the ladder and swung his leg around in a desperate search for the first rung. His breathing was already labored. His eyes grew wide and his pupils narrowed as he tried to suck oxygen into his lungs in defiance of his constricted diaphragm. His heart was pounding so hard that it reverberated in his ears. This was his worst nightmare—being swallowed by the earth and suffocating in the process. But now, Qazan was literally pushing him downward. The strong fingers that had encircled his arm were now pressing against the top of his head.

He was in a vertical shaft. He could feel the rock walls of the tunnel chafing against his back and hips. There was not an inch to spare. Each rung transported him closer to hell. His breath came in painful, short gasps. He wondered when the unholy flames might erupt and consume him, remembering the Quranic verse, "When they are flung therein, they will hear the terrible drawing in of their breath and loud moaning even as the flame blazes forth."

Just as he was on the verge of passing out, his right foot touched earth. He became aware that the rocks were no longer pressing against his back. And the hand that had pressed him downward was now pushing him to one side. As Valikhanov moved away from the ladder, Qazan planted his feet on the cool, earthen floor.

With a small penlight, Qazan illuminated a cord attached to a single bare bulb. As the bulb's light dispatched the darkness, he looked into the frightened eyes of Valikhanov.

"What the hell is wrong with you?"

Afraid to speak, Beibut remained silent.

"Speak, damn it. What is wrong with you?"

"I don't like small spaces," he said in an embarrassed whisper.

Qazan shook his head.

"I want you to listen to me carefully. It can make a life and death difference."

Beibut nodded.

"You are four meters below the grade of the street. Outside of the factory, this is the only place you can talk openly with Al Hameed. No RF signals can escape this room, so listening devices are worthless."

"I understand."

"Use the supplies here wisely. They will not be replenished."

Valikhanov's pupils finally dilated sufficiently to allow him a good view of the room. He determined that it was approximately four meters square. Packed into the tight space were two cots, two folding chairs, and floor-to-ceiling shelves stocked with military rations, plastic reservoirs of water, medical supplies, and other necessities. In one corner, there was a portable latrine. Across from it, on the far wall, was a door. It was secured with two steel bolts that ran directly into solid rock.

"What are you looking at?" Qazan asked in annoyance.

Gesturing with his head, Valikhanov responded, "Where does it lead?"

Qazan studied Valikhanov for a moment, still irritated by his irrational behavior.

"I should have been informed of your issues," he said with disgust. "You do understand that you could jeopardize this mission."

"I won't let anything jeopardize the mission," Valikhanov responded. "You have my word."

Qazan moved towards the door, slid back its massive bolts, and flung it open. With the flip of a switch, he illuminated a trail of lights running through the heart of a tunnel.

"It runs south for fifty meters and then splits. The left tunnel ends at the underground sewers. The right tunnel leads to another safe house. You are not to explore it. You are never to open this door. Am I clear?"

Beibut inhaled sharply, then let out a sigh, relieved to know there was a way out.

Before returning to the ladder, Qazan called Beibut's attention to one last item: a state-of-the-art air purifier that exchanged the carbon dioxide-laden air and pulled in fresh air from above.

"You need to be certain this is always working. If not, your time in this space is limited to one hour — no more."

With his instructions completed, Qazan tugged on the light cord and thrust them into darkness. A panicked Valikhanov shot up the ladder in seconds, his ISI handler shaking his head as he followed.

CHAPTER THIRTEEN

Faisalabad, Pakistan

AL HAMEED ARRIVED AT PRECISELY 8:15 PM the following evening. It was a time when families were finishing their evening meals and preparing to put their young children to bed. The street was empty.

Beibut opened the door before Al Hameed could knock. Almost merging with the darkness was a man wrapped in a black cloak, a hood enveloping his head. The jihadist seemed no more substantial than a shadow, a strangely ethereal creature roaming the night.

"As-Salam-u-Alaikum, wa rahmatullahi wa barakatuh," Beibut greeted his guest in a hushed voice.

"Wa Alaikum Assalam wa Rahmatullah."

"We will continue our conversation where it is safe." Beibut gestured for Al Hameed to follow.

Beibut felt his chest tighten and his heart begin to race as he approached the trapdoor, but he knew he had no choice but to proceed.

The men descended the ladder into the room below and sat in chairs facing one another.

"This is an interesting place to entertain guests," Al Hameed commented.

"ISI insists it is necessary for our protection," Beibut replied.

"Protection from whom? The Pakistani government?" Al Hameed quipped.

An awkward silence followed until it was broken by Beibut: "I am honored to be in your presence and to serve Allah through you."

"It is I who am honored. Many men are passionate in their resolve to destroy the infidels, though armed with little more than their emotions. You, on the other hand, possess not only the passion, but the knowledge and the tools to make such destruction possible. You will fashion the sword that I will brandish in our attack."

"What has al-Bakr told you?" Beibut asked.

"He has told me of your work in Russia and your accomplishments in modifying the genome of a very deadly virus . . . something your former employer did not fully appreciate. Apparently the credit accrued to another."

A cloud passed across Valikhanov's face. "Yes, and the man to whom the credit accrued no longer basks in *his* accomplishments," Beibut responded, without a hint of emotion.

Recognizing a kindred soul, Al Hameed laughed. "Yes, I understand he died a particularly hideous death. Marburg, wasn't it?"

Valikhanov smiled and nodded.

Al Hameed continued, "I was told that you are delivering a weapon of mass destruction capable of unleashing a fury like no man has ever witnessed—a fury that can only be described as Armageddon."

Valikhanov nodded, "A fury that will allow us to reclaim our rightful position in the world. Muslims will no longer bow to the oppressive regimes of the West, but rather bring them to their knees in submission!"

Al Hameed leaned back in his chair, sizing up the man with whom he spoke. Could he have found the perfect partner with whom to rain down hell? It seemed almost too good to be true. It had to be the invisible hand of Allah.

"Tell me of your work. I know of it in principle but not in specifics. Our leader is truly great, but his knowledge of molecular biology is limited. He has spoken of the cataclysmic power of this pathogen, but not a word about how the infection will be contained to the infidels."

Now it was Valikhanov's turn to lean back in his chair. "We have much to talk about. Surely your studies in America have made you quite aware of the tremendous gains that have been made in decoding and manipulating the genetic structure of viruses. My work, both in Russia and now at the factory, has focused on the genetic structure of orthopox viruses, specifically in manipulating members of that viral family—predominantly variola."

"Yes, but doesn't that weaken the virus?"

"That is the art of bio-weaponeering. It requires the precise placement of selective gene sequences to produce the sought-after characteristics without limiting the viability of the virus. Before there was success, there were many failures."

"How are you defining success, Beibut?"

"Success is a stable, hemorrhagic variant of smallpox with an average incubation period ranging from thirty-six to seventy-two hours instead of days or weeks, and a mortality rate that exceeds ninety percent. Success is a virus impervious to the millions of doses of vaccine stockpiled by the West."

"But won't it burn out as people succumb to the infection, as happens with Ebola?"

"That was the difficult part," Valikhanov said, puffed up with self-admiration. "We've improved upon its infectivity—raising it to that of measles. They will infect many others before dying, and it will spread like wildfire through the West."

"And what happens when it reaches our distant shores, shores that are mere hours away on a transcontinental flight from America, Canada, or Europe?" Al Hameed asked with growing concern.

"We will have a unique vaccine for those true Islamists whose lives are to be protected during Armageddon. It will be up to you to decide who receives it. I simply refer to them as the *Chosen Ones*."

"It will not be up to me to determine who comprises your so-called Chosen Ones," Al Hameed corrected Valikhanov. "It will be up to the Council."

Valikhanov continued. "When the virus eventually does burn out after a few years of global pandemic, the Chosen Ones will be the only people left standing. It will not be Christianity's meek who inherit the earth, but the bold and unapologetic jihadists who wield the sword of Islam!"

"How will you create such a vaccine in the laboratory?"

Beibut spoke as if addressing a fellow scientist. "As you know, humoral immune responses often rely upon the precise targeting of specific areas of a protein's surface or *epitopes*. We are developing recombinant vaccines based upon the heterologous expression of immunogenic proteins."

"Again, that's a grand theory, but what proof do you have of the vaccine's effectiveness?"

Without taking his eyes off of Al Hameed, Valikhanov rolled up his right sleeve until the top edge of his shoulder was revealed. A raised, circular wound stood out above his bicep. Though still a bit weepy, it was crusting over.

"I am proof that it works. Do you need something more?" Valikhanov asked.

"What if you had died? What if all the time and effort spent recruiting you, transporting you, and building a factory had been snuffed out by your dangerous experiment? What then?" Al Hameed asked sharply.

"But that didn't happen. I didn't do this in a foolhardy fashion, but after years of research, much of which occurred while I was at VECTOR. I just had to be certain. We will conduct one final test of the vaccine—to go from 99 percent certainty to 100. Now, let me explain what I need if I am to deliver upon my promises."

Valikhanov slowly began to enumerate what would be required to move from laboratory proof of concept to having a weaponized biologic agent capable of unleashing Armageddon, as well as millions of doses of vaccine.

"I don't know how many people will be among the Chosen Ones, but I have planned for approximately fifty million. I will need time to refine and produce the weapon and the vaccine, and that assumes hiring perhaps thirty to forty more people to work at the factory—people who will need to be carefully scrutinized."

"Once the vaccine is available, when will we begin the process of immunization?" asked Al Hameed. He assumed it would begin immediately.

"We cannot risk having our efforts detected, and I'm concerned that mass inoculations would raise many red flags."

"Why not inoculate people on their buttocks or hip, where it will be hidden from view?"

"But what of the inoculation process itself? Will it not garner the attention of others when millions of people are pulling down their pants or lifting their dresses to be jabbed repeatedly with an inoculation needle?"

Al Hameed conceded the point.

Valikhanov explained that inoculation would begin the day of the attack. "We will need a carefully orchestrated plan, but I believe we will have enough time before the virus reaches any of the Chosen Ones to immunize the vast majority of our followers. The vaccine allows a day or two of grace following exposure. It appears to markedly reduce the lethality of the infection if given prior to the presentation of symptoms. Once the prodromal period ends and symptoms begin, the efficacy of the vaccine in preventing death decreases dramatically with each passing hour."

"How long before the vaccine is ready?" Al Hameed asked with an eagerness bordering on impatience.

"That depends on staffing—we will need more people if you want our work to progress faster," Beibut explained.

"Then hire them!"

Beibut had delivered a long-awaited gift to Al Hameed—he was an ally with the means to destroy his enemy. And an ally who would not deprive Al Hameed of the full glory, but rather ensure the successful delivery of Armageddon.

Stiff from sitting too long in the hard metal chair, Al Hameed rose and thrust his arms high in the air. He proclaimed, "Your name will be praised in the centuries to come as part of the great liberation force that released us from the tyranny of the West.

"One more thing, Beibut. I want to see the virus tested on unvaccinated men."

CHAPTER FOURTEEN

Washington, DC
Washington, Virginia

THREE WEEKS LATER, on a crisp, early spring night, Commander Hart rounded the corner on D Street NW and pulled into the circular drive of the Marriott where Liz Wilkins was staying. It wasn't exactly the Willard, but it was close to FBI Headquarters, multiple metro stops, and plenty of good restaurants.

Before leaving to pick up his date, Hart had called Liz to ask if she minded a bit of a drive. She politely deferred to whatever he had in mind, within reason.

As Hart pulled up to the curb, Liz emerged from the lobby. He hastily jumped out of the car to greet her.

"Where are we headed, Commander?" she said with a mock salute, taking a seat in his black BMW.

"I'm setting a course for Sperryville, Virginia. ETA is about ninety minutes—or a lot less if you don't mind a fast ride," he smiled.

"It's your license."

"It's your life," he responded.

"I trust you." The words somehow escaped from her mouth before she realized what she was saying.

"Wow, that's something I don't hear from a woman every day."

"Be careful, Commander, you wouldn't want me to change my opinion of you, would you?"

"No Ma'am."

Twenty minutes past Dulles, the scenery changed from suburban sprawl to rolling countryside dotted by horse farms. It was hard to imagine that they were so close to the Beltway, yet so wonderfully removed from its chaos. Before she knew it, they had arrived, and John was awaiting the parking valet. Liz instantly recognized the restaurant—one that she had long heard of but never had the privilege of experiencing.

"The Inn at Fletcher Mill!" she exclaimed.

"I hope it's okay with you."

"Of course . . . I was just thinking something . . ."

"Simpler?" Hart asked. "Well, there's an Arby's about five miles down the road. Come on, Liz. You'll love it."

"Commander Hart, how nice to see you again, Sir." The maître d' extended his hand in greeting.

"Thomas, this is Dr. Wilkins. I'm looking forward to sharing your extraordinary hospitality with her."

"Welcome, Madame. I trust you will find everything to your liking. Please follow me."

As they followed the tuxedo-clad host to a quiet table tucked away in a far corner of the room, Liz could not help but notice her fellow diners. It made her feel both special and a little out of place.

Whispering into John's ear, she asked, "Did you see who's at that table? There are two Supreme Court Justices!"

"And do you know what they are saying to each other?" John whispered into her ear. "They're saying, 'Did you see who just walked in? It's Liz Wilkins!'"

Liz smiled.

"Is this table to your liking, Commander?" Thomas inquired.

"Exactly as I specified," he shook the maître'd's hand, discreetly depositing a twenty-dollar bill.

Liz felt as though she were in a nineteenth-century sitting room. She was surrounded by wall hangings laden with brocade, tables topped with vibrant flowers, and china fit for a queen. The setting was beyond romantic.

"You can't see them at night, but there are beautiful gardens just outside the window," John gestured to his right. "Perhaps you'll get to see them in the light."

Liz blushed, unsure of what he was implying, then reached for her menu.

As she opened it, John counseled her, "There is a prix-fixe dinner with many courses, some of which sound a little off-putting. You can order whatever you wish, but my bets are on the fixed dinner. If you'd like something a little lighter, they will gladly accommodate your request."

Just then, a man in a chef's uniform approached the table.

"John, I haven't seen you in weeks!" Finian, the brilliant chef who drew throngs of Washingtonians to this small town in Virginia, greeted him with a warm handshake.

"I've been traveling a lot, Finian. After a few weeks of military rations, I decided it was time for a real meal. Plus I wanted to share it with my friend. Let me introduce you to Liz Wilkins. Liz, Finian is the magic behind this place."

Liz extended her hand. "You have an extraordinary inn. I'm overwhelmed."

The genuinely humble host smiled. "The most important thing is for you to be comfortable and enjoy what we hope is one of the best dinners of your life. Perhaps I can help with some suggestions?"

"That would be wonderful," Liz said with relief.

"For starters, I suggest the chilled grilled figs with country ham and lime cream, followed by an asparagus salad with pickled quail eggs and beet vinaigrette."

"That sounds like a meal to me!"

"You have to try the rack of lamb we are serving tonight. It is encrusted with pecans, topped with barbeque sauce, and accompanied by shoestring sweet potatoes."

"John has told me that I should leave it to you . . . so I am in your hands, Finian."

"As am I, Finian," added Hart quickly.

Finian bowed to the couple before taking his leave.

"Okay, Liz, it's time to get down to business," he said as he reached across the table and unexpectedly took her hand.

Liz was surprised, but welcomed his warm touch.

"Alright Commander, let's get down to business," she matched his playful tone.

"Why is a beautiful, articulate woman like you spending her days in a Biolevel IV laboratory working with nature's most efficient killers?"

"Nothing like a light question to start the evening off right, Commander."

Hart reddened. "People tell me I'm a little too direct. Guilty as charged."

"I like men who are direct, so here's your answer. I'm fascinated by viruses—their simplicity, their adaptability—there is an elegance to their design. I don't focus on their ability to kill, but rather on the lessons they have to teach us about what constitutes life. Where do you think I should be, Commander, in the kitchen making casseroles?"

"Of course not, Liz. But I can see you running the CDC, not mired in the lab."

"But it's the lab that I love. I've passed on other opportunities at the CDC, albeit not quite so grandiose. I know my place, I know my passion, and that's where I hope to remain."

"It's good to know your passion," he said as he squeezed her hand gently and leaned in even closer.

Just then, the figs arrived, forcing John to relinquish her hand for the moment.

After a single bite, Liz looked at him with genuine amazement. "These are extraordinary!"

"Just wait . . . you can give me a final verdict after dessert."

"And now, Commander, I have a few questions for you," Liz said with a twinkle in her eye.

"Fire away, but from now on I only respond to *John*."

"Okay, John, I want the backstory—who are you, where did you come from, and what exactly do you do?"

"A few questions? You want my life story. Tell me, should I try to complete it before the salads arrive?"

"No, I trust we have plenty of time."

He wasn't getting off the hook, and the real question was what he would share with this woman. He wasn't worried about breaching security. Rather, he was afraid that an honest portrait of Commander John Hart might repulse her.

Unlike her, his days weren't spent in a pristine laboratory. They were spent navigating the gutters of the world, mired in refuse, as he chased down bad people who wanted to do bad things to this country. For now, he decided to give Liz the sanitized version.

"You know that I'm a SEAL. I wanted to serve my country, and I was privileged enough to be given an opportunity with the Navy."

"I heard a story that you set some kind of record as a SEAL."

"No big deal, Liz. I managed to score well on the Physical Screening Test. Truth is, I cheated, but don't tell anyone," he whispered with a smile.

She knew better. The proof could be seen at a glance.

Changing topics, Liz asked, "What about all of your schooling? It seems a bit incongruous with the life of a warrior."

"I don't see it that way. Just as you are fascinated by viruses, so, too, am I. Thanks to the United States government, I was able to attend medical school at Johns Hopkins. After completing a residency in infectious disease, I did a fellowship at USAMRIID."

"Keep going," she encouraged.

"So I put in my time, did a good job, and eventually ended up working within the intelligence community."

"Could you be a little more specific, Commander? What exactly do you do within the intelligence community?"

"A little of this, a little of that."

"Come on, John. You know I'm cleared."

"And you can probably imagine, much of what I do is compartmentalized. Let's just say that I'm focused on projects designed to improve our ability to detect, deter, or survive a biological attack, including an event using the nasty type of bugs you work with every day."

"Why haven't we run into each other before?" Liz asked.

"We have, Liz. You just didn't notice me. We both attended the briefings at the Agency in July on UIS's potential foray into bio-weapons. Before that, I was at the CDC for your briefing in May on the current state of genomic modification of Category A pathogens. Would you like me to keep going?"

"Got it. Just one more question."

"Shoot."

"Why do you spend so much time at the Agency?"

"Oh, let's not go there . . . let's enjoy this wonderful room, this extravagant food, the conversation," he said, once again reaching across the table to her.

"I'm giving you a pass on my last question . . . for the evening, *Commander*. But at some point, I want an answer."

"Whatever Madam wants, Madam should have."

She leaned forward and placed her other hand on top of his. He pulled her ever so gently into a kiss.

"John, will you excuse me for a minute?" Liz asked, slightly out of breath.

He stood, pulling the table back to ease her exit, then sat down, wondering if he had moved too fast.

A few minutes later, he felt the light touch of Liz's hand on his shoulder as she returned to the table.

Dinner went on for hours, and with each passing minute, Liz and John revealed more. Not about the intricacies of their work, but who they were as people.

As they prepared to leave, John thought about asking Liz if she'd like to spend the night at the Inn. Had she been like other women he had dated, he might not have hesitated. But she wasn't like anyone he had met before. She was smart and intuitive, and the last thing he wanted to do was blow it.

Delivering Liz safely home, John gave her a warm embrace and a lingering kiss.

"When can I see you again?" he asked.

"When would you like to?"

"How about breakfast!" Hart suggested, half in earnest.

"How about dinner tomorrow night? I'll fix you something. It won't be an MRE, but don't expect the Inn at Fletcher Mill."

"I'll tell you what. I'll plan on picking up dinner from Georgia Brown's. Okay with you?" Hart asked.

"Fried chicken and collard greens—oh, that sounds wonderfully unhealthy! You've got a date!" Liz said with enthusiasm.

So began a fierce courtship between Commander John Hart and Liz Wilkins. It wouldn't fizzle out quickly. In fact, it would have probably continued with incendiary heat had it not been for one thing—Liz's need to know what her lover really did for a living.

There were too many times when John vanished for days or weeks, only to reappear as if nothing had happened. Although she was falling in love with him, after six months of seeing each other exclusively, she brought it to an end. John had been gone for two weeks. She had no idea where he was or why he had to leave without explanation. When he returned late on a Saturday night, she was waiting for him in his apartment.

Surprised to find her there, Hart set down his bag and walked over to give her a kiss.

"Not so fast, Commander," Liz held up her hand like a stop sign.

"Don't I get a kiss?" he asked innocently.

"Not until I get answers," she responded.

John shook his head, as if to say "not again." They had been down this road many times since becoming a couple.

"I'm tired. I'm going to bed. I hope you'll join me," he said, moving past Liz towards the bedroom, unbuttoning his shirt on the way.

Liz trailed a few feet behind him. She started to speak, but then noticed a series of welts starting at John's waist and crossing his back.

"What the hell happened to you?" she blurted as she stared at his now bare back.

Hart walked into the bathroom, where there was a full-length mirror.

"Oh, I hadn't seen those. I'll have to be more careful next time," was all he said before stripping to his boxers.

"Tell me what happened to you, John! I don't hear from you for two weeks, and then you reappear looking as though you've been in a bar brawl."

"You should have seen the other guy," Hart said, hoping to defuse the confrontation with levity.

Instead, Liz picked up her purse and headed for the door.

He jumped in front of her. "Wait a minute. I'm sorry, Liz. You know I can't discuss my work with you. That's just something you're going to have to live with, Darling."

"No, John, it's not." With that pronouncement, Liz Wilkins turned and walked out the door.

A year passed before he saw her again. He received an invitation to the National Geospatial Intelligence Agency briefing hosted by Sue Goodman. Her name was on the attendee list. Hart rarely recoiled from pain, but he was dreading having to face Liz again.

CHAPTER FIFTEEN

Malé, the Republic of Maldives

THE UNITED ISLAMIC STATE WAS BIRTHED by Ibrahim Almasi al-Bakr when he consolidated the power of twelve tribal leaders under a single flag. The organization expanded rapidly through the recruitment of thousands of disenfranchised Sunnis. Its initial efforts were concentrated in war-torn Iraq, where al-Bakr preached a vision in which jihadists would no longer be unified only by ideology, but by the presence of a growing state destined to become the dominant power structure in the world.

The Council, as the tribal leaders came to be known, controlled vast swaths of land crisscrossing the borders of Afghanistan, Iraq, Syria, Libya, Somalia, Yemen, and Lebanon. In addition, UIS cobbled together a network of cells throughout Western Europe, the U.S., Indonesia, and Australia, where they would remain invisible until they were activated. There were few corners of the globe untouched by their efforts.

The Council became a major target for Western intelligence agencies. They knew of its shadowy existence, but not the names on its elite membership roster. Al-Bakr planned on keeping it that way.

Since its formation, there had only been one face-to-face meeting among the twelve leaders. The group had assembled to ratify its constitution, swear allegiance to UIS, and commit to a thousand-year war against the infidels. Since then, the threat of drone strikes had outstripped any potential gain achieved by consolidating the leadership in one location—until today. This second meeting was called to discuss the complete annihilation of the West.

Great care had gone into planning the meeting. The Council was sequestered in the home of one of al-Bakr's trusted jihadists, far from the battlefields of Iraq and Syria, in a place that would not be given a second thought by the CIA or its kindred organizations.

Despite counseling his protégé, Al Hameed, on the need for patience, al-Bakr had no interest in waiting for a war of attrition to wear down the West. He lusted for annihilation, and he was relying on Al Hameed to deliver it in the form of a single cataclysmic event that would reshape the world. But before that could happen, before a biological agent could usher in Armageddon, the group had a sacred obligation to determine who would be spared.

"Welcome, my brothers! You have my gratitude for making the long journey to this remote corner of the world, a corner far from prying eyes and, more importantly, from hovering drones!" al-Bakr roared.

"You have put great trust in me—a sacred trust that weighs heavily on my mind. I would not have called you together if the issue before us was anything less than momentous. In a minute, I am going ask Ahmed Al Hameed to address you, but before he speaks, there is something I must say.

"We speak of making the blood of the infidels flow like a river, yet our actions are little more than pinpricks on the fingers of the Great Satan. If we are to restore Islam, its laws, and the civility it demands, our sword must be more powerful than anything we have thus far imagined.

"Al Hameed confronted me with this truth. In response, I gave him the task of developing such a weapon, and he put a plan in motion. He has assured me that, within a relatively short time, we will be ready to strike. But allow him to tell you, in his own words, the details of his proposed attack," al-Bakr said, gesturing for Al Hameed to address the group.

Al Hameed stood. "Good evening. As al-Bakr has told you, I bring good news. For several years now, we have been developing a weapon of mass destruction. Today, we have that weapon—a virus of unimaginable destructive power. Unlike a nuclear weapon that unleashes tremendous fury but whose damage is confined to a single city, this devastating virus will spread throughout the western world.

"We will use the four busiest airports in America to disseminate the virus. Based upon our models, between 150,000 and 200,000 people will be traveling through each airport on the day of the attack.

"It takes as few as ten viral particles to infect a person, and there will be trillions of such particles floating through the air of the concourses. If we infect just one in a thousand, that's 200 new vectors or sources of contagion at each airport. Virtually all of them will die, but not before contributing to the exponential spread of the virus.

"Our jihadists will also board planes with a minimum capacity of 180 seats, and the infectivity rates among the passengers likewise should be very high. The shortest flight lasts two hours and the longest five. I'm projecting an infection rate of at least 20 percent, which means an additional 144 infectious people fanning out to all corners of the country."

"How quickly will it spread?" Sheik Mubarek Gilani, one of the more vituperative Council members, questioned.

"Each infected person will subsequently infect fifteen more people. So the 144 people infected on the planes will initially infect 2,160 new people. In the next wave of infection, they will theoretically infect 32,400 people. If the pandemic continues unabated, the next wave will involve 486,000 people—all traceable to the passengers on the four airplanes. And we haven't even begun to consider the massive number of infections contracted in the terminals."

"You are confident of these numbers?" asked Arun Khan, a swarthy man sitting closest to Al Hameed.

"As confident as I can be based upon stochastic models developed by the Russians to project the spread of a less virulent form of the disease. I can guarantee that within 180 days, two million Americans will be infected, 1.9 million will perish, and the virus will be reaching out to the far corners of the globe. The numbers will, in all likelihood, be vastly greater. That assumes that the virus spreads far and wide before quarantine measures are put in place.

"It will take twenty-four hours for the virus to incubate to the point of high infectivity, and an additional twenty-four to seventy-two hours for the person to become highly symptomatic. Death will follow quickly, primarily as a result of internal bleeding, but not before thousands of secondary infections could be started."

"What if health officials become aware of the virus shortly after its release?" the Council's representative from Yemen asked.

"If hundreds of patients flood local ERs, health officials will realize that some type of aberrant event is in progress. Of course, by then, infected passengers will have fanned out across the nation. ER doctors are not experts in exotic diseases—particularly ones that are not supposed to exist. So it is unlikely that they will recognize the disease in its early stages. There will be a delay as their Centers for Disease Control attempts to identify the pathogen."

"Is there a chance that the Americans will have an effective treatment?"

"Even if it is diagnosed in a timely fashion, little can be done to aid victims. The latest anti-virals, including Cidofovir, will be completely ineffective. At some point, they will attempt to use stockpiled vaccines, but that, too, will prove fruitless."

Khaled Mohammed, a Libyan whose girth approximated his height, interrupted. "We sit on the edge of the Western world, separated by mere miles of ocean. How quickly will this virus leap into our midst and begin to destroy our people?"

Al Hameed smiled briefly. "That is the great beauty of our creation. We are developing a vaccine that will protect those who have been inoculated against the virus."

Al-Bakr rose again, indicating with a quick gesture of his hand that Al Hameed was to remain standing. "We will call them the Chosen Ones. It is our sacred task, tonight, tomorrow, and perhaps the next day, to determine who will receive the vaccine—who will survive Armageddon—and we will not leave until that task is behind us."

Amar Dahesh, an Iraqi, was next to question Al Hameed: "Are we speaking of hundreds or thousands who will be spared? And what of the devoted millions who will succumb? How can we make such a sacrifice in the name of Allah?"

Al Hameed answered, "We are speaking of saving tens of millions of lives. As al-Bakr has told you, we are not yet ready to launch our plan. First, we must perfect the vaccine and then manufacture up to fifty million doses. Finally, there must be a plan for mass inoculations. We are well on the way to completing this work. Our efforts will ensure that fifty million holy warriors and their families will emerge from Armageddon unscathed. Billions of non-believers, however, will die!" he cried, with fist held high.

It was genocide and eugenics brought together in a way that not even Herman Göering could have imagined.

The men leapt to their feet, fists raised, and cheered.

Al Hameed shouted, "Death to America!" The cry was repeated by the group.

"Death to all infidels!" resonated through the room, before everyone resumed their seats.

Awad Rashid, a Sunni Syrian and one of the most powerful members of the Council, spoke to al-Bakr: "You have brought us a great gift tonight. We gave you our full trust based upon a vision. We didn't know if we would live to see the conquest of the West and the rise of our Caliphate. Tonight you have brought us hope that the vision is infinitely closer than we could have ever imagined. We praise you, Ibrahim, and your disciple, Al Hameed. We will work with you to identify the Chosen Ones."

Rashid turned to the group, surveying them man by man, as each nodded his head in agreement. It was unanimous.

After turning on the projector, al-Bakr began his presentation with a global view of his post Apocalyptic world. Areas shaded in bright red represented areas of mass casualties. Yellow signified regions with high levels of mortality but with a surviving population that would require conversion. Green denoted concentrations of the Chosen Ones. As he clicked the remote, an animation began illustrating how the destruction would grow exponentially before finally burning out.

Al-Bakr then brought up a more detailed map, where pins denoted centers for inoculation. Each was accompanied by a population statistic indicating the number of Chosen Ones targeted for vaccination.

Before bringing up the next slide, he intoned, "Unfortunately, there will be those who sacrifice their lives—not in direct confrontation with the West, but as unavoidable casualties of Armageddon." He pressed the remote, and small gray circles began to appear on the map, followed by larger ones. They dotted the U.S., Canada, Western Europe, Australia, and other areas where cells had been established. Adjacent to the largest of the circles were population estimates.

"We will make every effort to reach many of these cells, but I must confront you with the most onerous of potential scenarios."

Al Hameed tried to read the audience. It was difficult to discern whether their silence was a tribute to the level of planning that had been done or a comment on the projected consequences of a biological attack. Finally, Rashid spoke again. "Precisely how many true believers will be among the Chosen Ones?"

Al Hameed answered, "Our initial estimate of fifty million should be close. There are certain areas where our brothers and sisters may be difficult to reach in time to vaccinate—particularly in Indonesia. However, this very remoteness also means that the virus will be slow to spread, and that will afford us a grace period of weeks or months."

Upon a signal from al-Bakr, Al Hameed distributed briefing packets to the twelve attendees. "You will find everything that we've just covered in these briefing books. We will stop for the evening, but I suggest you spend several hours carefully reviewing the contents before you retire. We will reassemble in this room following morning prayers. We will then determine the degree to which we are in alignment, and whether we can return to our homes or have more work to do.

"Before we adjourn," al-Bakr added, "It is imperative that we maintain the element of surprise, for it is critical to our success. Secrets often unravel with time. This secret you must guard with your life." He paused to ensure that everyone was in agreement.

"We will not begin mass inoculations until the day the weapon is released. We cannot risk raising the specter of a biological threat in the minds of our enemies. The only exceptions will be for The Council and a handful of others integral to carrying out our mission. You will be vaccinated one month prior to the attack. Now, please go and study the material we have given you."

The attack was no longer a vision in the distant future.

CHAPTER SIXTEEN

Fort Belvoir, Virginia

"GOOD MORNING, COMMANDER." Sue Goodman, Deputy Director of the National Geospatial Intelligence Agency, welcomed her guest as he entered the conference room and took a seat. "I believe you know Dr. Elizabeth Wilkins from the CDC," Goodman gestured with her head towards the attractive blond seated across from Hart.

Hart's eyes remained fixed on Sue Goodman. "Yes, Ms. Goodman, Dr. Wilkins and I are acquainted," he responded without betraying any hint of the depth of their relationship.

"Well, then, let's begin. We have a situation that Dr. Wilkins and I believe to be worthy of your attention, Commander."

It was not the first time Goodman had briefed the commander on issues of grave importance to national security. Hart was well known among seasoned members of the intelligence community, especially those involved in bioterrorism. And he was hard to forget.

Goodman switched on a large, flat-screen monitor before continuing. "Two years ago, a snippet of intelligence set off major alarm bells within the intelligence community. One of the Agency's assets stationed in the northeastern industrial hub of Faisalabad reported that a pharmaceutical factory was being built on the grounds of an abandoned food manufacturing plant.

"As you know, Commander, history has taught us that such structures often bear an uncanny resemblance to chemical and biological warfare facilities; and some have proven to serve dual purposes, primarily in countries trying to evade the 1972 Convention on Chemical and Biological Weapons. Still, we were somewhat dubious."

Hart's question came fast. "Why the doubt?"

"Two reasons, Commander. The factory's sponsor is Rador Pharmaceuticals. That's a pretty stalwart firm to be involved in international espionage. Second, Pakistan is our ally."

"I'll grant you the first point. But, as for Pakistan's loyalty to the U.S., we both know better than to bank on that." Hart sat back in the chair, hands folded behind his head, wondering why the DDO had not mentioned the factory to him. He still had not made eye contact with Wilkins.

"Obviously, someone higher up agrees with you because we were told to initiate regular fly-bys using a high altitude long endurance RQ-4 Global Hawk."

He had his answer. Kahn was waiting for more definitive evidence before yanking his chain.

Hart was intimately familiar with the drone. It had proven its worth during Operation Inherent Resolve in Iraq, and he knew it would provide analysts at the National Geospatial Intelligence Agency with an on-demand view of the factory as it arose from the shell of a long-abandoned structure. If there was any hint of WMD, the Agency would be notified immediately.

Goodman continued, "The only problem was that, shortly after the walls were erected, a strategically placed metal roof obscured our view from space. As a result, everything within the facility was rendered opaque. Because we were blind to the inner workings of the factory, we were ordered to keep the drone on station."

"I trust your team came up with some way to peer into that factory or we wouldn't be meeting today," Hart suggested.

"Actually, we sat on our hands until the factory became operational. Then the team shifted its attention to analysis of the effluent gases coming from the factory's smokestacks. Using satellite-based infrared spectrometry, we were able to identify the principal organic and inorganic compounds being emitted, thus narrowing the range of deliverables being produced by the factory. Though a definitive evaluation could not be rendered, one thing was certain—they weren't manufacturing pharmaceuticals."

"And your confidence level in that conclusion?" Hart asked, knowing the stakes had just been raised considerably.

"Although I can't tell you specifically what is being manufactured in that factory, I can assure you with a ninety-five percent confidence level that it is not pharmaceuticals. However, there does appear to be a vaccine manufacturing process underway."

"What leads you to that conclusion?" Hart pressed.

Goodman turned to Liz Wilkins. "Dr. Wilkins, perhaps you'd like to explain?"

Goodman picked up on the unease between Hart and Wilkins. She didn't know what it was about, but she clearly saw Liz tense up before addressing the commander, and it wasn't because she was intimidated.

"Commander, one of the elements we identified in the effluent gases was mercury, which is a decomposition product of thimerosal. It seems logical to assume that the thimerosal is being used as an adjuvant in some type of vaccine."

Eyes on the screen, Hart asked, "Any thought about what type of vaccine, or whether they're brewing some new bug that should worry us?"

"No," Wilkins confessed.

"Let me get this straight. You are recommending that definitive action be taken based upon a fragment of data possibly related to an unknown vaccine hypothetically being produced in a suspected bio-warfare factory?"

Liz's mouth opened, but no words came out. Rushing to her defense, Goodman brought up the next slide: "It's more than a hunch, Commander. Here's a schematic of what we believe to be the inner workings of the factory. We've reverse-engineered the plant's layout based upon what we know about the physical footprint of the factory, combined with other data, of course. We are confident that our rendering is within a few linear feet of the actual layout. There's a copy in your briefing book."

"Okay. I'll give you credit for a nice schematic, Ms. Goodman, but what does it tell us?"

A second slide juxtaposed an image adjacent to the plant's schematic. She explained, "As you can see, Commander, aside from scale, these two drawings are virtually identical.

On the left is the Faisalabad factory and on the right is a VECTOR facility in Novosibirsk Oblast."

Hart's jaw tightened as the full impact of Goodman's conclusion registered. He turned once again to Liz. "Valikhanov."

Liz nodded her head in agreement.

"I'm sorry, I missed that, Commander. Did you say *Valikhanov,* as in *Beibut Valihanov?*" Goodman had obviously not been briefed.

"Yes. He disappeared some time ago and hasn't been seen since. He purportedly left VECTOR with one of their nastiest bugs. Tell me, Ms. Goodman, have you contacted Rador?"

"We had a local 'journalist' make the contact . . . looking for a lead on a business story."

"And?"

"They played along, saying it was a new division working hand-in-hand with Pakistan's Population Health Services to develop and manufacture vaccines and treatments for endemic viruses. They even offered to give the journalist a tour. It might explain the thimerosal, but not the parallel construction to VECTOR. No, Commander, I'm afraid they are just good at bluffing. It looks like you can stop searching for Valikhanov."

Goodman finished her briefing with a clear hand-off. "Commander, you are going to need to place someone on the ground inside that factory."

Inserting a covert operative into an environment where every employee would be rigorously scrutinized—let alone accomplish such a task in time to mitigate the potential threat—would be a Herculean challenge.

"So what you are telling me, Ms. Goodman, is that I need to identify an operative to send on a probable suicide mission deep into the heart of Pakistan, while ensuring that he can pass muster with the jihadi HR department." He added sardonically, "Anything else?"

Goodman gave him a wry smile. "I trust you've been in far tighter spots. Best of luck to you." She closed her portfolio and stood to leave. "We will be watching from above. Thank you both."

After Goodman left, Hart closed his leather portfolio, straightened his uniform, and walked out of the room. There were no good-byes.

CHAPTER SEVENTEEN

Washington, DC

THOUGH NOT A RELIGIOUS MAN BY NATURE, John Hart believed that only the hand of God could have caused a candidate to surface so rapidly in his search for a covert operative . . . even if that candidate was flawed.

Sayed Tamari was a young recruit, fresh out of graduate school at the University of Indiana. Though he spoke fluent Urdu and could blend effortlessly into the world of jihadists, Sayed was completely unproven in the field. That made him a tremendous risk to a vital mission. Before recommending him to the Deputy Director of Operations at the CIA, Hart needed to be convinced that Sayed was for real and that he was ready for deployment.

Hart and Sayed met in a cloistered office tucked away in the Walsh School of Foreign Service on the Georgetown campus, a short walk from the iconic spires of Healy Hall. The office was made available to the Agency as needed.

The night before Hart's arrival, a CIA team had waited for the janitorial crew to complete their rounds before slipping in and electronically sweeping the room. There were no windows in the office, so there was no glass from which the resonating sound waves could be read by a distant laser. It wasn't CIA headquarters, but it was pretty damn secure.

Hart introduced himself with a firm handshake and an unnerving stare, but Sayed didn't blink. Rather, he returned the look with equal intensity.

"We are taking a tremendous risk with you, Sayed."

"Why is that, Commander? Have I not been clear about my abdication of all that I was taught in the madrassa?"

"You've been quite clear," Hart said, holding up the transcripts from Sayed's initial debriefings. "But I want to hear your story, unfiltered by my colleagues' interpretations."

"I'm happy to speak with you, Commander, but I've spent hours being debriefed. Interrogated might be a better term. Most of that time, I was being polygraphed."

"Yes, I've read every word, but I need to know there's not a chance in hell that one corpuscle in your body remains loyal to your former masters. I need to know that, when I put the fate of this country in your hands, I'm not signing its death warrant. And finally, I want to be assured that I'm not going to have to hunt you down and kill you myself for betraying this organization. So, yes, you're going to answer my questions and ensure that I'm comfortable with the answers . . . or you can walk out that door."

"I'm sorry, Commander. I will be honored to share my story with you."

Sayed sat back in his chair, took a deep breath. "I grew up in Pakistan and was educated in a Saudi-funded madrassa near Quetta. It was a brutal place. Each day we were fed a diet of the most pernicious form of Islam you can imagine. Intolerance and hatred were prized virtues in my school—virtues that our teachers worked hard to inculcate in us, their Islamists in training."

Hart interjected, "It's my understanding that every madrassa follows a common core of teachings: *Hadith*—the teachings of Muhammad; *Fiqh*—Islamic law; and *Tafseer*—understanding and memorizing the Holy Quran. Are you saying that your madrassa was unique?"

"I am impressed Commander, even by your pronunciation. But I'm not talking about the core teachings, but of the true mission of my school—jihad.

"Beyond the holy books, we were required to read radical writing, like *The Management of Savagery, The Essentials of Making Ready for Jihad*, and *Introduction to the Jurisprudence of Jihad*. We learned that a war without mercy was needed to cleanse the planet of all but the faithful and restore it to a pristine state under which a new Caliphate could flourish. That's why our mentors brandished more than mere books. They carried Kalashnikovs and instructed us on how to assemble suicide vests."

Hart leaned forward until his elbows rested on the desk in front of Sayed. "No one has ever betrayed your school, nor any Saudi-funded madrassa, for that matter. The indoctrination is too profound, and the potential consequences too grave. So what makes you the lone exception among thousands of graduates, Sayed?"

Sayed turned his eyes away from the Commander and looked down at the floor.

"Two years before graduation, I was shown a series of photographs taken in the aftermath of a suicide bombing. The images showed bodies blown apart by the force of two kilograms of C4 packed tightly into a vest and surrounded by ball bearings and nails.

"Have you ever seen such images, Commander?" Sayed asked, his eyes once again riveted on Hart.

"I was in Mosul when a bomber struck. I was lucky; after crawling over bodies shattered by the explosion, I emerged with only a concussion and a broken eardrum. But I spent weeks trying to get the smell of blood out of my head. Does that answer your question?"

Nodding slowly, Sayed continued. "The first photograph showed partial limbs, fingers, and an ear scattered across the pavement a few feet from a blood-soaked torso. The second image revealed the distorted features of the bomber's head, which had been literally ripped from its body."

"And your point, Sayed?" Hart asked, though he knew from reading the dossier what would come next.

"Despite the blood and disfiguration, I realized this was not some unknown martyr but the remains of my brother, Kaleen."

"What did you say when you were shown these photographs?"

"At first, I said nothing. I was trying not to throw up. Then I realized that my teacher was staring at me . . . gauging my reaction to the news. If I didn't praise Allah upon learning of Kaleen's sacrifice, then I was an apostate. So I summoned what courage I could, looked directly into the soulless eyes of my teacher, and proclaimed: 'Kaleen is in heaven surrounded by seventy-two virgins. Allah Akbar!'"

"How did your teacher respond?" Hart asked.

"Apparently he was pleased. He told me that I had learned well and would someday follow in Kaleen's footsteps.

He reminded me that God tests us through loss and suffering and that I needed to remain strong and endure the
pain. Then he sent me home to my family."

"And then?"

"Once I was out of sight of the madrassa, I turned
off of the main street into a narrow alley. After a few
steps, I dropped to my knees and threw up in the gutter. I
retched until my stomach stopped heaving; then I wiped
my mouth on my sleeve and spit out the last remnants of
what had roiled from my belly. Is that enough detail for you,
Commander? I want to be sure you get a clear picture of
what it feels like to learn that your older brother, someone
you loved and looked up to, was eviscerated by a bomb."

"Got it, Sayed, but I already have my own picture. You
see, my brother was working on the ninety-first floor of the
south tower of the World Trade Center on the morning of
September 11, 2001."

"I'm sorry, Commander. It seems that we have both
suffered great loss at the hands of extremists."

"The difference, Sayed, is that I made a vow to my
brother to never let such a tragic event be repeated—not
on my watch."

"We both made vows, Commander, and we each seek
to strike a common enemy."

"I hope that is true, Sayed."

Sayed continued. "As I neared our home, I could hear
my mother crying out in grief. Opening the door, I saw
her huddled in a corner. My father knelt next to her, his
head slumped, an arm draped over her shoulder. Tears
were streaming down his cheeks. I had never before seen
my father cry.

"Later, as we were burying my brother's remains, I saw the funeral processions for the victims of Kaleen's bombing. *Shia apostates*, I had been taught, but the people looked no different than my family.

"Such thoughts, of course, were dangerous. My survival depended on not betraying my emerging contempt for jihad. I had to complete my education, bide my time, and hope that Allah would show me a path out of this twisted world of hate."

Sayed told a hell of a story, and Hart prayed it was true—that Kaleen's death had truly catalyzed such a profound transformation in this young man, who had once been a jihadist in training. His mind flashed back to Cory.

Cory had been the true intellectual all-star in the family. The two brothers had traveled very different paths. Cory Hart had become a highly successful investment analyst in a major brokerage firm. With three beautiful young daughters, an adoring wife, and a house in the Hamptons, Cory was living the life. Until one beautiful September day in 2001—a day marked by a cloudless, radiant blue sky in New York.

Hart had cobbled together the story of his brother's last day on earth based upon a disparate collection of facts, the most telling of which was Cory's cell phone call to his wife at 9:17 AM, forty-two minutes before the collapse of the south tower.

After dropping off his girls, Cory ascended the elevators to the ninety-first floor. Just as he sat down at his desk, the building shuddered violently, driving Cory to his knees. As he fell, his head struck the edge of the large mahogany desk, knocking him unconscious. When he came to, he struggled to regain his bearings. There was no power in the building. The sickly sweet smell of jet fuel was quickly permeating the air.

He called his wife, Catherine, to tell her what was happening. The call lasted barely a minute—Cory promising to call her again as soon as he was out of the tower. But Catherine never heard from him. Less than an hour later, the building collapsed, burying Cory and thousands of other innocent New Yorkers under tons of rubble.

Hart blinked slowly, wincing at the pain he felt every time he thought about Cory. It wasn't the first time he had lost someone he loved. Bringing himself back to the task at hand, Hart picked up Sayed's transcript, rapidly turning the pages, before focusing on the next set of events.

"How did you end up in Indianapolis?" he asked.

"I had another encounter with my teacher—the one who showed me the photographs of the bombing shortly before graduation. He told me that our family was being sent to America, where I was to continue my education. But that was only part of my mission. I was also told that I would become part of a vast network of sleeper cells—radical jihadists embedded within the fabric of American society who awaited orders to attack their host.

"When I asked how we would survive in a new country with no money, no relatives, and no way to make a living, I was informed that the madrassa would provide some money—not much, but enough for my father to start over. In return, the day would come when I would be instructed to take the proverbial dagger of Islam and pierce the heart of the Great Satan. He admonished me that, though I might not hear from the madrassa for a year, two, or even five, they would always be watching me.

"Two months after graduation, my family moved to Indianapolis. As instructed, I enrolled at the University of Indiana in Bloomington, a forty-five-minute drive from the two-bedroom apartment my parents had rented."

"That had to be a hell of a transition," Hart acknowledged, as he thumbed through the pages in Sayed's file. After pausing to read one of them, he instructed, "Tell me about Basheera and Jaleel."

"As you can imagine, Commander, Muslims were in short supply at IU, and not particularly welcomed. I had very few friends for a very long time. Then, during my junior year, I met a woman in my Islamic Studies class. She was of Syrian descent, her parents having immigrated when she was a small child. Her name was Basheera.

"You've seen her pictures, Commander. I'm sure you would agree that she is quite beautiful."

Hart had not only seen her pictures, but had met her on more than one occasion. He recalled her long, shimmering black hair and luminous green eyes. She was not someone easily forgotten.

"Yes, Sayed, she is beautiful." His tone had softened.

"We did not have the easiest of courtships. Remember, Commander, I was new to this country and its customs. When I saw Basheera, I was overwhelmed by her beauty but angered by her abdication of Muslim traditions. I wanted her to cover her bare skin, to shield her head. I finally worked up the courage to ask her why she did not cover her head and protect her virtue."

"I'm sure that went over swimmingly," Hart said, his sarcasm not lost on Sayed.

"She was shocked. She asked what gave me the right to question how she practiced her faith."

"And you told her . . . ?"

"I told her that the Quran was not subject to her interpretation. It was the direct word of God being communicated to her and that she sounded more like an apostate than a Muslim."

"Another big hit, I take it?"

"Surprisingly, she was not rattled, but seemed to find humor in my passion, however misguided it may have been. She admonished me to 'make some radical changes in the way I thought,' and then walked away. Fortunately, despite its chilly start, our friendship blossomed. I learned that, while she was assimilated in many ways, Basheera remained traditional in others. For this, I was grateful to Allah.

"Basheera opened up a new world for me. She introduced me to her friends from the Islamic Studies department. Among them, Jaleel was my favorite."

"Why Jaleel, Sayed?" Hart raised his chin and looked down his nose, trying to ferret out any discrepancy in Sayed's story.

"Because he reminded me of Kaleen. He was passionate about his beliefs—whether he was debating the fallacious theory that American imperialism fomented the rise of Islamic extremism or proselytizing about the merits of fighting radical Islamic terrorism."

"And he convinced you to join that fight," Hart said almost as a question.

"There were rumors about Jaleel . . . that he had ties to the CIA. Most people didn't take them seriously."

"But you did."

"Yes. When I asked him, he laughed at first, as did Basheera. When he saw that I was not laughing, he asked if such a relationship would end our friendship. I assured him that it would not. I asked if he was afraid that being affiliated with the CIA made him a target."

"How did he respond?" Hart asked.

"He told me that he lived one day at a time and that fear was a relative thing. He told me that he had far less fear of assassination than of having terrorists continue to pursue an unholy caliphate. I asked if I could join him in his efforts."

"That was a bit impetuous, wasn't it?"

"Funny, that's exactly the word Jaleel used. I told him that I was no more impetuous than he was methodical in his recruitment of me during my undergraduate and graduate years at the university. The point was made."

"Did Jaleel explain the risks to you?"

"He tried to dissuade me. He told me that I was entering a world far removed from the safe confines of the university. If I failed in this world, it was not a bad grade I would receive, but the sharp edge of a knife pressed against my throat seconds before it was slit. He applauded my enthusiasm but worried about my naiveté."

"He's in good company," Hart added.

"Commander, I endured the fanaticism of a madrassa. I saw my brother blown to pieces. Naïve? Perhaps in some ways, but certainly not in others."

"I think that will do for this morning, Sayed." Hart leaned back in his chair.

"Did I pass, Commander?"

"That's not my call. It's up to the Deputy Director of Operations."

"But he will listen to your recommendation, Commander."

Throughout the lengthy interview, Hart had sought to uncover any hint that Sayed's renunciation of his former extremist views was a sham. He needed to have confidence that there was zero possibility of Sayed serving two masters. The Agency had been gravely wounded by double agents in the past. Ames and Hanssen came to Hart's mind. Hart prayed he was making the right decision.

"My recommendation will be that you represent our best option."

CHAPTER EIGHTEEN

Faisalabad, Pakistan

A GROUP OF MEN, most of whom were Pakistani, was packed into a narrow, subterranean observation room deep beneath the streets of Faisalabad. It was a quiet refuge from the busy streets above . . . a place where secretive work could be carried out without fear of detection.

The observation room was adjacent to a medical isolation unit. A one-way mirror, hidden behind a curtain, allowed researchers to view the subjects of their medical experiments while remaining safely concealed.

Al Hameed turned to Valikhanov. "We will see how your test turned out." He then pulled steadily on a cord until the full expanse of glass was exposed, and the isolation room came into clear view.

Nine bodies lay in front of him—men who varied in age from mere teenagers to old men whose beards had grown white. They were face-up in their hospital beds, anchored to the mattresses by thick leather restraints at their wrists. Death had not been a peaceful passage. Rather, their contorted faces spoke to the horror of their final moments. Some of the victims had died with their eyes open and mouths agape, as if screaming in agony for an end that could not come soon enough.

A smile burst forth on his normally somber face. Giddy with joy, Al Hameed raised a clenched fist to his mouth and bit hard into his flesh until a small drop of blood appeared against his skin.

The bodies were in varying stages of decomposition, and all were covered with petechiae—small, purple spots of blood that peppered the skin. Some patients displayed large, dark bruises. The whites of their eyes had turned a reddish brown, and trails of blood drained from their noses and ears. All but one showed signs of extensive internal hemorrhage.

Al Hameed's eyes swept left to right, assessing the carnage, until they locked on a tenth man. He had emerged from some place deep below consciousness and was struggling to free his hands from the restraints. Al Hameed, who was standing mere inches behind the mirror, jerked back reflexively as the man's chest heaved upward, his neck straining as if to glimpse the monster that had inflicted such suffering. For a moment, Al Hameed felt the man's eyes lock on him, forgetting that the victim could see nothing more than a reflection. Then the patient's lips began to quiver before parting in a raspy plea for help.

Yet the only sound that could be heard was the insistent hiss of air being sucked into the negatively pressurized isolation room to prevent the escape of infectious agents. An even higher rate of exhaust would carry all of the viral particles out of the room, but only after first passing through a HEPA filter and then being exposed to ultraviolet irradiation.

The isolation unit had been built to exacting standards by Valikhanov. Neither he nor Al Hameed could afford any mistakes—particularly the accidental release of a deadly virus. He knew that something as simple as a defective filter could unmask his program, much as it had revealed a covert Soviet bio-weapons manufacturing plant at Sverdlosk in 1979.

There, a technician's mistake allowed anthrax particles to escape into the night sky. Those fine, invisible spheres of death, some as small as five microns in diameter, lodged deep within the lungs of employees working the night shift at adjacent Soviet factories. With the warmth of human bodies for incubation, the bacteria began to replicate. One hundred and five fatalities later, despite the relentless efforts of the KGB to cover up the tragedy, the world took notice.

The United Islamic State would not be so careless. The timing and location of the planned viral release was exquisitely important, and they were still months away from being ready for that world-changing event.

The ceaseless wheeze of the air compressor brought Al Hameed's mind back to the isolation room, back to the tenth man. Even though the air in the room was exchanged at a rate of twelve times per hour, he knew that the pervasive stench of death engulfed this man like a putrid fog.

The lone survivor appeared to be in his early thirties, though it was difficult to tell through the layer of filth covering him. He lay bathed in his own waste.

With a sudden shift in his mood, Al Hameed roared, "Who is this man, and what gives him the audacity to survive?"

Valikhanov stirred uncomfortably.

"He is one of the men we took from the market. His name is Kaisal."

"You did not answer my question!"

"I promised you a ninety percent mortality rate, not one hundred," Valikhanov reminded him.

Al Hameed drew a long, audible breath through his nose and released it slowly in sync with the sound of the compressor, as if to release the tension building in his body.

"How did you get him to cooperate?"

"The man lost his job months ago and could no longer feed his family. With a wife and three young daughters, he was desperate for work," Beibut answered.

"What did you promise him?" Al Hameed asked.

"We offered him a week's wages in exchange for participating in our vaccine research. We told him that it was safe and that he would he leave wealthier and healthier."

Al Hameed paused, reflecting on the virus's ninety percent kill ratio. One hundred percent was his goal, but he kept his thoughts to himself, realizing that ninety percent was good enough.

"Allah Akbar!" he said, thrusting his arms high in the air. "Allah has given us the sword with which to slay the infidels!" A chorus praising Allah erupted among the men behind him.

As the reverberations of the chant faded, Al Hameed turned towards the window and focused his attention on Kaisal. Reaching up, he grasped the cord and slowly closed the drapes. He watched as Kaisal, whose pleas for help had gone unanswered, relinquished the last threads of hope and sank into his bed.

Perhaps it would be one hundred percent after all.

CHAPTER NINETEEN

CIA Headquarters, McLean, Virginia

THE DEPUTY DIRECTOR OF OPERATIONS did not share Commander Hart's confidence in Sayed, nor in the mission. He questioned Sayed's purported conversion from a radical Islamist to an Agency operative, he objected to his profound lack of training and experience, and he thought his cover was weak. Furthermore, he could not understand how Hart could plan a mission in which key elements were out of his control, including the need for Sayed to be hired by the factory.

His tone sharply critical, Marvin Kahn addressed Hart. "John, you're usually far more buttoned down than this. I don't get it. You're asking me to sign an order authorizing the insertion of an operative whose very veracity we question, not to mention the deep concerns we harbor regarding his skills and survivability. And as though that's not enough, there are no guarantees that Sayed will even get into the factory."

"I understand your concerns, Sir, and I share them," Hart began, but Kahn cut him off.

"Then what the hell are you doing? We can't send this guy in there!" Kahn exclaimed with unbending conviction.

Kahn had come up through the ranks, starting his career at the Agency shortly after the Iran Contra debacle. He had survived nearly impossible situations in the field and was not going to let the poor judgment of one of his agents undermine his division.

But Hart was not about to capitulate. "We have to, Sir. You've seen the report from NGA. The factory is operational, and God knows what they are churning out. Before we learn the hard way, we need an asset on the ground to confirm our suspicions and to provide the justification for intervention."

"Then get me someone with experience, someone in whom we can have confidence!"

"I'd like to, Sir, but that's a tall order on short notice. We both know that time is of the essence, and finding someone with the characteristics required for this mission is almost impossible. I spent hours considering the risk before making my recommendation to you."

"I'm sure you did, Commander," Kahn reluctantly acknowledged.

Hart continued: "Not only are we working against time on the potential deployment of a biological weapon, but we assume that the factory will be fully staffed soon, based upon their recruitment activities. If we're going to stand a chance of placing an operative on the factory floor, they need to be standing in line now, hoping to get a job."

Kahn picked up his pen. "I'm going to sign the order, Commander, based solely on my confidence in you. Let's pray your intuition is right."

Minutes after walking out of the DDO's office, Hart called Sayed on a secure line.

"Good morning, Sayed."

"Good morning, Commander. I hope you bring good news."

"I'll leave that up to you to determine. You said you wanted a chance to avenge Kaleen's death. Well, we are going to give it you. Meet me at the Agency tomorrow morning at 0900 hours. I'll brief you then."

The next morning, Hart wasted no time bringing Sayed up to speed. "We have a potential situation emerging in Faisalabad. It involves a newly constructed pharmaceutical factory that appears to be producing more than just aspirin. There's mounting evidence to suggest that biological agents are being produced—as well as vaccines." Hart dropped a high res image from the Global Hawk in front of Sayed. "We've been down this path before, during Mr. Tenet's tenure. I'm sure you were briefed on the Agency's grand blunder relative to Iraq's purported WMD program."

"Yes, everyone in the Muslim world is aware of it."

"What you don't know is that the Agency was forced to manipulate its own intelligence to support the recommendations of a group of neocons hell-bent on the destruction of Iraq. Some of us believe it was the unholy trinity of Rumsfeld, Wolfowitz, and Cheney that fabricated the myth of WMD in the Middle East, not the CIA. Sayed, not all the bad guys are Islamic terrorists. We've got our fair share. That opinion stays in this room.

"What we are talking about today is very different. No one is seeking to gain political clout or trumpeting the need to invade a sovereign nation due to the perceived presence of WMD. This one is off the radar screen and will remain a compartmentalized mission on a need-to-know basis."

"What do you need from me? I am no expert in biological weapons," Sayed said quietly.

"I need you on the inside of that factory, working hand-in-hand with the jihadists and finding the proof we need to justify intervention. According to your file, Sayed, you were being trained for an eventual suicide mission. Well, this may be it . . . at least you will be dying for a just cause."

"Commander Hart, we all believe our causes are just at the time. I was fortunate to be given a window through which to gain a very different perspective on my early training, though at the cost of my brother's life. I have no interest in dying, but I do have a passionate hatred for what the jihadists have done to my religion, my family, and my country."

"Is that hatred sufficient motivation for you to get inside the factory and get the critical information we need?" Hart awaited the response that would determine if his mission was a go or a bust.

"Yes, Commander Hart, and, God willing, I will get out. Your help will be appreciated in that regard."

"What will you say to your former masters, who believe they are still pulling your strings, Sayed? How will you explain your return to Pakistan?"

"I will tell them that I need a break from this despicable country and from Basheera. I will tell them that I have grown lax in my practices, and that time spent in Pakistan will reinvigorate my passion for jihad. They will welcome me back with open arms. Call it a sabbatical, if you will.

And if I happen to find a job at a certain factory, they will consider it to be Allah's will."

"Good. Their reference may prove critical in getting a job at the factory. Security will be the overriding concern with anyone they hire. We've learned that they are accepting job applications one day a week—on Mondays. You'll be arriving on Saturday. Get situated, and then be damn sure you get yourself over to that factory first thing Monday morning."

"What guarantees do we have that I will be hired?" Sayed asked the Commander.

"None," Hart responded abruptly.

Hart handed Sayed a manila envelope. Inside was a plane ticket to Faisalabad, a little over four thousand dollars—an amount that Sayed could have reasonably saved working part-time—and the name of a contact that he was to memorize and then destroy. He would be leaving in two days.

"What do I say to Basheera?" he asked.

Hart lowered his eyes.

Before he could speak, Sayed said, "I know, Commander. I realized it a very long time ago. It was simply too fortuitous that Basheera and Jaleel were friends."

"Does she know that you know?" Hart questioned.

"She knows that I joined Jaleel in his efforts but not that I am aware of the role she played as his co-conspirator in recruiting me. I'd prefer to believe that she truly fell in love with me, not that I was an assignment.

"So, for now, it will remain the unspoken secret between us."

"Tell her you cannot discuss why you are going abroad. She understands compartmentalization. If she is asked about your departure, she should intimate that each of you needed time apart to reassess things before committing to spending your lives together. If pressed, she can speak to your yearning for the traditional beliefs in which you were raised," Hart advised. "Sometimes it's not wise to get too close in our line of work, but I trust you know that," he added.

A small voice in his mind chastised Hart for having the audacity to offer advice on personal relationships. Love interests were not Hart's strong suit. Though his romances began with intensity, they dimmed quickly. The invincible SEAL had a fatal flaw—he failed to understand the toll that secrets take when kept from loved ones. His secrets weren't about infidelity or other transgressions, but they were barriers nonetheless to the intimacy needed to nourish a relationship.

Hart almost always emerged unscathed, but Liz Wilkins was the sole exception. He had fallen head over heels for her and was deeply wounded when Liz ended their relationship. She had grown tired of the incessant secrets surrounding her lover's life. Hart inhabited a very different world—one that required illusion, deception, even killing in order to maintain peace and security. Hart, who was first and foremost a soldier, accepted this reality without question. But Liz did not.

Reflecting on that meeting, Hart thought about the sorrowful look in Liz's eyes as he walked out without uttering a word. Perhaps he was not the only one who was suffering.

Snapping back to the moment, Hart gave Sayed a final word of advice: "Your flight leaves for Pakistan in less than 48 hours. If you feel compelled to return to Indianapolis, I suggest you get on a flight today. Take care of your business, and then move on. This mission must stay on schedule. I'm sure Basheera will be waiting for you when you return."

"You mean, *if* I return," Sayed corrected Hart.

"No, Sayed, I mean when we bring you home."

CHAPTER TWENTY

Faisalabad, Pakistan

SAYED ENDURED AN INTERMINABLY LONG FLIGHT from Indianapolis to Faisalabad, all the while crammed into a coach seat and unable to sleep. He finally arrived, exhausted and wanting nothing more than to crash for a few hours. But he knew there was work to be done. At the top of his list was finding a decent place to live.

Sayed took out his laptop, logged on to Zameem.com, and began to search for an apartment to rent. He found a small apartment on Canal Road in Farooqabad. It wasn't the best of locations, but the price was right—12,000 rupees a month, about $115 U.S. And though substandard when compared with American apartments, Sayed knew it would more than meet his needs. Most importantly, it wouldn't raise suspicions.

The next imperative was to secure a job at the pharmaceutical factory. It could be any job, as long as it got him under the roof and with access to the inner workings of the plant.

On Monday morning, Sayed arose shortly after 5:30 AM, eager to be the first in line at the factory. After a quick breakfast, he walked twenty minutes, arriving at the factory at 6:15. People were already queuing up at the gate. A security guard told them to be patient; it would be 7:30 before HR started processing them.

At 7:30 AM, all of that day's applicants were shown into a conference room near the entrance to the building. None of the factory's inner workings were visible . . . just a corridor leading to a second set of doors. Sayed took a seat in the middle of a long table and began filling out the application. It was surprisingly detailed, particularly the section labelled *Personal History*. Thirty minutes passed before Sayed reached the final section requesting references.

As Hart suggested, Sayed printed the name and title for the headmaster of his madrassa, Dr. Wazir. He had emailed the man prior to departing the states, informing him, in detail, of his plan to return to Pakistan. Dr. Wazir was empathetic to Sayed's need to reconnect with his people but was also clear about his expectation that Sayed would return to the States after an appropriate sojourn. The madrassa had invested too much in the young man to take him out of play for long. Sayed understood and agreed.

When he was finished with the application, Sayed handed it to a staff person. He was told that he would receive a call within the week if an appropriate position was open.

Two days later, Sayed's cell phone rang. A man introduced himself as the director of human resources and told Sayed he wished to interview him. He asked Sayed to come in that afternoon.

At 3 PM Sayed appeared at the factory, where a guard escorted him to an office. For the first time, he was able to get a view of the factory floor, although the unfamiliar

machinery gave him little clue as to what was being manufactured. As they approached the office, a man in a
business suit greeted Sayed. He explained that he, not the
director of HR, would be conducting the interview and
apologized for any confusion. When Sayed asked him his
title, he answered, "Director of Security."

A wave of panic shot through Sayed at the thought that
his cover may have somehow been blown.

The man lit an offensive smelling Turkish cigarette,
then leaned in towards Sayed. "I've looked at your work
history, Sayed, and you've never worked in a manufacturing
plant. Nor do you have any medical or scientific training.
It looks like the only place you've worked is a restaurant.
So perhaps you can explain what has brought you to the
doors of our factory."

Working to slow his breathing, Sayed responded, "You
are correct. My parents moved our family to America after
I graduated from our local madrassa. They believed that
there were greater opportunities for the family abroad.
My father opened a small restaurant in Indianapolis called
Chacha Khan. Thanks to Allah, it has done very well." Sayed
paused. "My father needed my help, but he insisted that I
go to college. So I attended the university near our home.
I returned home on most weekends to help out."

"Waiting tables is a humbling profession. Did you enjoy
your work?"

"Most of my family's patrons were kind, with their words
and with their money. A few, however, were pigs—glad
to consume my family's food but intolerant of our faith."

"Why have you returned to Pakistan, Sayed?" The man
asked, stubbing out his half-burned cigarette.

"I felt I was losing my way. I needed to reconnect to my people, to my faith."

"Is there anything you are running away from, Sayed?"

Sayed felt his heartbeat accelerating.

"Only the decadence that surrounded me," he replied earnestly.

The man put down the folder holding Sayed's application and closed it before speaking. "Your conviction is admirable, and I trust that your faith will be replenished, as will your appreciation for the values you were taught. But still, I must ask: Why should we hire you when there are many other people, just as hungry as you, but more qualified?"

"Because I will work harder than any man on your team."

"Words come easily to you, Sayed, but can you live up to your promises?"

"I suggest you ask my references." Sayed pointed to the first name he had listed as a reference—Dr. Wazir.

The director glanced at where Sayed was pointing and then said, "We've already spoken with Dr. Wazir. He thinks quite highly of you. He indicated that you were a man we could trust. He also told us that you would be returning to the United States at some point in the future."

"That is true, but not for some time. I have signed a year's lease on my apartment. I hope that will provide you with some assurance of my intent to remain in Pakistan for months to come."

"Dr. Wazir and I have known each other for many years, though it has been quite some time since I was in Quetta. His word means a great deal to me."

The man then shifted from questions to statements, signaling that the interrogation was over. Sayed's heart rate began to slow for the first time since the beginning of the interview.

"We will start you out on the factory floor. You will be paid 80,000 PKR each month. If you perform as promised, there will be other opportunities. If you wish to take the job, I need your answer now."

Not wanting to appear overly eager, Sayed responded, "I do not wish to seem ungrateful, but may I take just a moment to reflect on your gracious offer?"

"I will return in fifteen minutes. I will expect your answer then," the Director acquiesced. "May I ask, Sayed, why the hesitation?"

"It's just that the salary is less than I had hoped. I trust that my hard work will be rewarded and greater opportunities will await me."

"That much I can promise you. We will review your performance in ninety days." Pausing at the door, the director asked, "Do you still need a moment to consider the opportunity?"

"No. Thank you. I accept your gracious offer." Sayed smiled and extended his hand to consummate the deal.

"We will expect you to report on Thursday. It's the first day of the month. You do understand that you will be living on our campus."

"No one mentioned that to me." Caught off guard, Sayed hoped his voice did not betray his dismay.

"All employees live in factory-provided housing adjacent to the facility. It is one of our benefits that helps offset what you deemed a less than ideal salary. There is a cafeteria where you can take your meals. All at no cost," the director explained.

"And what if I wish to maintain my apartment?"

"Then you will need to find a different job."

"But what of my rent? I just signed my lease two days ago."

"I understand, but I believe it's a job you want . . . not a small apartment. We will speak with your landlord. For now, assume there is no issue and that you will be released from your obligation. Are we still on track for you to start Thursday?"

"Yes. And thank you. I am indeed grateful."

"Before you leave, there is some paperwork you must complete for HR. Someone will be in shortly. When you arrive on Thursday, you will be issued photo identification. Never be without it, Sayed. We take security very seriously. Do you understand?"

"Yes, but why are such precautions necessary?" Sayed asked.

"You are a bright man, Sayed. Have you not heard of corporate espionage? We develop and manufacture unique drugs and vaccines. The formulations are worth hundreds of millions of rupees. There are many companies that would pay dearly for our secrets. Is there more you wish to know?"

"No."

So began a trickle of information flowing through a circuitous channel from Sayed to Commander Hart. Both men knew they had to proceed with extreme caution or face discovery, which could result in Sayed's beheading. More likely, his betrayed compatriots would find such punishment to be too quick and merciful a death. Sayed had seen videos of UIS's more heinous solutions, including burning a man alive as he thrashed about in a steel cage.

Sayed's work at the factory was menial. He monitored the temperature of what were referred to as reactor vessels, to ensure that the broth-like liquid contained within them remained in a steady state. Respirators and Tyvek worksuits were required when entering the factory floor, a precaution that Sayed pretended not to understand. Nor did he appear to understand the need for a vaccination, particularly one he was told might make him ill. Indeed, it had—Sayed spiked a high fever and missed two days of work.

When he asked for an explanation, he was told that workers could easily contaminate the drugs during production, particularly if they carried certain common infections. Such an accident could close down the factory. And if that happened, Sayed and everyone else would be searching for a job.

Once on the job, it took little time for Sayed to identify Al Hameed and Valikhanov, whose photos had been shared by Hart during his briefing. Like a pair of magnesium flares, the two names that appeared in Sayed's report brilliantly illuminated the threat facing Commander Hart.

Until the meeting with Sue Goodman and Liz Wilkins, Hart had never considered the two men coming together like some unimaginably horrible chimera. As information continued to accrue over the ensuing months, a clear image of what was happening under the roof of the pharmaceutical factory began to emerge. But before he could act, he needed proof that weapons of mass destruction were being assembled in the purported pharmaceutical factory. That meant obtaining biological samples revealing the precise nature of the threat.

That became Sayed's pressing assignment—to procure a small amount of the pathogen for safe transport to the

CDC. In addition to the ever-present threat of discovery, he would risk exposure to whatever pathogen was being cultivated. Hart assumed it was hemorrhagic smallpox. But Sayed never fulfilled the mission.

One day, shortly after beginning his shift, Sayed was called to the plant office by the foreman—a burly, dark-skinned Pakistani whose thick eyebrows merged in the middle of his forehead. Two other men were present. Sayed recognized one of them as the Director of Security with whom he had first interviewed.

Before his boss could utter a word, Sayed spoke up nervously: "Am I in trouble?"

"Should you be?" asked the foreman.

"No, I do my job well. I don't complain."

"You do complain about one thing," the foreman countered, "You complain about the imperialistic West and the need for its total destruction. Do you not realize who consumes our drugs? Without America, how would we exist?'"

Sayed hung his head, not knowing how to respond. The precarious game of deception required of field agents was still so new to him. Yet the assignment, as well as his life, depended upon how he managed the next few seconds with this man.

Sayed raised his eyes and looked directly at the foreman. It was a look imbued with hatred. "The Americans are imperialistic pigs. I will not apologize for praying for their destruction. If that means that I can no longer work for you, so be it!" he said defiantly.

The foreman returned the stare, letting Sayed dangle for a few seconds before bursting into laughter.

"When we first met, you said you wanted to be rewarded for your hard work," the Director of Security reminded him. "How would you like a very big promotion?"

"I don't understand," Sayed confessed.

"We are all on the same side, Sayed. We share your contempt of the West and work towards its destruction. Before I say more, you must know that the promotion of which I speak requires an oath of silence. If you betray it, it is more than just your job that you will lose. Do you understand?" the director asked.

"Yes, I understand. But why does Rador insist upon an oath? Does not my work itself speak to my dedication?"

"It is not Rador for whom you work, Sayed."

Sayed shook his head. "What? Once again, I am confused. I was hired by Rador Pharmaceuticals."

"You have been working for the United Islamic State. And the position to which you are being promoted is critical to our mission."

Sayed was told he would remain at the factory for a period of time before being sent to a training camp. From that point on, the details were fuzzy . . . but he knew it would be a one-way journey in the name of Allah.

Hart soon learned from Sayed's handler in Faisalabad that his deeply planted asset was being sent to a remote area in Pakistan for training—presumably in anticipation of an operation. That meant they were close to deployment. If they were going to strike the United States, it would come within days or weeks of the completion of Sayed's training.

Hart moved quickly to apprise the Deputy Director of Operations of the information coming out of Faisalabad. The commander explained how his intelligence findings had advanced from suspecting that a bio-warfare factory was under construction in Faisalabad to the visual confirmation of Beibut Valikhanov and Ahmed Al Hameed on site at a probable bio-warfare facility. Hart stated that, though they had yet to procure a sample of whatever was being brewed within the factory, immediate action was required to prevent a potentially catastrophic release of a pathogenic agent against the West.

Hart was shocked by the Deputy Director of Operation's under-reaction to the evidence suggesting an attack was imminent. Kahn informed Hart that he was not about to raise the alarm to a presidential level without irrefutable proof of the presence of a WMD. It was up to Hart to assemble a team capable of providing such evidence of a clear and present danger.

CHAPTER TWENTY-ONE

CIA Headquarters, McLean, Virginia

HART COULD BE STUNNINGLY IMPATIENT. It didn't arise from intemperance. It was simply a by-product of his intellect. The clock speed on his internal processors ran at a blistering pace. Sometimes he could muster a modicum of tolerance, but not now—not with the threat they were facing.

Everyone arrived promptly for the 10 AM briefing scheduled in a windowless conference room on Sublevel 1 of the old building at Langley. One person was lingering by the door as Hart approached.

Stepping directly into the commander's path, Liz Wilkins addressed him. "I'm surprised you put me on the team. You couldn't even look me in the eye at Sue Goodman's briefing." Her tone was hurt and angry.

Grasping her arm firmly, Hart steered Liz clear of the conference room. Once they were out of earshot, he responded: "How I feel about you is irrelevant. I picked the best people I could find. No one understands the magnitude of the threat we are facing better than you."

"Is that an attempt at an apology, Commander?"

He squeezed her arm gently before letting go, then looked directly into her eyes. With a brief smile, he gestured towards the conference room, "Yes it is, and for right now it's the best I can do. Now, shall we?"

Once inside, Hart made a quick visual sweep of the room to confirm that everyone was present. He pressed a key on his laptop and the wall-dominating image of the Agency logo faded from view. In its place was a slide that read:

Operation Wildfire
TS/Compartmentalized

"Good morning. The briefing you are about to receive describes an existential threat to the United States and its allies around the world. It is a threat of unprecedented magnitude and one that requires an almost instantaneous response."

There was a moment of silence. The tension in the room was palpable.

"Some time ago, our colleagues at National Geospatial Intelligence Agency identified a suspicious structure taking form in Faisalabad." An image appeared on the screen of a large pit with a supporting foundation arising from its depths.

"A high-flying bird was feeding NGA analysts images of an emerging factory . . ." Hart clicked the remote to show a partially completed factory. ". . . Until a roof went up, obscuring whatever was happening under its cover." He clicked it one more time, revealing the gray metal roof.

"Here is a street-level view of the facility. As you can see, an 11-foot security fence, topped by razor wire, encircles it. The only access is through a gate guarded by a heavily armed security detail. This place is more secure than some federal prisons.

"When the factory finally became operational, NGA started monitoring the effluent gases from the smokestack. And, to no one's surprise, the proclaimed pharmaceutical factory did not appear to be in the drug business.

"Though we suspected a bio-warfare factory, we couldn't be certain without someone on the ground. It took us a while to identify a covert operative with the requisite bona fides to pass muster with paranoid jihadists. The good news is that we found him. The bad news is he's found an abundance of evidence to confirm our worst suspicions.

"Our operative identified two men associated with the factory." Hart brought up a picture of a heavy-set man in a Russian uniform. "The first, Beibut Valikhanov, was a rock star in the former Soviet Bioprepart. He was last employed by Russia's VECTOR but disappeared under mysterious circumstances. You should note that Valikhanov is a devout Muslim originally from Kazakhstan."

He then projected a photo of a man who appeared to suffer from something akin to albinism, which made his Arabic features all the more dramatic. A buzz suddenly engulfed the room; it appeared that the man needed no introduction. "I trust you all recognize Ahmed Al Hameed," to which Hart received a flurry of nods.

"Apparently he has partnered with Valikhanov to usher in some kind of unimaginable hell. Our job is to make sure it never happens."

A female senior analyst raised the first question: "Do we know what Valikhanov was working on at VECTOR?"

Hart gave a measured response. "We believe that he was last working on a genetically-modified form of hemorrhagic smallpox."

From the opposite side of the room, a man dressed in black fatigues, asked: "Commander, when was our last contact with the operative?"

Hart pursed his lips and furrowed his brow. "That's another problem. He's not checked in for several months."

"How do you know he is still alive?" the man asked.

"Shortly before we lost touch with him, the bird spotted him in a courtyard adjacent to the factory. He had his belongings with him. He got into the back of an SUV, accompanied by another worker. We don't think he would have had his bag with him if they were taking him out into the desert to cut off his head."

"How do you know he hasn't turned?" another member of the fatigue clad group of three asked.

"We don't," replied Hart. "A high-flying bird transmitted an image of him being transported, but we don't know where. Our hope that it was a training camp, but even so, there are hundreds of such camps, and we've not been able to locate him via satellite."

"I know that most of you have worked together on various occasions, but several of you are new to the team. Let me introduce our next speaker, Dr. Elizabeth Wilkins."

Hart turned to his right and directed his attention to Liz. "Welcome, Liz," he said with a measure of warmth.

"Good morning, Commander."

Turning back towards the group, he continued: "Dr. Wilkins joins us from the CDC, where she is in charge of the BL IV laboratory. As you know, that's where all the fun happens. Dr. Wilkins gets to work with Category A biological threats—Ebola, Marburg, smallpox, and other incurable and inevitably fatal diseases. Prior to the CDC,

Liz worked at Fort Detrick , where she did groundbreaking work on the pathogenesis of some nasty bugs. Right, Liz?"

Liz half-smiled, "Only if you consider Ebola, smallpox, and SARS to be nasty. I find them simply to be adaptive . . . well, maybe not Ebola . . . it kills too efficiently for its own good."

"Liz, I expect you to take the lead in identifying whatever bugs we're dealing with. You will also play lead on triage and treatment. Until we have reliable containment strategies in place, you'll probably have your hands in that, too."

An older man, who was sitting at the far end of the table, spoke: "That assumes we will be unable to stop an attack. Is that what you are implying, Commander?"

"I think we have to assume a worst-case scenario and work towards a best-case solution."

The man asked, "Are we contemplating any type of vaccination strategy?"

"We don't know for certain what we would be vaccinating to protect against. Once we have confirmed the specific bio-agent, vaccinations will be on the table for consideration."

"And if we don't find out until after an event?"

"Then we will determine if a post-exposure vaccination campaign brings any meaningful hope of reducing the toll taken by the infectious agent."

Needing to adhere to schedule, Hart clicked on an icon and brought up Liz's briefing on the laptop and handed her the wireless remote.

Liz began with a short history lesson: "Gentlemen, to date, the largest bio-terrorist attack in the U.S. occurred more than thirty years ago, when followers of cult leader Bahgwan Shree Rajneesh contaminated a salad bar in The Dalles, Oregon, with salmonella. Though hundreds of people became quite ill, there were no deaths.

"By comparison, what we are potentially looking at today is your worst nightmare. In all likelihood, a sophisticated organization such as UIS would deploy a Category A pathogen. Depending upon which one they select and the method of dispersal, the casualties could number in the hundreds of thousands, if not millions. There are no effective treatments for many of these pathogens, particularly if they have been genetically altered."

One of the men wearing fatigues asked, "What is the probability of a genetically engineered pathogen, Dr. Wilkins? Isn't that technology a bit beyond the capabilities of Islamic terrorists who are still focused on shoe-bombs and exploding underwear?"

"There are libraries of information on the genomes of pathogens, as well as common working knowledge of how specific modifications can influence a variety of factors, from infectivity to mortality rate. I would assume that UIS has these capabilities. Frankly, I'd be stunned if they didn't."

"If I may continue," Liz said, bringing up an image of a man's torso and face covered with a concentric rash of raised pustules. "The most likely weapon of choice will be smallpox. Since no one has been immunized against it in nearly forty years, there's virtually no immunity to it within our population. Furthermore, if it is genetically modified, the vaccine would probably be rendered ineffective.

"There are two limiting factors, however," Liz explained. "The mortality rate for the primary type of smallpox is only thirty percent. That's low by UIS standards—those bastards want a total kill. Second, once you ignite the fire, it's hard to stop it. There is nothing to keep it from eventually reaching their shores. All it takes are a few infected people on airplanes traveling to the Middle East, and soon you have hotspots in the middle of jihadi-ville."

Hart was quietly laughing to himself. This was classic Liz—a wonderful combination of extraordinary intellect and sarcasm, her dark side emerging when he least expected it. He had not seen the complexities of Liz's personality when they first met, but he had quickly learned to appreciate her wicked sense of humor.

Liz turned up the volume. "If they have selected a hemorrhagic variant of smallpox and further altered its genetic structure, we could be looking at biological Armageddon. I don't want to sound theatrical, but an apocalyptic scenario is quite possible. I'll spare you the details regarding protein-signaling mechanisms relative to coagulation and the other mumbo-jumbo that we know about hemorrhagic diseases. All you need to know is that ninety percent of the people who contract such a disease will die." Liz scanned every face in the room to ensure that her point had been made before taking a seat.

Hart rose. "Thank you, Liz, for that enlightening and upbeat assessment of what we may be facing."

He nodded his head towards a tall, slender man seated across the table from Liz. "Dr. Thomas Scanlon joins us from the PROPHECY division at DARPA, where he and his colleagues are working on cutting-edge ways to outsmart even genetically modified bugs. Have I got that right, Tom?"

Scanlon smiled and nodded in agreement.

"Colonel Scanlon is not a desk jockey. He built his reputation in the field while serving as one of the early virus hunters. Dr. Scanlon helped track down and identify filoviruses before anyone had an inkling of what they even were. I've had the privilege of working with him on numerous occasions. Frankly, Tom, I wish I didn't have the privilege of working with you on this assignment," Hart said, as he handed him the remote.

"The feeling is mutual, John. I don't think there is a great deal that I can add to the excellent briefing by my colleague, Dr. Wilkins. DARPA is working on transformative methods of either preventing or treating deadly viruses, but much of the work remains embryonic. So, don't count on life-saving solutions from DARPA—not yet."

Scanlon continued, "We're going to have to hope that this is a normal bug—likely smallpox—and rely on rapid inoculations post any potential exposure. We have an adequate supply of vaccine for virtually any imaginable scenario. The challenge will be rapid identification of the bio-event, followed by the logistical challenge of administering tens of thousands of doses of vaccine within a short period of time following the event. I will be working closely with Dr. Wilkins on event identification and management, including medical response and containment.

"One final note," Scanlon added. "I have a meeting scheduled with an old friend, Dr. Anatoly Belikov. As you may remember, he was one of the leading figures employed by the former Soviet Bioprepart before he defected to the U.S. in 1992. I will find out what, if anything, he can add to this party."

As Scanlon sat, the man at the far end of the table rose. He was stocky and appeared to be of Middle Eastern descent. "I've not had the pleasure of meeting most of you. My name is Omar Warum, and my job is to understand events unfolding in pivotal Middle Eastern countries at a ground level. I look forward to working with each of you, and to preventing the scenario that Dr. Wilkins described."

As he took his seat, Hart quickly interjected, "Omar is being far too modest. Mr. Warum is our leading expert on Muslim extremist groups, several of which he has successfully infiltrated in the past."

"Yes, and my face bears the scars of groups that ensured my fidelity with the sharp blades of their knives," Omar added.

Deep, long rivulets of scar tissue crisscrossed Warum's face. It was common practice with certain groups to take draconian steps to ensure that new recruits were not operating under a separate agenda.

"Most importantly," Hart added, "Omar is quite familiar with Al Hameed, al-Bakr, and UIS operations."

"Yes, Commander, al-Bakr has long been a focus on my attention, as well as my prayers . . . prayers that we bring a swift end to his reign."

"Agreed."

Before adjourning, Hart acknowledged the three men in fatigues, who snapped to attention, their hands clasped firmly at their backs. "James, Seth, and Andrew will help ensure the team's safety when in the field, as well as lead interdiction if and when we encounter any type of potentially adversarial force. I've worked closely with each of these men before, know their capabilities, and can assure you that you are in good hands."

CHAPTER TWENTY-TWO

Faisalabad, Pakistan

THE LINCHPIN OF ARMAGEDDON LAY in the novel vaccine engineered by Valikhanov. It was the proverbial sheep's blood that would allow the messenger of death to pass over the Chosen Ones while claiming the lives of all of infidels and apostates. Without it, three years of work would be down the drain.

There was to be one final test before moving forward with the planned attack, and Al Hameed had returned to Faisalabad to view the results.

As he stood inches away from the windows of the observation unit, a strong sense of déjà vu carried Al Hameed back to his first exposure to the devastating effects of the virus. What would be revealed when the drapes obscuring the medical isolation room were opened? Would he be greeted by nine decomposing corpses or would the vaccine prove successful?

Valikhanov thrust open the drapes, allowing Al Hameed's eyes to soak in the glorious results. In front of him were a group of men whose greatest malady appeared to be boredom. Some lay shirtless on their beds, reading or watching television, while others talked or played cards. To a man, they seemed healthy and strong.

"The Chosen Ones!" Al Hameed proclaimed as he turned to face Valikhanov.

Valikhanov nodded with pride.

"How long ago were they exposed?"

"Fifteen days. They were exposed to an overwhelming viral load. We are a minimum of ten days past the incubation period, and the only symptom we've observed is a mild fever in three of the patients," Beibut assured him.

"How long before we have the required doses of vaccine?"

"You will have them shortly. We began production long before the results were in. It was the only way to stay on schedule. We're fortunate that the vaccine exceeded our expectations."

"And what about the package we plan to deliver to our friends in the West?"

"Yes, it, too, is ready for delivery upon your instructions."

"Then I must talk with al-Bakr and apprise him of our plans."

CHAPTER TWENTY-THREE

Abbottabad, Pakistan

As the blindfold was removed, Al Hameed raised his hand to shade his eyes from the harsh glare of the mid-morning sun. Squinting, he could make out the figure of his teacher standing before him, extending his arms in welcome.

"Welcome Ahmed. I am sorry for the precautions," al-Bakr said, "But we fear the Americans may be close at hand."

Al Hameed did not step forward to accept the welcome, but instead spoke: "My teacher, do you not trust me? It is I, the man in whom you have entrusted the future of Islam, who stands before you. Am I not worthy of knowing where you reside?"

Al-Bakr lowered his head in deference to Al Hameed. "That was never my intent. You have my apology. Look around, Ahmed. You are in the courtyard of a compound located less than a mile from the Pakistan Military Academy in Abbottabad. If there is more you wish to know in order to reassure you of my absolute trust in you, please tell me."

"That will suffice," Al Hameed said as he stepped forward and kissed each of al-Bakr's cheeks.

"So what have you come to share with me, Ahmed? I trust that you and Valikhanov have worked through the details of a plan and are ready to move forward."

"With your blessing, of course."

"Let's go inside. You can walk me through the details, none of which are too small to warrant my attention."

The two men entered the house and climbed stairs to the third floor. There, al-Bakr led the way to a balcony surrounded by a seven-foot privacy wall.

"Are you not concerned about the Pakistanis—particularly being so close to a major military facility?" Al Hameed inquired.

"Not as long as our interests remain aligned with those of ISI. I am their guest, and it is through their grace that I live my days in relative peace. But those days may be numbered. They are becoming increasingly focused on sectarian concerns, not problems that lie across vast oceans. All the more reason why we must not waste precious time." Al-Bakr gestured for Al Hameed to begin.

Al Hameed leaned forward as he began to speak. "We have completed our work in Faisalabad. Within two weeks, we will be prepared to launch. Like a multi-headed hydra, we will strike numerous cities at one time. If everything goes as planned, the devastation will be unimaginable. Even if problems arise, there will still be catastrophic damage wrought upon the Great Satan," Al Hameed said, more as a promise than a statement.

"Our primary target has always been the West, but it is not merely the Great Satan that we wish to destroy.

Ultimately, it is infidels and apostates throughout the world," al-Bakr interjected.

Al Hameed was delivering on his promise to unleash the perfect weapon. "As you will see, there will be a great cleansing across the globe in preparation for the new Caliphate."

"Beibut and I will leave Pakistan shortly for America. On the way, we will enjoy an extended layover in London."

"Ah, to visit our friend in the import/export business." Al-Bakr's inflection suggested a question.

"Indeed, he will be instrumental in transporting our materials to the U.S. and through customs. Although I am leery of a man who makes his living providing services to the CIA, he appears to represent our best option."

"Being alert is being wise, but you needn't worry about Umami. He's proved himself time and again."

Al Hameed continued, "There will be four jihadists—one to attack each of the four busiest airports in America: Atlanta Hartsfield, Chicago O'Hare, Dallas/Fort Worth, and Los Angeles International. You identified two of the men who will commit jihad. The other two came from within the factory. You would be surprised what a good recruiter of Islamists Valikhanov has proven to be."

"Surely you are joking."

"We were able to identify two men at the factory who were passionate in their hatred of America and conviction that its people must die. They were jihadists who simply needed training and a target."

"How did you handle it, Ahmed?"

"Beibut said that I commandeered them. I'd prefer to think of it as having arranged additional training that made the men more valuable. We took the most passionate and capable of his workers and sent them to the mountains for a few months. It was also a good test of their loyalty."

Al Hameed stated, "With the men now trained, we are ready to deploy them. Each one will go to a separate city in the Midwest. They will arrive at their initial destinations one day ahead of Beibut and me. They will be given a day of rest—a Sabbath, if you will—the last Sabbath before the wrath of God is delivered upon the infidels!"

"Go on."

"On November 22, we will converge in Missouri at Babur and Sarah Qaisrani's home. There we will arm the four jihadists with bio-weapons and instruct them as to their targets. The following day, each man will travel to his final destination. Then, on one of the heaviest travel days of the year, the day before America's Thanksgiving, the hydra will strike, unleashing its venom."

Al Hameed paused to ensure that every detail was being absorbed by his mentor.

"Let us take a moment," al-Bakr said as he poured them each a cup of thick, acrid coffee from a small pot. "Did you see Sarah in the courtyard?"

Al-Bakr's question caught Al Hameed completely off-guard, "No, my teacher. If I may ask, why is she here?"

"Her value far exceeds her role as the dutiful wife of Babur. She will be a gracious hostess to you, but she will also be instrumental in covering your tracks and ensuring that nothing stops you."

"I'm glad you have such confidence in the woman," Al Hameed could not conceal the contempt that now laced his voice.

"I recognize talent, Ahmed. That's one of my gifts. It doesn't matter if the talent comes in a thobe, a burka, or a skirt. Furthermore, she carries a U.S. passport. Need I explain the utility of that to you?" Without waiting for a response, he concluded, "I will expect you to speak politely to her before leaving."

"Yes, my teacher. May I continue?"

Al-Bakr waved his hand, "Yes, I wish to hear the details of the attacks."

"The four jihadists will be on-site at the airport terminals at precisely 6 AM local time, just as the morning rush is getting into full swing. Each will carry a leather briefcase that contains two liters of the deadly bio-weapon."

"How will they clear security with such a weapon?" al Bakr asked.

"They won't. There is no need. Tremendous damage can be done simply by walking through non-secure areas, such as the ticket counters and food courts."

"How will this weapon be disseminated?"

"As they activate a small switch on the handle, a pump will silently feed the liquid medium into a fan at the base of the case. It will instantly aerosolize and be carried on air currents throughout the facility. All our attackers need to do is mill about for an hour."

"The Americans will be on guard for young Muslim men milling about in an airport," al-Bakr objected.

Al Hameed had anticipated his mentor's objection. "Since 9/11, every young Muslim sporting a beard and wearing traditional clothing looks like a terrorist to the Americans. That is why our men will be clean shaven and dressed in business suits. They will have gone without their beards for a month, a sacrifice they will gladly make as an act of taqiyya."

Al-Bakr continued his scrutiny of the planned attack. "The Aum Shinrikyo developed a similar, albeit flawed device, though it was never used. As you know, they came under tremendous scrutiny following their failed attempts to attack the Tokyo subway using Sarin nerve gas.

"It takes a great deal of confidence, Ahmed, to model your attacks on a group with such spectacular failures," al-Bakr cautioned.

"I trust in Beibut's judgment . . . as did the leaders of the former Soviet Union."

"What happens after they successfully disperse the agent?" al-Bakr questioned.

"At precisely 7 AM, the men will go into specific restrooms within the terminals. There, a confidant will await them.

"Each man will step into the handicapped stall, use the bathroom, and leave his briefcase behind. The confidant will step in immediately afterward, flush the toilet, and take the briefcase. They will wait an extra minute before exiting the bathroom to give each jihadist time to clear the area and head for security lines. When the jihadists reach security, they will be carrying nothing more than their boarding passes and a fountain pen. Meanwhile, the confidants will have exited the airport with the briefcases."

"What are you talking about?" al-Bakr raised his arms in confusion.

"The second wave of the attack, my teacher. Each man will have an innocuous looking pen. Each pen contains a sealed ink cartridge. The dark blue liquid is, in reality, the liquefied bio-agent. The weapon will not become active until the base of the pen is turned firmly clockwise, puncturing the small reservoir. The 'pen' is capable of atomizing a small amount of the liquid when the clip is pressed for two to three seconds.

"They will reach up to adjust the air vent with the pen in hand. An undetectable squeeze of the pen's clip will aerosolize an invisible mist of viral particles that will move quickly through the plane.

"According to Valikhanov, the virus will ride on the circulating air currents and be dispersed throughout the plane. When inhaled by an unsuspecting victim, the virus will implant itself in the nasal pharynx, where it will go to work on the mucous membranes, and later the lymphatic system. From there, it will be a precipitous descent into hell for those afflicted with the virus."

"Ingenious, Ahmed!"

"Thank you, my teacher. It will be a proverbial *one-two punch*, to borrow an American expression: First create mass exposure at the airports, where a small percentage of a very large number of people travelling that day will be infected. Second, use the planes like human greenhouses to infect a larger percentage of a smaller population.

"Do I have your blessing, my teacher?"

"Yes. You must strike now, before we risk having our plan discovered."

CHAPTER TWENTY-FOUR

Faisalabad, Pakistan

CLOISTERED IN THE HIDDEN ROOM beneath his house, Valikhanov was holding a rectangular metal container about the size of a two-liter milk carton.

As he spoke, he pushed it towards Al Hameed. "The virus is quite stable while housed in its sealed container," Valikhanov explained. "There will be no deterioration or weakening of the bio-agent prior to its dispersal and certainly no leakage."

"I will take your word for it." Al Hameed gestured for Beibut to move the vessel from in front of his face. He was amazed and terrified at how cavalierly Valikhanov handled the most destructive weapon on the planet.

"As you can see, the containers are equipped with a small threaded attachment which connects to a hose within the aerosolizing device. Four containers, each holding two liters of the deadly bio-weapon, are ready for transport upon your orders."

"But Beibut, the containers are large and heavy. They must be disguised, even if it is but a thin veil."

"Did you notice the two large pieces of luggage upstairs?"

"Yes. I assumed they were yours."

"In a sense, they are. The containers conform precisely to the dimensions of false compartments in the luggage. Since the luggage is worn and battered, I don't think anyone will be rifling through it looking for something to steal. However, the hidden containers can be detected by x-ray."

Al Hameed knew this was a significant point of vulnerability in a plan that could afford no errors. There were other methods of transportation—including by ship—but each brought their own set of challenges. In the end, he had accepted the risks and sought to mitigate them by ensuring that the luggage would never be inspected.

"If there is a weakness to our plan, it is in the transportation of the weapon. There are too many elements out of our control—times when we must have faith in our friends and allies to come through. Failure at any point in the chain could disrupt years of planning," Al Hameed commented.

Valikhanov agreed. "I'm concerned about our friends at ISI, particularly with its recent changes at the top. As you know, General Pasha has been replaced by General Ul-Sharif. General Ul-Sharif was recruited by the head of the Army, General Malik, with instructions to rebuild the tattered relationship with American intelligence."

"Don't concern yourself," Al Hameed counseled. "Al-Bakr has spoken with Ul-Sharif about his obligations and allegiance to General Malik, and he has received assurances that nothing would change in the relationship between ISI and UIS. Ul-Sharif described it as a marketing campaign by ISI to placate the Americans after they were caught playing host to Osama Bin Laden. A smokescreen, if you will."

"Let's hope that is true." Beibut sounded doubtful.

"We have a common purpose and shared values—beginning with a strong hatred of the U.S. I believe that our cargo will be in good hands on its journey out of Pakistan."

"You are the one who raised the doubts, so who are you attempting to assure—me or yourself?" Beibut asked. "Either way, I will pray you are right about ISI."

Al Hameed said, "Ahmed al-Shishani and Kameel Imad al-Din will take the containers by train to Karachi, where they will board a Gulf Air plane bound for Bahrain. There they will catch a connecting flight to London. ISI has ensured safe passage through the Karachi airport.

"The Gulf Air flight from Karachi departs for Bahrain at 9:05 PM on Friday, November 18. They will change planes there and arrive in London at 7:45 AM on Saturday. Since luggage transferred from one international flight to another is not subject to inspection in Bahrain, it should arrive untouched and undetected at London's Heathrow Airport."

"Assuming it arrives in London untouched, as we both hope, how will you get it to the U.S. and through customs?" Beibut asked.

"Once in London, the luggage will be collected by our dear friend, Mohammed Umami, whom you will meet shortly."

A wave of panic shot through Beibut's body. He had no plans to leave Pakistan and was not one to enjoy surprises—particularly if they cast him in a role for which he was ill-prepared.

"Why am I going? I am not a jihadist!" he cried out.

"Do you not wish to serve Allah? And what were you doing in the factory if not preparing for jihad?" Al Hameed demanded.

"There are many ways to serve Allah," Beibut replied tersely. "As his servant, I use my humble intellectual gifts to forge the weapons that will be carried by those stronger than me. Based upon what you have said, your teacher appreciates those gifts."

"Relax, Beibut, I am just toying with you."

"I don't find it amusing," Valikhanov said, shaking his head.

Ignoring Beibut's irritation, Al Hameed continued, "You will not have an active role in the attack, other than to help ensure that our vision is realized. Now, if we are done with this foolishness, let me tell you of our plans.

"You and I will travel to London, where we will be the guests of Mohammed Umami. He will be responsible for couriering the package from London to Detroit. We will stay with him until the package is safely on its way."

"What is our final destination?" Valikhanov asked.

"Initially, Detroit . . . but we will be there only long enough to collect the package, then sleep.

"On November 22, our team will converge at a safe house in the middle of the country. It is from there that the four attacks will be launched.

"Once we know that our four jihadists have arrived safely at the hotels adjacent to their targeted airports, you and I will depart for Pakistan via Chicago O'Hare. Our job is to leave without a trace."

"You've still not answered my question," Beibut pressed.

"You've not given me a chance. Patience, Beibut. It is a virtue you must acquire," Al Hameed admonished before answering the question: "Umami is an interesting man and one of great wealth and influence. His wealth has been acquired through trafficking in various forms of illicit cargo, primarily weapons. His principal client is the CIA. One of his planes will be departing for Chicago at 12:30 PM on the day we depart Heathrow. The bags will be on it. It will be hand-couriered to a safe house in Detroit by the pilot."

"And if the canisters are discovered?"

"Hopefully that will not happen. If it does, we will still have our pens. As they say, 'the pen is mightier than the sword!'"

CHAPTER TWENTY-FIVE

Jinnah International Airport, Karachi, Pakistan

AHMED AL-SHISHANI AND KAMEEL IMAD AL-DIN, al-Bakr's men entrusted with transporting the bio-weapon, arrived in Karachi two hours before their flight was scheduled to depart for London via Bahrain. Thanks to first class tickets, they bypassed the long lines at the check-in counter and went to a private area.

After reviewing the men's travel documents, the ticket agent looked at their large, leather suitcases and then directly into the travelers' eyes.

"You will have to take those bags to security to be x-rayed," he informed them.

A wave of panic pulsed through al-Shishani as he spoke, "As first class passengers, we understood that our bags would receive priority handling," he politely informed the man.

"Is that so," the agent said dismissively.

"Yes, it is so," al-Shisani said more forcefully than he had intended.

"Let me see your passports again," the ticket agent demanded, reaching out his hand.

With no option but to surrender them, al-Shishani and Imad al-Din complied.

A furtive smile crossed the man's face. "Ah, Mr. al-Shishani and Mr. Imad al-Din, how foolish of me. Of course, we will handle your baggage from here," the ticket agent's tone was now officious.

Confused, and wary of what might follow, Imad al-Din spoke.

"My camera and film are packed inside. Will they be safe going through x-ray?"

"You still use film? I have not had a passenger raise such a concern in a long time."

"I find that film offers a finer image than a digital camera, and, in any case, I am too thrifty to spend hundreds of dollars on a digital Nikon," al-Din continued.

"But you will spend thousands of dollars on a first class fare?" the agent inquired.

Before Imad al-Din could respond, the agent handed back their passports and said, "Relax, Gentlemen, and enjoy your flight. Your baggage will be safe. You have General Malik's word on it."

It was unsettling to be toyed with in such a fashion. And despite the agent's reassurance, neither al-Din nor al-Shishani could relax until many hours later when they received confirmation that the package had arrived in London safely . . . ahead of Al Hameed and Valikhanov.

CHAPTER TWENTY-SIX

London, England

IT HAD BEEN A LONG TRIP from Faisalabad to London. The last leg was in a taxi, which eventually deposited the travel-weary Al Hameed and Valikhanov at the estate of Mohammed Umami.

Umami had begun his professional life as a rug merchant, selling only the finest Persians. He had an eye for beauty, whether in rugs or women. He also had a knack for making money. He had realized decades ago that certain commodities were far more profitable to import and export than rugs. Drugs, while lucrative, offended his sensibilities. But weapons—that was another matter.

Unusually tall and slender for an Arab, Mohammed Umami radiated a sense of optimal physical conditioning. None of the unattractive bumps and bulges that often accumulated by middle age were visible through his perfectly tailored Burberry suit.

Despite making a living as an international arms dealer, Umami's passion was unarmed combat. Al Hameed knew that his host was among the most lethal men he had ever met. Yet, adorned with a Hermes tie, he looked the picture of affluent civility. What he lacked in mass he made up for in velocity. Lightning fast with his feet, he could bring down an attacker with a side-kick so swift that the air would audibly snap like the crack of a whip.

Al Hameed had witnessed a demonstration of his prowess at a training camp in Afghanistan, where Umami was delivering a shipment of AKs. The camp was run by a petulant former Iraqi Army captain. The man, whose square body looked like that of a professional boxer, was well aware of Umami's reputation. Still, he found it hard to believe that this genteel man, with his expensive silk shirts and refined sensibilities, could hurt anyone. That was a serious mistake.

He challenged Umami to a sparring match. When Umami politely declined, he began goading him. After a handful of insults, Umami reluctantly consented.

The entire camp witnessed the match, which lasted only a few seconds. That's how long it took for Umami to draw a bead and plant his heel in the center of the man's forehead. The kick literally lifted the man off his feet and propelled him a good three meters. When he landed, he was out cold. Fortunately, he didn't die, though he suffered a severe concussion.

Al Hameed had congratulated him on the swift and decisive battle, but Umami turned away, ashamed that he had allowed this man to goad him into a fight.

"Why do you not raise your fist in celebration of your victory?" Al Hameed asked.

"When a mad dog barks at you, is it better to kick it or simply move away?" he responded.

"I'm afraid I don't understand."

"Nor did I the first time my master posed the question to me."

Umami's biggest client was the CIA. From the Agency's perspective, they were his only client. In reality, they provided a useful—albeit unrecognized—cover for his true work. He supported al-Bakr and UIS, as he had since its inception. He supplied money, arms, and safe haven. His loyalty to the movement was beyond reproach, and that meant he would be loyal to Al Hameed.

Exiting the taxi, the two men climbed a short set of limestone stairs leading to an Elizabethan mansion. Al Hameed had barely rung the bell when a butler appeared at the door. He inquired as to who was calling.

Umami appeared behind the man, put his hand on the butler's shoulder, then spoke. "It's alright, George, these are the friends I've been telling you about—Mr. Habib and Mr. Saleh. They will be staying with us for a few days. I trust their rooms are ready."

"I will make sure of it, Mr. Umami. Gentlemen, please excuse me." George lowered his gaze and tilted his head subserviently before moving towards the stairs leading to the estate's eight bedrooms.

Mohammed Umami had changed in the five years since Al Hameed had last laid eyes upon him. His long, angular face was still accented by a closely trimmed beard, but it had grown white since their last encounter. His eyes, however, remained impenetrably black, peering out from deeply recessed hollows above his sunken cheeks.

"While George checks on things, may I take a moment to acquaint you with my humble home? After that I will let you get settled before afternoon tea."

Al Hameed and Valikhanov had rarely seen such wealth. The furnishings were lavish and looked as though they could grace the Palace of Versailles or the great estates of the Romanov Czars at Tsarskoe Selo. Every wall was covered with paintings, tapestries, or mosaics.

The two men were simultaneously seduced and repulsed by the level of extravagance. Squelching any sense of temptation, Al Hameed wondered if this might be Umami's fatal flaw—the failure to recognize that great wealth cannot be accrued here on earth but only bestowed by Allah after one's ultimate sacrifice. It was a thought he would store away for another day, part of the vast catalogue of vulnerabilities he maintained on all who surrounded him.

Beyond its furnishings, Umami's estate was also home to an extraordinary collection of Middle Eastern antiquities. As they walked into the drawing room, a bronze statue caught Al Hameed's eye. It was no more than eighteen inches tall and centuries old. A fierce warrior held a curved sword in one hand and the severed head of his victim in the other. He recognized the figure immediately as Shahbab-ud-din Muhammad Ghuri, a legendary Muslim hero.

"He was a great general," Umami said.

"Great indeed! A thousand years after his conquests, we still revere his accomplishments," Al Hameed added.

"It's as if you know him," Umami observed, with a glint in his eye.

Flattered, Al Hameed elaborated. "There's much to be learned from the man who brought broad swaths of India under Muslim control . . . a man whose ferocity in battle became legendary, thanks to the hundreds who fell to his sword. Yet the warriors who fought at his side, including thousands of slaves, knew Ghuri to be a loyal and kind master."

"I have rarely seen you speak of the dead with so much passion, Ahmed. Perhaps your soul and Ghuri's are one." Umami fed Al Hameed's hunger for praise.

"I have been to his grave at Damik. It's where his life was snatched away by a cowardly assassin. He struck while Ghuri was deep in prayer. I have prayed to Allah to guide me as he guided Ghuri in his conquests."

Umami concurred, "Indeed! There is much to admire about General Ghuri, as well as those who follow in his footsteps. May you enjoy the fruits of conquest, and be watchful even when you pray. I have lost too many friends through the years. I do not wish to visit your grave.

"Perhaps at your next visit, we can discuss repatriating India." Umami's comment elicited a smile from Al Hameed, who was still staring at the statue.

Beibut worked to stifle a yawn. He was fatigued, and there were still many hard days ahead of them.

"Gentlemen, George will show you to your rooms. I will look forward to seeing you in a few hours. Please tell George if there is anything he can do to make your stay more comfortable." Umami bowed and transferred custodial responsibility for Mr. Saleh and Mr. Habib to his butler.

The short time spent at Umami's estate was intended to be relaxing, yet the awesome responsibility of what awaited them weighed heavily on Al Hameed and Valikhanov. They were eager for the time to pass and their operation to begin.

The next day, they took a short trek from the village of St. James into the city, walking from Buckingham Palace past the Queen's Gallery and on to Westminster Abbey.

Hundreds of inconspicuously mounted video cameras captured their every movement. Al Hameed knew that the feed from those cameras was being processed in real time through facial recognition software. Even without the aid of such software, his stark white skin made him stand out in a crowd.

But no one in MI-6 was looking for Al Hameed in London. Once identified, British intelligence would conclude that he was there on a scouting expedition and ramp up the threat level across the U.K. By that time, they would be in the U.S.

Nor was anyone looking for Valikhanov, though that would change. Information regarding his disappearance from VECTOR had not been shared by the CIA with other agencies, including MI-6. As such, his image failed to score a hit. It would prove to be one of those costly errors that came from not trusting one's compatriots in the intelligence game.

CHAPTER TWENTY-SEVEN

London, England

IT WAS NOT UNTIL THEIR LAST NIGHT in London that Al Hameed, Valikhanov, and Umami finally got down to business.

Sitting at a dining room table capable of holding a multitude, the three men huddled at one end. Umami had given the staff a night's leave so he and his guests would be undisturbed.

"Tell me of the packages that arrived earlier," said Al Hameed.

"They have been here since shortly before your arrival," Umami explained. "It was the safest place for them. When you leave, they, too, will leave on one of our planes bound for Chicago. The flight is scheduled to depart Heathrow mid-day. It will be carrying a large shipment of telecommunications equipment, at least according to its manifest."

"And in reality?" Al Hameed inquired.

"In reality, it will be loaded with heavy wooden cartons filled with Israel's greatest contribution to mankind—the Uzi. The Agency seems to have an insatiable appetite for them these days, despite the availability of more sophisticated weapons."

"What happens when this flight of yours lands in Chicago?"

"Thanks to our friends at the CIA, ground control will divert the flight from the international arrival area to the private aviation terminal, allowing it to bypass customs. All of its cargo will be off-loaded onto unmarked trucks, except for the worn leather suitcases carried by the pilot. They will disappear into the trunk of his car and reappear wherever you wish."

This was Al Hameed's cue to reveal the address of the first safe house, but he hesitated. Al-Bakr had always stressed the importance of compartmentalization, confident it was the surest way to keep secrets. But this was a secret he knew he must reveal.

"This is the address where we will be tomorrow night. It is imperative that nothing delay the arrival of the package. It is a five-hour drive from O'Hare to Dearborn without traffic. Are you certain your man can be trusted with this critical task?"

"You have my word," Umami said, raising his hand to his heart.

"Tell your pilot that, when he arrives, he will be greeted like a relative returning home after a long trip. We will help him carry the bags into the house, where he will spend a couple of days before departing. That should quell any anxiety among curious neighbors who may wonder who is arriving late in the night."

"He's not slated to fly again until the weekend, so that should work out well," Umami agreed.

Al Hameed's words gave no hint of the fate that awaited Umami's pilot following the safe delivery of the bio-weapon. Al Hameed would be forced to tidy up loose ends. The safe house in Dearborn was too important to risk discovery. He knew that when the pilot failed to report to work the following weekend, Umami would grow suspicious. But by that point, it would be a minor detail in comparison to the unfolding terror in America.

Before retiring, Umami tried to end the night on a more familiar note. "Will you see your family when you return home, Ahmed?"

"No, nor will I be able to warn them of the coming Apocalypse. Consider yourself lucky, Mohammed, that you were one of the first among the Chosen Ones."

"Have they not received the vaccine?"

"No. They know nothing of our plans."

"And how, my friend, do you reconcile these facts, if I may be so bold?"

"I do not try to reconcile them. It is with a heavy heart that I send my parents to be martyrs in the kingdom of heaven."

Standing so as to end any further discussion, Al Hameed thanked Umami for his hospitality and excused himself. Valikhanov followed close behind.

While Al Hameed fell quickly asleep, Valikhanov fell prey to the ghosts that inhabit the night. It happened often: He would dream of Irina's abandonment. He would relive his confrontation with Kurtova. Other nights he was greeted by the corpulent face of Bucherov and watched as it gradually morphed into an unrecognizable corpse. But the dreams that disturbed Beibut the most were of his mother.

She would call out to him, as she did this night, her voice growing ever more desperate. But something kept him from answering her.

He bolted awake, the sheets soaked with perspiration. He had not spoken to his mother since departing Kazakhstan. He wondered if she was still alive. If so, he prayed that Taras was honoring his pledge to care for her as a son would care for his mother. Though he yearned to reach out to her, to comfort her, he knew she would be under the scrutiny of Russian Intelligence. They would lay in wait for an opportunity to repatriate their former scientist.

The next morning, Al Hameed and Valikhanov bid their host good-bye. "Jazak Allah Khairan (may Allah reward you with blessings)," repeating the phrase almost in unison as they moved towards the waiting Bentley.

"Wa Antum Fa Jazakumullahu khayran. Fi Amanillah (And may Allah reward you, too, with good and Protect you)," came the response from Umami.

"There is one thing more before you leave." Umami turned, withdrew something heavy from a box, and handed it to Al Hameed. "A small gesture of gratitude for our friendship."

Al Hameed could not believe that he was holding the statue of Muhammad Ghuri that he had so admired. But he could not accept it, certainly not now.

"I am overwhelmed by your generosity. I will not insult you by refusing your kindness, but will ask that you keep it for me until I next return."

"As you wish. But let's not allow another five years to pass before we see one another again."

It was 2:35 PM when they finally departed London for Detroit. The Virgin America flight would take 8 hours and 51 minutes—putting them on the ground at 6:26 PM, Allah willing.

CHAPTER TWENTY-EIGHT

Alexandria, Virginia

ANATOLY BELIKOV HAD SPENT MONTHS following his defection from the former Soviet Union being debriefed by Colonel Tom Scanlon. Each day, they met in an office housed in a drab beige building not far from Tyson's Corner. The sign on the office door, "Prometheus Cremation Services," was obviously the product of an Agency employee with a dark sense of humor and too much time on his hands.

Over the span of a few short months, Belikov proved to be the CIA's dream come true. He was a virtual encyclopedia of knowledge regarding the inner workings of the former Soviet biological warfare apparatus known as *Bioprepart.* But it was more than his knowledge that made him valuable to the Agency. He was equally masterful as a storyteller and regaled his interrogators with first-hand accounts so chilling they virtually guaranteed that the Agency's requests for bio-defense funds would pour in. All that was needed was to invite a few members of the Senate Select Committee on Intelligence to listen in.

Whether some of the stories were more fiction than fact was a question that always haunted Scanlon, though he knew better than to openly question Belikov's integrity. Still, he wondered. Was it conceivable that the former Soviet Union had manufactured smallpox virus and anthrax spores by the metric ton in complete violation of all injunctions against the use of chemical or biological agents? For the sake of national security, he had to assume the stories were true. Belikov certainly lent them a great deal of authenticity by providing cogent, scientific explanations for how various technical challenges had been overcome when creating the weapons.

Once Scanlon and a host of Agency personnel were confident they had extracted all vital information from Belikov's memory, he was free to create a new life in America. The Agency called in a favor, and a teaching position was created for him at the American University.

Belikov and his wife gradually settled into upper middle class lifestyle within the Beltway, occupying a modest and perfectly groomed two-story brick house with freshly painted black shutters on a quiet street in Alexandria. Their neighbors remained blissfully unaware of the role Belikov had played in planning the total and complete annihilation of the United States. According to the Belikovs' cover story, he was a political dissident once exiled to Siberia. And Russia wouldn't touch him. It was an unspoken rule in the spy trade that such assassinations carried the threat of severe repercussions.

A broad smile broke out on Belikov's face the moment he opened the door and saw his old friend, "Scanloon," standing there. "Thomas, Thomas . . . please . . . come in!" Anatoly bellowed, before calling out to his wife, "Valeriya, Thomas has come to visit—please say hello."

An aging but elegant woman emerged from the kitchen still wearing her apron. She gave Scanlon a warm embrace. "What brings you to our home, Thomas? We haven't seen you in such a long time."

Scanlon looked to Belikov for a quick escape.

"Come, come, my dear . . . no reason to ask *why*, when a gift has been delivered to our doorstep."

"Of course," she smiled. "Forgive me. But please, don't be such a stranger! Anatoly and I miss you. Perhaps the three of us can share a glass of wine when you and Anatoly are finished with your business?"

"I would like that," Scanlon responded.

"Why don't we take a walk," Belikov suggested. "One never knows who might be listening," he said gesturing around the edges of the room as though there might be listening devices.

"Who are you afraid of—our side or yours?" Scanlon asked with a smile.

"Both!"

The two men exited the home and walked in step, as friends do, the three short blocks to a nearby park. Belikov eyed a bench that was far enough removed from a throng of children playing on swingsets to conceal their banter and provide the anonymity he knew Scanlon desired.

"We've got a situation, Anatoly," said Scanlon. "I can't go into detail, but it involves the potential manufacture and release of a bio-agent believed to be genetically modified smallpox."

Extracting from his breast pocket a slightly out-of-focus photograph taken at a distance with a telephoto lens, he handed it to Belikov. "This man appears to be running the factory where we believe the bio-agent is being produced.

He is working under the direction of a man known as Al Hameed."

"This is not good, my friend. No, this is very, very bad. Of course, I know of Al Hameed, and I also know this man quite well. His name is Beibut Valikhanov."

"Yes, apparently Commander Hart knows him, too. But, as you are aware, Anatoly, I'm a giant step removed from the field of spycraft. Who is he, and why should we be so concerned?"

"He was one of the chief scientists at VECTOR. He was the first person to create a recombinant vaccinia virus that incorporated DNA from Venezuelan Equine Encephalomyelitis virus. From there, it was a small step to learn how to manipulate the variola virus."

Scanlon interjected, "As Werner Herzog said, 'It's a small step from insecticide to genocide.'"

Belikov grunted his acknowledgement, then added, "You always struggled to believe my stories about hemorrhagic smallpox, my friend."

Scanlon started to disagree, but Belikov shushed him with a lift of one hand.

"I don't blame you. Had I been in your position, I would have found the stories to be preposterous, as well. But it is imperative that you believe me now. Valikhanov was working with a genetically modified variant that further suppressed the host's innate immunologic response to the virus and resulted in mortality exceeding ninety percent."

"I suppose that's the good news," Scanlon said, afraid of what might follow.

"There is more. Our Kazakh friend relishes a relatively quick kill, so he worked to shorten the incubation period by increasing the speed with which the virus propagates. He dropped it from as long as two weeks to as little as a day or two. Finally, he worked on the R value. He's been trying to increase its virulence to approach that of measles or SARS. The infectious dose for this new variant of hemorrhagic smallpox is as little as ten viral particles.

"I am confident he would have copied VECTOR's full genomic library onto a flash drive and taken it with him to his new home—probably accompanied by a few carefully pilfered viral samples. So, Thomas, Valikhanov has the recipe and ingredient. It sounds like the Pakistanis have provided the kitchen."

"Did I mention anything about Pakistan?" Scanlon asked, wondering if he had let something slip.

"Thomas, we are both a step removed from the field, but I occasionally hear things."

"We should still be interrogating you!"

"Yes, you should. But even if you did, I would have trouble explaining how Valikhanov got from VECTOR to Pakistan. Here is what I can tell you. Beibut is what you Americans call a hard-liner. He became frustrated when the Cold War began to thaw. Glasnost and Perestroika were anathema to him. After all, he had devoted a lifetime to developing weapons that he envisioned being put to good use."

"We've got our share of hard-liners," Scanlon admitted, "but they usually don't join forces with terrorists in a third-world nation."

"There's another matter we should discuss pertaining to his wife. You see, the Siberian winters didn't agree with everyone, including Mrs. Valikhanov. There was much bickering—enough to become an official part of his file. In Russia, that is not a good thing.

"Apparently, Beibut came home one day to an empty house. Even the cat was gone. Beibut blamed Mother Russia. Imagine that," Belikov said, with a roll of his eyes.

Picking up on the story line, Scanlon concurred: "So he was vulnerable to recruitment, and that's presumably what happened."

"That's what I've heard through a very long grapevine. You know, it used to be far more direct," Belikov said wistfully.

"What can we do, Anatoly?"

"You must trust what I have told you regarding the devastation that can be wrought by this disease. It will spread with a vengeance. Anti-viral therapies will be worthless. Your only hope will be if Valikhanov has continued his work on a vaccine. That work was in its preliminary stages when he was still employed by VECTOR."

"What do you mean by preliminary stages?"

"Simple—it was still far too dangerous to use in mass vaccinations. It kept causing an aberrant level of postvaccinial central nervous system disease and killing our test subjects. If Valikhanov has overcome that complication, he has created the perfect tool for genocide."

"This information cannot travel back across your grapevine, Anatoly," Scanlon said with sudden seriousness.

"Of course not. Now, let's join my wife for that glass of wine and hope that we will share many more glasses of wine in the future."

Three wine glasses were waiting on the coffee table when they returned to the house.

"You two must have had a lot of catching up to do," Valeriya said, more as a question than a statement.

"Two old warriors far from the field of battle—of course, there is always much to talk about," Anatoly responded.

"I understand you have a new grandchild since we last saw one another," Scanlon said in an obvious effort to redirect the conversation.

Valeriya was far too gracious not to accept the course correction. "Yes, and he's adorable. Of course, no more adorable than our eight other grandchildren," she smiled, pointing to a photo on the coffee table.

"It's a good life, Valeriya. I'm happy that you and Anatoly have adapted so well."

"Thomas, if only ordinary Russians could see what a wonderful country America is—except maybe for McDonald's. You can keep your fast food. I'd rather have boiled potatoes and a pot of borscht."

"On that wonderful note, I'm afraid I'm going to have to say goodbye and get back to work."

"But you've barely touched your wine!" the Belikovs said in synchrony.

"That was a very heavy pour—one that would last me the balance of the afternoon. I'll tell you what—I promise to call and set up a dinner date soon."

"We're going to hold you to it." Anatoly raised a fist and gave it a quick twist, as if to seal the deal.

The half-hour they had spent leisurely consuming wine had pushed Scanlon's anxiety level off the chart. He knew they were in a race against time. As soon as he had said his goodbyes, he jumped into the car and headed to the Agency. He called Hart en route.

"It appears that our fears are well placed," he said, knowing the line was secure. "I suggest you bring in the team. They need to hear this now!"

CHAPTER TWENTY-NINE

Tribal Region, Pakistan

THE SUN WAS JUST BREAKING over the tops of the mountains as Sayed and Tariq Abu al Khayr prepared to leave the remote training camp that had been their home for two months. The camp, which was little more than a collection of tents, lean-tos, and latrines, was run by Tehrik-e-Taliban—a group that shared ideologies and resources with UIS.

Two hours earlier, Sayed and al Khayr had been summoned to the leader's tent, given a fresh change of western clothes, and told to prepare for the long journey ahead. They knew better than to ask questions, for there would be no answers.

The two men had undergone a metamorphosis since arriving from the factory. The 110-degree days spent under a sweltering sun had burned away all remnants of body fat, leaving only highly efficient killing machines.

Flanking Sayed and al Khayr were two men new to the camp. They introduced themselves simply as Hamzah and Jamal. Their manner was curt and their authority clear—communicated by locked and loaded AK-47s. Wordlessly, they pointed to an aging Toyota Land Cruiser and gestured for the men to get in.

Minutes later, the SUV was careening across the rough desert terrain headed to Karachi. If Sayed's memory was correct, they should pick up the semblance of a road in ten or fifteen miles. Still, it would be a long, dusty, and often brutally rough ride.

Sayed reflected on what he had learned over the last two months. He had risen each morning for prayer, after which there had been long lectures. Once the temperature had risen above 95 degrees, they would move outside and begin physical drills, starting on a makeshift range used for weapons training.

Their goal was to achieve maximum killing power with an AK-47. It was not an easy task with a gun that was less than accurate. Its popularity was due to three factors: It was cheap to manufacture, readily available, and more reliable than the M-16. Plus, at close range, you didn't need a great deal of accuracy with a firing rate of 600 rounds per minute.

Mistakes were not tolerated. When one trainee failed to dislodge a misfired bullet jammed in his gun, his trainer slammed the butt of his rifle into the back of the man's knee. He let out a sharp cry and went down fast.

The message was clear—don't screw up, even for a second.

Beyond the AK-47, trainees had to demonstrate proficiency with a variety of handguns, RPGs, and PK machine guns. It was evident to Sayed that his trainers had vast experience with every weapon—and not just on the range. These were war-hardened jihadists—the kind that had recruited and trained his brother, Kaleen.

In the afternoon, two hours were reserved for instruction in unarmed combat. It was an unorthodox mix of karate, Muay-Thai boxing, and taekwondo, but it was remarkably effective in taking down multiple attackers. Sayed's kicks and strikes progressed from sloppy and imprecise to focused and powerful.

When the other trainees were given a break from the exhausting, non-stop routine, Sayed and al-Khayr were taken to a separate area for specialized training. There, they were shown the rudiments of a system that could aerosolize and disperse a continuous, invisible cloud of biological agent. The equipment and their trainer had been provided by the factory.

By the end of each day, they would drag their limp, sweat-soaked bodies back to their tents for an hour of rest before the evening program began.

After evening prayers and dinner, they received lessons on Western customs, colloquialisms, even humor, all of which were viewed as important tools to help lower the enemy's guard. It was remarkably sophisticated training, considering the setting. Moreover, it was delivered by American and British jihadists with names such as Jim, George, and Jake, though they preferred their Arabic noms de guerre.

One trainee had made the mistake of maligning Tom, one of the Americans. Before he knew what hit him, the recruit was flat on his back with the sharp tip of a knife blade pressing against his Adam's apple. The point made, Tom slowly withdrew the knife and helped the man to his feet. It was a mistake that would not be repeated.

Most nights concluded with videos depicting the atrocities of the infidels, including videos from prisons such as

Abu Ghraib. Explanations were given as to why Holy Jihad was needed to purge the earth of apostates and infidels. The videos were expertly produced, as was most UIS propaganda. Such propaganda was essential to the success of UIS's recruiting efforts.

The SUV lurched to a stop, snapping Sayed back to the present moment. Traffic had come to a momentary standstill. As he stared out of the window, he realized how far they had traveled while he was absorbed in reflection. Desert brush had given way to dirt roads, then to gravel and rock, and ultimately to the paved highway they were now on.

The traffic jam cleared, and soon they were cruising at 100 kilometers per hour. A scant three hours later, Jamal broke the silence.

"Karachi!" he exclaimed, pointing to faint lights on the distant horizon.

Karachi was the seventh largest city in the world, with much of its growth occurring over the past decade. In addition to being home to twenty-five million people, it housed Pakistan's most important corporations and financial institutions. It was also the country's primary port.

As the outline of a massive city rose from the surrounding desert scrub, Sayed understood why it was often referred to as the City of Lights. It glistened like bright specks of quartz against a matrix of muted rock.

When signs for the airport appeared, Jamal spoke again, this time in flawless English. "Here are your travel documents. The four of us are traveling to New York's JFK airport via two different connecting flights in London. We will enter the airport separately. We will not sit together on the planes, nor even acknowledge each other's existence. In fact, we will not speak again until after we clear United States Customs and Immigration. Do you understand?"

Tariq and Sayed nodded in unison.

CHAPTER THIRTY

Karachi, Pakistan
Indianapolis, Indiana

TWENTY-FOUR HOURS AFTER DEPARTING Karachi International Airport, Sayed stood in a long line waiting to clear U.S. customs and immigration. As the queue snaked slowly forward, he wondered which required more time—a flight from the other side of the world or gaining entry to the United States. As if someone had read his mind, a handful of additional agents entered to man the empty immigration stations.

The pace picked up, and soon Sayed was cleared for entry. He navigated through the international terminal towards Terminal 2. As instructed, he proceeded to the Buffalo Wild Wings adjacent to Gate 26 and waited. Within minutes, he could see Jamal striding towards him. He greeted Sayed with the warmth normally reserved for the closest of friends.

"Smile, Sayed, and act as though you are glad to see me."

Jamal's tone dropped to a whisper, "Listen to me. Your flight leaves in forty minutes. You and I will be joined at the hip until you climb on board that plane."

The service was slow, and Sayed kept looking at his watch as the minutes ticked by. When fifteen minutes remained, Jamal stood up abruptly, threw some money on the table, and said, "Let's go."

They walked a short distance to Gate 30, where a final call was in progress for all passengers departing for Indianapolis.

"I will be leaving you at the gate for your next flight."

"Where am I going?" Sayed asked.

"Indianapolis. I believe you know it well. When you arrive, someone will meet you. That's all you need to know for now."

A dozen yards ahead of them, Sayed glimpsed a similar scene unfolding with Tariq and Hamzah.

"Where is Tariq going?" Sayed asked.

"St. Louis," came the quick response. "No more questions. Just do your duty," Jamal said as they closed in on Sayed's gate. "I will stay at the gate until your flight departs."

"That's really not necessary, I . . ."

Jamal cut him off. "No more discussion." His tone was now firm, almost menacing.

Once safely ensconced on the plane, Sayed turned his full attention to what had been tormenting him for hours. He had to get a message to Commander Hart—but how? His cell phone had been confiscated, and Jamal had not let him out of his sight while in the terminal, making it impossible for him to use a pay phone.

As the flight attendant was instructing passengers to power down their cell phones, Sayed turned to his seatmate. "Can I please borrow your phone? I just need to send a quick text."

"Don't you have a phone?" the man griped, clearly irritated by the request.

"I left it on my last flight. Please, I'd be most grateful!" he implored of his less-than-receptive neighbor.

"Fine," the man relinquished his grip on his phone and handed it to Sayed. "Be quick. I don't want it taken away!"

Sayed entered Hart's phone number, then texted: *Arriving in Indianapolis at 12:30 PM—being met at the gate. Will call when I can. Not feeling well—there may be some bug going around. Sayed.*

As he handed back the phone, the man next to him couldn't help himself. He glanced at the message. Startled, he began looking around for an open seat, preferably as far from Sayed as possible. Eyeing one, he stood up and said, "Thanks, buddy. I don't have any interest in getting the flu!" and squeezed past him into the aisle.

If you only knew, Sayed thought.

CHAPTER THIRTY-ONE

HART SENSED THE VIBRATION IMMEDIATELY. A single pulse meant a text message, not a call. And though it would undoubtedly prove not to be urgent, he nonetheless removed the cell phone from his breast pocket and looked at the screen.

He stared at the message for a long time—and was grateful that Sayed was alive. He assumed that Sayed's words were a clear pronouncement that a biological attack was imminent.

Hart thanked his host, then excused himself from the reception he was attending at the Ritz in Pentagon City. He moved quickly to the hotel's garage. His black BMW was parked facing out towards the exit, as was Hart's habit. It took him just seconds to clear the property. At the same time, he placed a call to Phil Esposito in the Counter-Terrorism Center.

As he merged into the traffic on Hayes Street and headed for Army Navy Drive, Esposito answered. Hart quickly explained that he needed Esposito's help deploying a welcoming party for Sayed—one that would remain safely undercover with instructions simply to follow Sayed and whoever was meeting him at the airport.

"John, I wish I could help you, but we're stretched to the max. Plus, I don't know how I would field a team that quickly," Esposito said, trying to punt responsibility to TSA.

"Phil, don't make me turn to TSA. God knows what will happen to Sayed in that case. If TSA can't detect ninety-five out of a hundred weapons passing through airport security, how can I trust them with my most precious asset?"

"Okay, point taken. I'll get a team dispatched right away."

"The *right* team, Phil."

"Of course, the right team."

CTC would mobilize two of its best agents, Gina Harmon and Alex Ross. They were based in Carmel, which was close enough to Indianapolis International Airport to arrive ahead of the flight. Esposito made it clear: They were to observe, not close in. If they were detected, the consequences could be catastrophic.

Posing as husband and wife and dressed as if they had just left the hills and hollers of Kentucky, agents Harmon and Ross arrived at the terminal thirty minutes before Sayed's flight was scheduled to land.

From a safe distance, they watched as Sayed deplaned. He walked through the gate and towards the main terminal, where a man slowly began to walk towards him . . . soon matching him stride for stride. The agents followed at a safe distance.

As they walked past baggage claim, the man grabbed Sayed's arm and pulled him through an exit door. The swift movement almost caused Sayed to lose his grip on the wheeled carry-on bouncing behind him. Barely holding onto the bag, he was shoved into the back seat of a nondescript maroon Camry, which sped off before even a single digit of the license plate could be captured.

Harmon and Ross stood with their mouths open. Sayed had once again vanished.

Esposito would be furious. Hart would be beside himself.

Once they were miles from the airport and closing in on an exit for I-70 West, the man driving the Camry pulled off at a rest stop. Parking next to a silver Accord, he handed the keys to Sayed along with directions to Sarah and Babur Qaisrani's house near Columbia, Missouri.

"Your exit is one mile ahead. Good luck, Sayed, and may Allah smile upon you."

As he turned to leave, the man said, "There's just one more thing."

With that, a man who had sat silently in the backseat reached up and put his hand on Sayed's shoulder. "I will be accompanying you for the ride, Sayed . . . just to make sure that you arrive safely at the Qaisranis," he said, effectively eliminating any opportunity for Sayed to reach out to the commander.

There was nothing he could do. Sayed calculated that, even at a modest pace, he would complete the drive from Indianapolis to Columbia in less than seven hours. That was nothing compared to the past seventy-two hours, during which he had been transported from the primitive austerity of a makeshift training camp in remote Pakistan to the commercialism and decadence of America. After two months of immersion in the camp, the culture shock was overwhelming.

Fifty miles ticked off on the car's odometer, putting them close to Terre Haute, while Sayed replayed the past. It was a way of keeping his mind occupied and his fate at bay. But his mind kept returning to the imminent attack. Soon he would receive his final instructions before being sent off to unleash a living hell on the Americans. There was no turning back, nor turning away.

CHAPTER THIRTY-TWO

Detroit, Michigan
Columbia, Missouri

AL HAMEED AND VALIKHANOV ARRIVED at the safe house at 8:20 PM. It was eight blocks from Ahmed's childhood home on Hartwell Street. A part of him yearned to be home. He imagined sitting with his father at that moment, explaining to him the role he would play in ushering in Armageddon. He ruminated over the necessary sacrificial role befalling his family.

At 10:30 PM, Jarod Hartman arrived at the safe house. Umami's pilot was an unimpressive college drop-out who craved a meaningful identity. He had found one as an Islamic sympathizer with aspirations of being a jihadist.

The process had begun four years earlier, when he had been recruited by a group of Islamists attending flight school near Delray Beach, Florida. Following his training, his recruiters had provided an introduction to Umami, who offered him a job. Hartman began flying short missions to remote locations. Over time, he proved his competency and won Umami's confidence. Then he began to take on increasingly important assignments.

As promised, Al Hameed and Valikhanov enthusiastically welcomed him. After ushering him into the home, they excused themselves momentarily to retrieve the suitcases from the trunk of Hartman's rental car. The package had survived the dangerous journey from the factory in Faisalabad to the heart of America. Soon its contents would be transferred to the hands of jihadists ready to inflict a mortal wound to this country. Al Hameed deposited the suitcases safely in the bedroom and returned to Jarod.

Putting his hand on Jarod's shoulder, Al Hameed praised him for his service to Allah: "You've heard that seventy-two virgins await martyrs in paradise, but I have one awaiting you now in the basement. Consider it a gift for your hard work." He smiled and guided the man towards a set of stairs leading to an unfinished basement.

It was an unexpected but welcome surprise for the young American pilot, whose wife was far more interested in tending to the needs of their small children than to the passions of her husband. She will never know, he thought, as he let the excitement of the imminent conquest fill his mind.

As they reached the bottom of the stairs, Jarod looked around but saw nothing except shelves loaded with plastic bins, an old washer and dryer, and a stack of yellowing newspapers. Turning back towards Al Hameed, he caught the briefest glimpse of the barrel of Al Hameed's silenced 9 mm Sig Sauer pistol before two hollow-point bullets were embedded deep in his brain. One bullet careened through the back of his skull, creating a massive exit wound and scattering bone fragments and brain across the floor and wall. Eyes wide open and unblinking, Jarod's body crumpled onto the cold concrete floor.

Al Hameed climbed the stairs, where he was greeted by his host, Fuad Areem.

"I'm sorry, Fuad, to have made a mess of your clean basement. If you would be so kind as to give me some trash bags, a saw, and some bleach, I will clean up after myself."

"You have done the difficult part. Allow me to do my small part. After all, you are protecting me and this house from discovery."

"So be it," Al Hameed said, with a quick nod of agreement. "Beibut and I must rest and pray. We will speak to you in the morning."

"Before you retire, there is still one thing we must do," Fuad said as he led them into a small unfurnished bedroom. Instead of a bed, there was a seamless backdrop, lights, and a digital camera sitting atop a tripod.

"I need a few pictures. I also need a sample of your signatures."

In the morning, Fuad Areem began doling out identification. First came the Michigan drivers' licenses bearing their newly taken photos and signatures. They were also given credit cards and passports.

Areem shoved a key ring across the table to Al Hameed. "The pickup is in the driveway. It's full of gas and ready to go."

Exiting the house, Al Hameed and Valikhanov found an aging truck. The once bright red Ford 150 had seen years of hard service marshalling through the snow and salt of Michigan winters. Rust had eaten through the front bumper and was now going to work on the wheel wells. An empty gun rack was visible through the back window, and on the rear bumper, a faded but still legible sticker proclaimed: "America, Love It or Leave It!"

"I would have preferred a Mercedes," Al Hameed said to his host.

"German cars are as welcome in Detroit as jihadists. I thought you would want to vanish into the landscape, and I have provided you the perfect car for doing so," came Areem's quick response.

The driver's side door opened with a grating creak, causing Al Hameed to raise an eyebrow as he lifted himself into the cab. To his surprise, it fired up with the first turn of the key.

After thanking Fuad, Al Hameed and Valikhanov headed for I-75 South towards Toledo. There was no straight shot to Columbia, Missouri. Rather, their route would cut diagonally across Ohio and Indiana, where they would pick up I-70 towards Illinois.

"How long is the drive?" Valikhanov asked a scant thirty minutes later.

"Ten hours, maybe a few minutes more. Are you in a hurry or just eager to see the fruits of your labor spread across this massive nation?"

"I will rest easier when the team is assembled and we know that everyone and everything is in place," Beibut confided.

"Spoken like an anxious woman," Al Hameed chided his companion.

"No more anxious than you," Beibut countered, "just more willing to admit it."

Both men laughed. They knew the victory they had so long awaited was finally at hand.

"So tell me again, how confident are you in your projections regarding the spread of the virus?" Al Hameed said more seriously.

"As confident as I can be with a novel pathogen that has never been proven in the field. Rest assured, the logic underlying the mathematical model is solid. If there is a miscalculation, it is tied to how long people will remain ambulatory after infection. As you've seen, it is a horrific infection with a brief prodromal period during which victims appear to be well. Once patients are symptomatic, they begin to suffer. The rate at which that suffering escalates to the point of incapacitation is the variable in question."

"Why did you not rely on existing scenarios to predict the virus' progression? The U.S. government spent millions formulating such models."

"Yes, and they reflect the linear thinking of the U.S. government. They failed to consider that the virus might be altered."

"Go on."

"Their scenarios rely on a normal variant of smallpox, not a genetically modified hemorrhagic virus. As such, the prodromal period used in their projections may be as long as seventeen days. The mortality rate is a mere thirty percent, and the level of infectivity is markedly lower. It is apples and oranges, to borrow an American phrase."

"Your one caveat—how long victims remain ambulatory once the symptoms appear—how significantly could it impact the projected spread?"

"By orders of magnitude, but I believe I have been conservative in my estimations. As I've told you before, the virus will roar through the unprotected population like a wildfire during a drought."

"I'm counting on it," Al Hameed said with a tone and look that made Valikhanov squirm in his seat.

As they spoke, a highway patrol car slowly passed them. Al Hameed glanced quickly at the speedometer—precisely sixty-five miles per hour, no reason for concern. Even so, he couldn't help but glance at the trooper, whose broad-brimmed hat seemed oddly comical.

The trooper did not return the glance but waited until he was well past their truck before switching to the right lane. Al Hameed was forced to follow him, at a short distance, for the better part of an hour before the trooper finally turned off just south of Holland, Ohio.

The remainder of the trip was uneventful. It was the Midwest—no mountains, no ocean, nothing to gaze upon in awe. Just mile after mile of farmland, silos, and occasional patches of timber. Yet it was part of the vast continent that would become their spoils, a land that would someday form the western edge of the Caliphate.

A little after 5 PM they turned off I-70 onto Missouri State Highway 179 South, about twenty minutes west of Columbia. They were closing in on their final destination—a farmhouse in Pierpont, Missouri, where their comrades awaited them.

CHAPTER THIRTY-THREE

Pierpont, Missouri

GPS WAS AMONG THE GREATEST GIFTS bestowed upon the civilized world by the infidels, Al Hameed concluded as the navigation unit guided him flawlessly past Rock Bridge Memorial State Park to where Route N and Highway 163 coalesced in Pierpont, Missouri. Without it, he could easily have missed this speck of a town and its rectangular green sign proclaiming a population of seventy-seven.

Al Hameed and Valikhanov continued south until the road terminated, at which point the GPS unit went from being a remarkable aid to a repetitive annoyance, as it obsessively chanted *recalculating*. Shutting off the now useless unit, Al Hameed removed a scrap of paper from his pocket and unfolded a small map with hand-written directions. As described, a dirt road could be seen ahead on the right. It was largely obscured by overgrown brush and thus could be easily missed. Once on it, Al Hameed followed the road until it dead-ended after a mile.

Where the road ended, tire tracks continued, forging a rough path through prairie grass and rock-hard mud. After a couple hundred yards, the car cleared a small rise to reveal a meticulously maintained nineteenth-century stone farmhouse.

Having heard the approaching car, Babur Qaisrani and his wife, Sarah, stood ready to welcome their guests.

After a traditional greeting, Al Hameed surveyed the surrounding land. "You have a beautiful piece of property, and it appears to be far from prying eyes."

"It's been in my family for more than six generations. I'm just the current custodian," Sarah said. "As for privacy, we've got a section of land—640 acres—a square mile of privacy. And you are standing right in the heart of it."

Sarah and Babur relished their seclusion. The couple had been married for nearly twenty years. Sarah met Babur while she was a graduate student at the University of Missouri, and, much to the chagrin of her conservative parents, began a relationship with her Pakistani instructor. He taught her not only an appreciation for eastern literature, but a reverence for the spiritual richness of Islam. With it came a deep contempt for any threat to their religion or their radicalized version of its ideology.

Together, they formed an important cell in al-Bakr's network. Their loyalty to UIS was unquestioned. Both Babur and Sarah enjoyed an unusually close relationship with al-Bakr. Whereas Babur was an invaluable propagandist and ideologue, Sarah was a warrior, capable of being every bit as barbaric as the most ruthless jihadist.

Clear proof could be seen in her relationship with her parents, who had been an ongoing source of friction for the couple since they were first engaged. Sarah tired of her parents' relentless prejudice against anyone non-white and non-Christian . . . including and especially Babur.

While most young people would deal with the situation through simple but effective avoidance, Sarah was not nearly so genteel.

Sarah's father had been the first to go. It had been a tragic accident, the kind that happens from time to time on farms. Heavy machinery and drinking don't mix, and George Bonner was known to drink. So it came as no surprise when neighbors heard the horrifying news that George had been caught in the combine. Apparently he had not fully disengaged the gears when he jumped down from the cab to clear something from the combine's path. When Sheriff Bill Tilson arrived on the scene, he was greeted by a limbless torso, its face an unrecognizable mass of shredded flesh.

Unimaginable was the way the sheriff had described George's body, complete with a quiver of his lower lip. He chose wisely not to give any more details to the press. A grieving Sarah had been called in to identify him. Had it not been for a small tattoo of SEMPER FI that remained unscathed above his right breast, the job would have been nearly impossible. Every deputy in the department was touched to the core by the long, piercing wail that emerged from Sarah that day.

When her job was done, she shuffled out of the room, crying softly. Once out of sight, Sarah wiped the tears from her face, saying under her breath, "One down and one to go."

She waited eighteen months before tackling her next task. It was rendered easier by the increasing spite with which Sarah's mother's castigated them in the months after her husband's death. She held them accountable for George's death—not literally, of course. Not even Mary

Bonner could have imagined such evil. George's drinking, long under control, had started up again during his daughter's courtship by that dark-skinned professor. Her husband had kept his hatred bottled up as long as he could, but eventually it overtook him, as did the bottle itself.

Sarah called 911 on a fateful October day when she found her mother dead. Next to her was a note asking for her daughter's forgiveness. Mary Bonner's note explained that, without her devoted husband, life was no longer worth living.

It had not been an easy suicide for Sarah and Babur to execute. They had come to Mary the previous night seeking a truce and asking what they could do to win her favor and make up for the hardship they had helped to create.

Dubious at first, Mary reluctantly let them in. As they sat in the parlor, Sarah offered to get everyone something to drink.

"There's a pitcher of fresh lemonade in the icebox," Mary offered.

"That's perfect, Mother," Sarah said, excusing herself.

Into Mary's glass, Sarah poured a small amount of gamma hydroxybutyric acid. It was just enough to sedate her mother, but not enough to remain detectable in Mary's bloodstream if or when an autopsy was performed.

"Here, Mother," she said, handing Mary the glass of the tainted lemonade.

Within minutes, Mary's eyes were fluttering. Then she leaned precariously forward, forcing Babur to catch her before she fell. They carried the semi-conscious woman up to her bedroom and placed her on the bed. Sarah wrote her mother's suicide note, carefully matching Mary's penmanship letter for letter. She ensured that it slanted to the left, that the loops were of the appropriate diameter, and that certain words were misspelled, just as they always were in her mother's correspondence.

Content with her handiwork, Sarah searched through her mother's medications until she found the bottle of OxyContin that Mary had received following a hip replacement. Afraid that she might become addicted, Sarah's mother had taken the pills only when her pain reached a nine out of ten on the scale the doctor had given her. At least fifteen remained in the orange plastic container.

Sarah went to the kitchen and carefully crushed them, then mixed them with a little of her father's bourbon. Returning to the bedroom, she had Babur hold Mary's head back while she poured the lethal concoction down her mother's throat.

Sarah and Babur each pulled on a pair of surgical gloves and proceeded to wipe their fingerprints from the bottle and the glass before taking Mary's hand and wrapping it around the tumbler and the pill bottle. The crime scene didn't have to be pristine; after all, the sheriff would be responding to an apparent suicide in Sarah's family home. But neither could it suggest the possibility of murder.

In the small town of Pierpont, everyone's heart cried out in sorrow for the massive loss that Sarah and Babur had experienced. People wondered how Sarah possessed the strength to go on after losing two parents under such devastating circumstances. Clearly Sarah had a source of deep strength, which most God-fearing people in this part of the country attributed to her Christian upbringing, completely unaware of her ties to radical Islam.

Al Hameed stepped closer to Sarah and Babur. "I understand you recently played host to some friends of ours?" Al Hameed asked, although he knew the answer.

"Yes, our friends from Jamat ul-Fuqra were here for two weeks of training. Nothing too exotic and certainly nothing too loud that would attract attention. After all, we must maintain appearances," Sarah said with a smile.

"I trust it went well?"

"I assume so. Babur and I were surprised and pleased when Sheikh Mubarak Ali Gilani thanked us for our support."

Gilani was not an easy man to please. He was ruthless, particularly when it came to Jews. Gilani had purportedly been complicit in the death of journalist Daniel Pearl. As such, he commanded Sarah's respect. She knew that Al Hameed was every bit as ruthless, and she seemed to feed on this knowledge in her uniquely perverse way.

As they spoke, Al Hameed's eyes were drawn to spots on Sarah and Babur's upper arms. Close to their shoulders were circular ulcers in the final stage of healing. Valikhanov, observing the glance, nodded to Al Hameed, "They were inoculated with the experimental vaccine three weeks ago."

"Beibut, how did you get the vaccine here?"

"It was part of a shipment of medical supplies being transported by our friend in London. Once the shipment cleared customs, it was an easy task to mail the vial of vaccine to our friends."

Returning his attention to Babur and Sarah, Al Hameed smiled. "It's good to see that you are among the Chosen Ones."

Babur bowed before speaking. "We are grateful to serve UIS in some small measure, and we are grateful to be among those privileged to bear witness to the conquest of the infidels."

Al Hameed slapped Babur on the back. "And now, may we greet the other guests?"

Before they entered the house, Al Hameed removed the suitcases from the trunk of the car and carried them up the walk. As they entered the house, the din of conversation could be heard from the back of the house. A small crowd was congregating on the flagstone patio.

Al Hameed studied the group before joining it. He was relieved to see that every piece had fallen neatly in place. The bio-weapon that had begun life in a former Soviet laboratory was now safely on American soil, as were the tools of its delivery. What the Soviets had begun, the United Islamic State would finish.

Sayed and Tariq stood closest to him as Al Hameed stepped onto the flagstones.

"I understand that you were exemplary in your training exercises," he said, gesturing to both men.

"We are grateful to have been selected. We worked each day to honor you and Allah," Sayed said, speaking for Tariq and himself.

Next he greeted Ahmed al-Shishani and Kameel Imad al-Din, acknowledging the vitally important role they had played in transporting the bio-weapon from Karachi to London.

"I understand that ISI played a game with you at the airport in Karachi," Al Hameed suggested to the men.

"Yes, they tested us," al-Shishani confirmed.

"You might take some pleasure in knowing that the ticket agent who *tested* you has gone missing. Apparently, he has not shown up for work since the day after your flight." Al Hameed smiled briefly before moving on.

Finally, Al Hameed was introduced to the two remaining men: an engineer responsible for the aerosolization devices that would disperse the agents, and a scientist responsible for safely transferring the biological agents from the suitcases to those devices and ensuring that everything was fully operational.

Formalities behind them, Babur directed their guests to the dining room, where Sarah had prepared a feast. It was the food of a faraway land, food that would bring both satiety and great comfort. They began with tabbouleh, several flavors of hummus, babaghanooj, fresh pita, and dishes over-brimming with various types of olives. Next came roasted legs of lamb, kofta kabobs, and shish tawouk, all served with rice. For dessert, there would be ample baklava. It wasn't the fattening before a kill but the celebration of the coming transformation of the world and a restoration of its appropriate balance.

"I feel like I've died and gone to heaven," Al Hameed said in praise of Sarah at the conclusion of dinner.

She heard something dallying in his comment and allowed herself to flirt with the idea of what it would be like to make love to such a man. A dangerous proposition based not only on Al Hameed's temperament, but also the punishment for adultery under Sharia law. She would let it go, for now. He was not worth pursuing as long as al-Bakr remained in charge.

After dinner, the tone shifted from one of celebration to a more somber and reflective one. It was time for the final briefing.

A prayer was said, after which Al Hameed and Valikhanov reviewed all the details of the mission with the assembled team. Each member was given a dossier on their selected airports, with reconnaissance photographs illustrating the most heavily trafficked yet unsecured areas of the terminals. They were also given instructions on precisely where to drop their equipment when they were finished dispersing the agent and prior to clearing security for their flights.

"Good night, my brothers. You should sleep well knowing that tomorrow you will leave the warmth of this home to do God's work. We will awaken you at 5 AM and expect you to be on the road by 5:20. Are there any questions?" Al Hameed paused momentarily. "Good, then. I will see you in six hours."

CHAPTER THIRTY-FOUR

Pierpont, Missouri

THE CLOCK INSIDE SAYED'S HEAD ticked incessantly. He knew that, with every passing second, the likelihood of stopping Al Hameed's plan grew dimmer. And he knew that, if he was caught, he would die the excruciating death of a traitor. Still, he had to get word to Commander Hart.

It was 2 AM before the stillness of sleep had finally descended upon the home of Babur and Sarah Qaisrani. The three men with whom he shared a room lay motionless. Two were snoring gently, a reassuring sound. The bed sheets covering the third man were rising and falling with rhythmic regularity. Sayed prayed that he, too, was deeply asleep, as he carefully slipped out of bed.

He picked up his shoes, then clothes, and began sliding his bare feet, inch by inch, across the wood floor. He was one creak away from discovery. He made it as far as the hallway door without a sound. His escape route was now only a few feet away.

The door to the bathroom had been left open by an earlier visitor. Sayed stepped in and shut it slowly so the hinges on the old door would not sing out in betrayal. Without turning on the light, he threw on his clothes. As his eyes adjusted to the darkness, he could make out the details of a window frame on the far wall. He pulled the window open and gazed into the black night.

Standing with one foot on the toilet and a hand on the sink, he raised his right leg and thrust it through the window frame. Shifting his grip, he repeated the action with his left leg. Soon he was sitting on the sill with both legs dangling. He launched from his perch and landed on soft, moist grass. Reaching up, he pulled the window closed, then broke into a full sprint towards the edge of the woods.

Three hours passed before Sayed's absence was detected. It was 5 AM, and Al Hameed was rousing the men from their deep sleep.

"Where is Sayed?" he demanded furiously.

The men looked at one another dumbfounded and then to the ground. It would be unwise to make eye contact with Al Hameed, whose eyes blazed with fire.

"He's either a traitor or a coward," Al Hameed shouted, as though Sayed might hear him. "Either way, his soul will burn in hell!"

"Let us find him!" one of the men called out.

"No, there's no time. He won't get far, and even if he does and tells a fanciful story, who will believe him? It will be the ravings of a lunatic!" Al Hameed said, more to console himself than the others. But he was not finished.

"Someone must take his place," Al Hameed commanded.

Babur responded instantly, "I will do it. It was on my watch that he betrayed us."

He bowed reverently as he approached Al Hameed. "You are far too important to risk being a casualty of this mission. I will go gladly in Sayed's place."

Al Hameed realized that, lacking Sayed's photo identification, Babur would not be able to board his intended flight. Even so, it was a minor glitch. The destruction Babur would wreak in the DFW terminal would still be profound.

"Thank you, and may Allah grant you success with your sacred mission," Al Hameed said, embracing Babur.

Al Hameed would not tolerate any further disruption of his plan. He expected everyone to be ready at 5:20 AM as planned, even Babur.

Before he could leave their bedroom, Sarah took Babur by the hand.

"I'm so proud of you, Babur. It is a truly selfless act that you are committing in the name of Allah."

"It is what must be done, Sarah, nothing more, nothing less."

"Your humility comes from your heart, a heart I hold immeasurably close to mine. Go, and may Allah watch over you until we are reunited on this earth or in heaven."

Babur's eyes moistened as he realized that this moment might be their last together. "You know how much I love you. Only for Allah would I make such a sacrifice."

Sarah knew nothing of being selfless, though her acting talents were beyond reproach. Even her husband of many years failed to recognize her duplicity. While she touched Babur's heart, her own heart remained stone cold. Even as the tears welled in his eyes, Sarah was revisiting how she might seduce Al Hameed once Babur was gone.

Man by man, the jihadists began to file out. The first to leave was Ahmed al-Shishani, who began the 2 ½-hour drive to Kansas City International Airport, where he would catch Delta flight 889 to Atlanta's Hartsfield. If everything proceeded as planned, he would check into Atlanta Airport Marriott Gateway, just a half mile from the terminal, by mid-afternoon.

Next, Kameel Imad al-Din headed east to St. Louis. With Lambert Field located on the west side of town, he should make it door-to-door in under two hours. From there, he would catch American 2022 to LAX, scheduled to depart at 10:30 AM, with a 12 PM arrival time. He would settle into the Concourse Hotel and patiently await his destiny.

Tariq Abu al Khayr headed northeast to Chicago, while Babur headed to DFW—Sayed's intended target. Both men had long drives ahead of them, though each found it gratifying not to rely on the airlines to deliver them to their targets. This, too, had been part of Al Hameed's fail-safe plan—a modification made after witnessing how computer glitches had temporarily shut down all Delta and Southwest flights the previous summer.

By 5:22 AM, only Al Hameed, Sarah Qaisrani, and Valikhanov remained in the house.

"Before you go, would you like me to show you where your compatriots trained last week?" Sarah asked softly of Al Hameed, communicating far more with her eyes than with her words.

Valikhanov, still bitter from his own wife's betrayal, pretended not to notice the look in Sarah's eyes.

"Perhaps another time," replied Al Hameed, averting his eyes from her steadfast gaze.

The two men thanked Sarah for her hospitality and walked out the door. They, too, were destined for Chicago, but it was only a stepping stone before their long flight to Pakistan. They would be far across the Atlantic before the attack even began.

All parts were now in motion, and Al Hameed allowed the impending glory from the imminent attacks to momentarily quell his anger at Sayed. He would find him eventually and deal with him. But nothing was going to take away from the triumph that lay ahead.

In the morning, Armageddon would begin—not with thunderous explosions, but with a sweet whisper, as an invisible mist of biological agent was released and carried throughout the terminals by a confluence of air currents.

CHAPTER THIRTY-FIVE

Columbia, Missouri

SAYED RAN UNTIL HIS LUNGS WERE CRYING OUT for air before he stopped, gasping. He estimated that he had covered at least six miles over the past hour. That left six more miles to Columbia. He wanted to move faster, to run at breakneck speed, but it would be foolhardy in the near pitch-black countryside, scarcely illuminated by the sliver of a partial moon. One misstep and a broken ankle could bring him to a crawl. He had already stumbled innumerable times, twisting his ankle in the process.

Sayed's only hope of averting the multi-pronged attack was to reach the local police and convince them to contact Commander Hart. It was a long shot. He had no idea where the police were located or if he was even moving in the right direction. He also knew that a man of Middle Eastern descent showing up unannounced in the early hours of the morning on the sheriff's doorstep might not sit well. But he had little choice.

By the time Sayed reached the outskirts of Columbia, his right ankle was swollen and throbbing. His clothes were soaked with perspiration, and his mind was dancing wildly. He was thankful that the months spent at the training camp had taught him how to manage pain. He climbed up a shallow embankment and onto the shoulder of a two-lane road. A sign indicated it was Missouri State Highway 201. Dawn was breaking, and Sayed began walking towards town.

As morning dawned, pickup trucks and an occasional car drove past. He stuck out his thumb, as he had seen Americans do in movies, and was surprised when an old truck stacked with hay bales stopped ahead of him. The driver of the truck hesitated for a moment, seemingly caught off guard by his foreign appearance, but then thrust open the door and told Sayed, "Come on now, get in."

The man, who was twice Sayed's mass and wearing bib overalls, asked, "Where you headed?"

"I need to get to the police as quickly as possible. Can you help me?"

"What kind of trouble are you in?" the farmer asked, his tone changing from congenial to suspicious.

"I am not in any trouble!" Sayed said emphatically. "I'm trying to prevent a problem."

"You're sure you're not in any trouble?" the man repeated.

"Yes, sir, I am not in any trouble."

They drove on silently for the next twenty minutes, finally arriving at a single-story brick building that housed the Boone County Sheriff's Department.

"Go on now, tell the sheriff whatever it is you need to get off your chest," the farmer said, reaching across Sayed and pushing open the door.

"Thank you," Sayed managed to call out before the truck trundled off down the road.

Relief surged through Sayed as he approached the building. Surely there would be time now to get word out and stop the unimaginable carnage that would otherwise occur.

As he neared the building, he glanced at a sign proudly proclaiming the department's mission: "Lead the fight to prevent crime and injustice. Enforce the law fairly and defend the rights of all. Partner with the people we serve to secure and promote safety in our communities."

As Sayed opened the door to Sheriff Bill Tilson's department, he suddenly stopped in his tracks. Sarah Qaisrani was standing next to a man whom he presumed to be the sheriff.

Equally surprised to see Sayed, she pointed to him and exclaimed, "That's the man I was telling you about, Bill! He broke into our house in the middle of the night, scared the living hell out of me and my husband, and then took off running into the woods."

The sheriff approached Sayed cautiously as he removed the guard on his holster, "Turn around very slowly and put your hands behind your head," he instructed Sayed.

CHAPTER THIRTY-SIX

Columbia, Missouri

"You've got to listen to me," Sayed implored. But Bill Tilson wasn't interested.

"I'm going to ask you one more time," he said with his gun now out of its holster and pointed squarely at Sayed's chest.

Sayed slowly raised his arms and placed them behind his head. Sheriff Tilson spun him around with one hand and pulled his arms down behind his back. Holstering the gun, he handcuffed him, then shoved him towards a holding area.

"Sheriff, you have to listen to me. This woman is part of a conspiracy to destroy this country."

"Really," Tilson said. "A conspiracy to destroy the United States. Sarah, I never knew you were so dangerous!"

"Looks can be deceiving, Bill," Sarah said, as they both laughed at the ludicrous tale being spun by this crazed man.

"Listen here, fella, I've known this woman all of my life, and I'd bet everything I own that she's telling the truth. So no more crazy talk, okay?"

A deputy appeared and took charge of Sayed, who was still pleading to be heard. They passed through a heavy metal door, which slammed behind them with a loud thud. Sayed fell silent.

Sarah said, "Thanks, Bill. I think this guy is nuts and maybe dangerous. Well, I guess he's your problem now."

"I'm going to need you to press charges, Sarah."

"Not a problem, I'll come back tomorrow morning, if that's okay."

"Could you bring Babur with you? We'll need his testimony, too."

"Babur left this morning for a business trip. I can try to reach him by cell, but I doubt he's in range. He'll have to come in when he returns in a couple of days."

"That will be fine." Tilson tipped his hat to Sarah as she turned to leave. He would never see her again.

Sarah headed back to the house, but only long enough to activate a delayed fuse on an incendiary device Babur had buried in the basement of the old farmhouse. It would give her eighteen hours to reach the Canadian border, then vanish before all remnants of her former life were consumed in a vicious conflagration of flames. Babur was supposed to have accompanied her, but that was before Sayed suddenly changed their plans. Still, there was a chance he would make it out of DFW and head for Matheson Island. If so, Sarah would plan a special welcome for him.

Sarah planned to stop mid-way and check into a cheap motel. She would catch a few hours of sleep, then shear her long auburn hair and dye it black. Finally, she would exchange the conservative dress that covered virtually every inch of her body for a short, provocative skirt and open blouse. That, she trusted, would douse any idea that she was a Muslim extremist.

She was headed to Matheson Island—a dot in the province of Manitoba along the narrows of Lake Winnipeg. Its population of 117 barely exceeded that of Pierpont. It was close enough to the U.S. border to provide ready access when needed, yet far enough removed from civilization to provide a healthy degree of anonymity.

Sarah opened the doors on her aged barn, revealing a vintage Land Cruiser. She and Babur had been storing it there for years, awaiting the day when they might be discovered and have to flee. It bore Canadian tags and was registered to a Rachel Carson Patel, who lived on Matheson Island. She checked the glovebox one last time to ensure that Rachel's passport and driver's license were safely stowed.

She quickly exchanged her Honda for the Land Cruiser, knowing that the barn, too, would be consumed in the inferno that was soon to come. Climbing into the spacious SUV, she headed towards Minneapolis. When she arrived there, she would be halfway home.

CHAPTER THIRTY-SEVEN

Columbia, Missouri

BY MID-AFTERNOON, SAYED WAS WORN OUT from hours of shouting in desperation. It did not matter what he said, nor how passionately he said it. Every word coming out of his mouth was ignored.

Now he watched as the bright red second hand on the clock measured off the final hours until Armageddon. Just a few minutes shy of 5 PM, the metal door swung open, and Bill Tilson walked in.

Tilson stood near the cell door, safely out of Sayed's reach. "I'm going home. You've made it a hell of an interesting day, I must say. I'll be back at 7:30 in the morning. We'll talk about what we're going to do with you then. In the meantime, shout your heart out if you want. No one is going to hear you, and even if they do, no one cares about what you have to say."

"Please give me five minutes . . . just five minutes," Sayed begged, but Tilson had already turned around and was walking out the door.

Sayed dropped onto the metal bed in his cell.

Before leaving, Tilson left a clear order with his deputy: "No one is to talk to the prisoner until I return."

The night seemed without end as Sayed replayed all the events leading up to his arrest. Berating himself, he wondered what he could have done differently to avert the tragedy that was now unfolding.

Per the sheriff's instructions, no one entered the holding area until shortly before 7 AM, when Sheriff's Deputy Carl Taylor stepped in to check on the prisoner and bring him breakfast. As he slid a tray of powdered eggs and toast under the bars of the cell, Sayed jumped off the bed.

"You've got to listen to me . . . please. Many people are going to die if you don't. It may already be too late."

But the deputy simply stepped back, ignoring Sayed's plea.

"Please, I'm telling you the truth. Something horrible is about to happen. You have to let me make a call!"

The deputy had questioned Tilson about the prisoner's right to make a call, but Tilson had made it clear that the prisoner had no rights.

Tears were now streaming down Sayed's cheeks.

Whether true or not, it was clear to Deputy Taylor that Sayed believed his rants, despite his boss's misgivings. Even so, he walked out without ever making eye contact with the prisoner. It's what Tilson had ordered.

Sayed felt his stomach turn, much as it had the day he was shown photos of the aftermath of his brother's suicide bombing. He hung his head over the steel toilet in his cell and threw up.

Thirty minutes later, the door swung open again. Carl Taylor stood motionless, staring at him.

"Every prisoner gets one phone call. You never got your one call, did ya? Well, better give me the number."

Returning to his desk, Taylor picked up the phone, held it for a few seconds, and then put it down. He repeated this action three times before finally dialing the number. Just as it was beginning to ring, Bill Tilson walked in. It was 7:18 AM, and he was twelve minutes early.

"Who're you calling, Carl?"

The guard handed the phone to the Sheriff. "It's the number the prisoner asked me to call."

Tilson reached over to hang up, but Carl covered the cradle with his huge hand. Incensed by his deputy's insubordination, Tilson glared at Carl as the sheriff slowly raised the receiver to his ear. He was in no mood to be kind and gentle to whomever answered the phone.

A gravelly male voice on the other end was repeating a question: "How can I help you, officer?"

"What the hell!" Tilson exclaimed involuntarily. Caller ID was blocked on this phone.

"Who is this?" he demanded.

"Officer, you are on a restricted line and are being recorded. Please state your business," came the response.

Tilson vacillated. Should he simply hang up, slamming the receiver down on Carl's hand if necessary? Something stopped him. It was a niggling fear, deep down, that he should have listened to the prisoner.

"This is Bill Tilson, Sheriff of Boone County, Missouri. I've got a prisoner in my jail who insists that we call this number. I don't know who the hell you are, but I'm only calling because this whack job keeps screaming that all kinds of shit is about to hit the fan. He says he has to talk to Commander Hart."

"What is the prisoner's name?" came the monotone response.

"He calls himself Sayed."

"Do nothing. Do not approach the prisoner or engage with him again until you hear back from us," the gravelly-voiced man instructed.

Hanging up the phone, Tilson sat down, resting his elbows on his legs and covering his eyes as if to blot out the world. "What the hell is going on, Carl?"

"I don't know Sheriff, but I know that this man believes he's telling us the truth."

Eight minutes later the phone rang. "This is Commander Hart. How long have you been holding Sayed?"

Tilson, having regained a small degree of composure, had questions of his own. "And who the hell are you?"

"I'm your worst nightmare, Sheriff Tilson, if you don't start answering my questions. Let's try this again. How long have you been holding Sayed?"

The color drained from Tilson's face and he began to sweat. He hated dealing with the feds. It always brought problems.

"He came in yesterday morning. One of our locals identified him as the man who had tried to break into her house last night, so we made him comfortable in one of our finest cells. Only the best accommodations for his kind. I'm sure you understand."

"No, I don't understand! What I do know is that your delay may have cost more than you can imagine. I need an

ID on your local. A photo would help. Can you do that, Sheriff, or am I asking too much?"

"I'll get on it," Tilson said a bit too slowly for Hart's taste.

"Do it now. And put Sayed on the phone and show him every imaginable courtesy unless you want to be facing federal charges."

"For what?" Tilson challenged.

"For illegally incarcerating a federal agent. Am I clear, Sheriff?"

"Crystal," came the chagrined response, as Bill Tilson motioned nervously for the guard to bring Sayed from his cell.

It was 7:30 AM when Sayed picked up the receiver.

CHAPTER THIRTY-EIGHT

LAX, DFW, ORD, ATL

THE FIRST JIHADIST TO STRIKE was Ahmed al-Shishani, who arrived at Atlanta's Hartsfield International Airport at precisely 6 AM on Wednesday, November 22—the day before Thanksgiving. Within seconds of stepping off the hotel shuttle and entering the terminal, he activated the switch on his briefcase and began disseminating a silent mist of death that would sweep through the massive structure. Countless travelers, whose primary concern was making it home safely before the holiday, were exposed to the virus.

Al-Shishani made his way to the Delta ticket counters, where he loitered near monitors showing flight status. The lines were already immense, even at this early hour. It was Allah's will, he reasoned.

After canvassing the full length of the ticket counters, he moved towards the food court. The longest line was at Starbucks, so he started there. He pretended to wait in line before moving on. He would repeat this cycle several times over the course of the next hour before taking the escalators down to baggage claim.

In a far corner of the lower level of the terminal were two infrequently used bathrooms. Al-Shishani entered the men's room at precisely 7 AM and proceeded to the furthest stall on the left—a handicapped stall. It was empty. Directly across from it, a man stood next to a sink, combing his hair in front of the mirror.

Al-Shishani entered the stall, took care of business, flushed the toilet, and exited. He left the briefcase against the far wall of the stall under the toilet paper dispenser.

The minute he left, the man at the mirror stopped his grooming and entered the stall. He emerged a few minutes later, briefcase in hand. He then exited the terminal to dispose of the now empty briefcase.

Free of any type of luggage, al-Shishani navigated his way to security. Though the lines were long, they moved rapidly, thanks to additional TSA personnel brought in for the holiday. He laughed to himself as the woman ahead of him was given a hard time for inadvertently leaving a bottle of water in her carry-on. In another line, he watched bemused as TSA officers patted down a woman in her eighties. Only in America, he thought.

He cleared security without incident in just over fifteen minutes, then boarded the tram for Terminal C. His flight, Delta 809, departed for San Francisco at 7:45 AM from Gate 16. By the time he arrived, the boarding process had begun.

Due to a minor runway delay, the flight was not actually airborne until 8:15 AM Eastern. At 8:30, he reached up to open his air vent. Squeezing the clip of the fountain pen he was holding close to the nozzle, al-Shishani released a stream of viral particles that flooded the cabin within minutes.

His job was done.

Tariq Abu al Khayr entered Terminal 1 at O'Hare airport at 6 AM Central Standard Time. At the same time, nine hundred miles southwest of O'Hare, Babur Qaisrani was entering the main terminal at DFW.

Each man went through the same ritual as had al-Shishani, though Babur was less scripted in his approach due to his abbreviated instructions. Each unleashed devastation throughout the terminals before they completed their work.

Al Khayr cleared security at 7:20 AM Central Standard Time and boarded a flight to Boston at 7:40 AM, twenty minutes prior to the scheduled departure. Everything had gone according to plan.

As he worked his way down the aisle looking for Row 22, the captain spoke over the intercom: "Ladies and Gentlemen, I know you are all eager to get home for the holiday, but we're going to have a short delay. We have a warning light in the cockpit. And even though we are confident it is a false alarm, we are legally obligated to check it out. We'll keep you apprised."

At 8:10, the captain came back on: "Ladies and Gentlemen, the problem has been fixed, and we've been cleared for take-off."

The flight attendants cheerfully rushed through their standard safety instructions, and by 8:20 the aircraft was headed east and climbing rapidly. At 8:32, fifteen minutes after take-off, al Khayr used the viral cartridge loaded in his pen to unleash a second wave attack. The virus would have several hours in which to do its work.

For Babur, there would no second phase of the attack. Without a plane ticket in his name, his mission had been limited to striking the terminal. With that task completed, the only thing left to do was leave quietly and begin the long trip north to Canada. He could not wait to put his arms around Sarah, knowing that she would be so proud of the job he had done.

The fourth terrorist, Kameel Imad al-Din, completed the attack on LAX at 7 AM Pacific. Before he could board a flight scheduled to depart for Denver at 7:30 AM Pacific, the security lines were shut down without explanation. Kameel moved rapidly towards an exit, only to find it—and every other door—guarded by TSA personnel and law enforcement officers armed with automatic rifles. He was frantic to get out, but his training taught him to appear calm until he could formulate a plan.

The worst terror attack ever launched against the United States had begun and ended without spilling a single drop of blood. Each of the terrorists had been armed with nothing more than a briefcase and a pen. And yet they had wandered nonchalantly through terminals, killing time and killing people. It would be a day or two before the first symptoms of Valikhanov's deadly pathogen began to appear.

CHAPTER THIRTY-NINE

CIA Headquarters, McLean, Virginia

By the time Sayed and Hart finally connected, three of the four jihadists had completed the first phase of their missions. They would also be too late to stop Kameel Imad al-Din's attack on Los Angeles International Airport.

Bill Tilson, still smarting from Hart's harsh rebuke, handed Sayed the phone as instructed.

"Commander, I'm so sorry, I . . ." but Hart stopped him.

"No time for apologies. I'm in a conference room at Headquarters, and I've got you on speakerphone. Everyone in the room needs to hear what you have to say. Let's begin with a high-level overview of what's coming down and when."

"Four simultaneous attacks on airports—Chicago, Dallas, Los Angeles, and Atlanta—are underway," Sayed said. "I was to attack DFW. You should assume that some-one has taken my place."

"Go on."

Sayed proceeded to walk Hart through every detail of the planned attacks.

Hart looked up at the clock in the conference room. It was 8:39 AM Eastern.

"When was this to occur?"

"Our missions were to begin at 6 AM local time. We were to begin clearing security at 7 AM. All of our flights departed between 7:30 and 8 local time, giving us a tight window to get through security and board the plane."

"It's 7:40 AM in Chicago and Dallas, and 5:40 in Los Angeles—maybe we can limit the damage," but Hart knew in his heart that it was too late. They might stop the final phase of the attack in L.A., but that was about all they could hope for.

"I'll call you from the air," Hart said. "Put the Sheriff on."

"Sheriff, we will be en route in twenty minutes. We will give you more instructions from the air. Let me make one point very clear: You and your deputy need to take good care of Sayed. Do you understand?"

A nearly paralyzed Bill Tilson muttered, "Yes, Sir."

CHAPTER FORTY

Washington, DC

"WE'RE MOVING OUT!" Hart shouted to the team. "Seth, you're driving. James, get on the line to the FBO. Tell them we're taking the G550 and to file a flight plan for Columbia Regional Airport in Missouri. They can direct any questions to Mr. Kahn's office. I want wheels up in twenty minutes . . . and I want to know everything we've got on the local woman."

Descending two levels to the garage, the team piled into a black Suburban. A minute later they were on Colonial Farm Road headed for Route 123. Seth waited until he hit traffic before flipping on the red and blue strobe lights concealed behind the front and rear grilles. Then, with the short burst of a siren, he pressed the pedal to the floor. Soon they were flying past cars veering to reach the shoulder so as not to impede the speeding vehicle. It would be a quick trip to Reagan National.

Hart was too absorbed in thought to notice as Seth careened sharply in and out of traffic and he struggled to determine the shortest path to shutting down four of the nation's busiest airports, as well as dealing with potential contamination aboard airplanes. Protocol demanded that the president or his surrogate—who, in this case, was the National Security Advisor—be notified. But protocols are laborious, almost by design. Right now, seconds mattered. Hart had no choice but to report up.

He called CIA Deputy Director Kahn on his private line.

Kahn answered on the first ring, "Commander, I'll have to get back to you." But Hart cut him off.

"I'm sorry, Sir. This won't wait."

"Go ahead, then," came the testy reply.

"We have credible evidence that there has been a major biological attack against the nation's four busiest airports, as well as a number of commercial flights. We need to shut down the terminals immediately and hold the flights on the tarmacs. We can't risk allowing anyone who may have been exposed to the biological agent out into the community."

"How do you know this, Commander?" Kahn's tone was dubious.

"Sayed, Sir. He's resurfaced. He was chosen to be one of the jihadists responsible for the attack, but he managed to escape. Unfortunately, he was unable to reach us in time to prevent the attack."

"Perhaps that was his intent," Kahn suggested.

"No, Sir. I don't think so. I don't have time to go into detail, but he was detained against his will by a sheriff in Columbia, Missouri."

"What exactly are you recommending, Commander?"

"An emergency briefing with the president, Sir," Hart responded.

"And what action are you suggesting the president take as a result of this briefing?"

"Sir, I need the president's authorization to work with DHS and TSA to confine the passengers until we learn more. We both know that a number of key people will need to be brought up to speed quickly. I'm not asking for a blanket authorization, but if the president could give me enough leash to move forward, I can provide him with a detailed briefing and recommendations within the hour."

"Alright, Commander, I will set up an emergency briefing with President Conner," Kahn replied. "Await my call, and do not contact anyone until you hear from me. Is that clear, Commander?"

"Yes, Sir."

The nation was unknowingly in the emergent phase of catastrophe, and there was nothing Hart could do but pray Kahn would be successful. With every passing second, he knew another exposed person could be walking out of one of the four airports. Although they would not be immediately infectious, they would disappear from view, only to reemerge when in the throes of a deadly and highly contagious disease.

Sixteen minutes elapsed before Kahn returned Hart's call.

"You've gotten what you asked for, Commander. The White House will notify DHS and DoD that they are authorized to take the requisite defensive action based upon their judgment and your guidance. President Conner wants a comprehensive briefing directly from you, Commander, once the emergent needs have been satisfied."

"Thank you, Sir."

"Don't thank me, Commander. If you're wrong on this one, I don't need to tell you the hell you will have to pay."

"I understand, Sir, but it would be a small price compared to the hell I fear our country is about to pay."

Not wanting to waste another minute, Hart dialed Dottie, executive administrator to Joe Blevins, Secretary of DHS.

"Hello, Dottie. It's . . ."

"Commander, how nice to hear your voice. We haven't seen you in a long time."

Dottie was a fixture in the department—a lifer in the federal government who had begun her career working in the mailroom of the Treasury Department. She was as good an admin as one could find and highly valued by Joe Blevins. Plus, she had spunk and charm, which endeared her to Hart.

"I'll try to correct that," he said. "Dottie, I need to speak with the boss."

"He's in a meeting for the next two hours. May I have him call you then?"

"It won't wait. I hate to make you do it, but the secretary needs to take the call now. In private, of course."

Dottie adopted a new tone of formality, "Please hold, Commander, for the secretary."

Though it was only ninety seconds, it seemed like an eternity before Joe Blevins finally picked up the phone.

"What swamp have you been hiding in, John, and why in God's name are you pulling me out of a meeting with the director of TSA?" Blevins said with the unmistakable drawl of a man raised in Mississippi and proud of it. "I trust this is in regards to an urgent matter?"

"Joe, I'm calling in a favor . . . and it truly is urgent."

"I'm listening," Blevins said, waiting to be hit squarely with whatever Hart had uncovered.

"I need to shut down four airports—LAX, ORD, ATL, and DFW."

"Have you lost your freaking mind, John?"

Just then, Dottie interrupted, "I'm sorry Secretary Blevins, but I have the White House on the line."

"Hold on, John, I'll be back to you in a minute," Blevins said as he put Hart on hold and took the pressing call. The voice on the other line was that of Aaron Littleson, the National Security Advisor.

"Joe, it's Aaron Littleson. We've got a situation involving bioterrorism. The President's point person is Commander Hart—I trust you know him."

"He's on the other line, Aaron."

"Hart doesn't waste time, and from what I've gleaned, we need to be moving at breakneck speed on this one."

"What does the president want me to do?" Blevins asked.

"Whatever Hart advises as necessary to protect the country. Just work with him, Joe, and do the best you can. Hart will be giving the president a full briefing within the hour."

Blevins ended his call with Littleson and returned to Hart.

"Sir, I trust that was the White House authorizing us to speak on this matter?" Hart asked.

"Yes, Commander. You were just telling me that we needed to shut down the four busiest airports in the nation. Is there more?"

"Yes. We need you to ground all flights from those airports, as well as any planes that have departed the four airports since 6 AM Central. You should start with LAX. TSA also needs to initiate a search of the terminal for a man of Arabic decent, a Saudi national, who is carrying a briefcase. Tell them he will be in a non-secured area, so don't waste time checking the gates right now. If they are fortunate enough to find him, he needs to be contained immediately, and I need to be called."

"Closing airports, terminating flights, and finding a needle in a haystack. And would you like for me to arrange for the second coming of Christ, while I'm at it? Jesus, John, what are you thinking!"

"If we fail to accomplish these objectives, you will likely bear witness to a Biblical Armageddon, courtesy of the United Islamic State," Hart admonished.

Although he had participated in countless bio-warfare exercises, nothing had prepared Joe Blevins for this call. He grimly wished the Commander good luck before disconnecting.

Blevins opened the door to his office and called out, "Dottie, I need to see Mr. Haroldson now! He's in the conference room. I need to have a private conversation with him, and I don't want a bunch of TSA staffers at his side."

A moment later, a startled looking Arnold Haroldson sat across from Joe Blevins.

"Arnie, we've got a situation that demands immediate action. Am I clear? We need to shut down LAX, DFW, ORD, and ATL—now. You can close your gaping mouth. I'm not finished.

"Simultaneously, we need to ground all air traffic on the tarmacs, as well as redirect any plane that departed from one of the four airports since 6:15 this morning. Let's ID the flights, let them land at their intended destinations, then hold them on a side ramp of the tarmac. Under no circumstances are passengers allowed to deplane," Blevins instructed.

"That's going to create some very unhappy travelers on the day before Thanksgiving, Mr. Secretary," Haroldson responded.

"I don't give a shit, Arnie. Let's get it in motion while we work on a longer term solution. One more thing—we need a sweep of the public access portions of LAX. We're looking for a Saudi national carrying a leather briefcase. We're confident he hasn't cleared security."

"Sir, you still have not told me why we are doing this."

"UIS hit the four airports with a bio-weapon this morning. It sounds like the result may be catastrophic."

"Is the president aware of what you are requesting?" Haroldson questioned.

"Yes. I received a confirmatory call from the White House authorizing us to proceed as indicated."

"Understood, Sir."

"Jot down a list of the key staffers who need to be briefed. I'm assuming no more than four or five of your best. As soon as you're done, I'll give it to Dottie to call their admins and get them into a secure conference room. We also want to conference-in Don Needham at FAA.

"Now, Arnie, don't go wandering off anywhere. I expect this to take less than five minutes."

"Can I go down the hall, Mr. Secretary?"

"After you give Dottie the list," Blevins said.

CHAPTER FORTY-ONE

Reagan National, Washington, DC

THE G550 WAS PARKED ON THE RAMP awaiting the team's arrival. The plane, which comfortably seated sixteen, would be carrying only seven passengers: Commander Hart, Colonel Scanlon, Dr. Wilkins, Omar Warum—plus Seth, James, and Andrew, the team's heavily armed escorts.

Thanks to a priority clearance, the jet was airborne in under two minutes. Once they had cleared 10,000 feet, the pilots began to throttle back the jet's massive Rolls Royce engines. With the noise level reduced from a roar to a low growl, Hart picked up the secure line and called Sheriff Tilson.

He answered on the first ring.

"Sheriff, we will be arriving at Columbia Regional's private aviation terminal at 10:20 Central Time. We've arranged for an agent from the Jefferson City field office to meet us there. He will be accompanied by a forensics team."

"No need," the sheriff replied, "The house went up in flames early this morning. There's not much left. It took out the barn, too."

"What about bodies?" Hart asked.

"None, but that fire was mighty hot," Tilson replied.

A flashing green light momentarily distracted Hart. The secure fax linked to Langley was signaling an incoming transmission.

"Hello . . . hello?" came a tinny voice from Hart's speakerphone.

"I am here, Sheriff," he responded curtly. "I need you to wait a moment."

The fax spit out three pages, beginning with a Top Secret cover sheet. The second page had originated from the Boone County Sheriff's department. It featured a photo of a woman accompanied by her name, SSN, birth date, and driver's license number. There was no arrest record. The third page was from the agency. Analysts had run the woman's profile through its databases and hit pay dirt.

The wholesome farm girl in whom Bill Tilson placed his complete trust had been identified as a known Islamic sympathizer with connections to al-Bakr. A recent entry indicated that the FBI had surveilled a visit to her home by Jamat ul-Fuqra.

What a pity, Hart mused, as he considered the massive gaps in cooperation and information-sharing among governmental organizations. Why hadn't the FBI made local authorities aware of their concerns, he wondered. And yet, who could blame them—Hart certainly had no interest in cooperating with the inept sheriff.

Hart ordered, "You will bring Sayed to the airport, then escort us to the house where Sarah Qaisrani, your trusted friend, recently hosted a jihadi party.

"And I need you to do one more thing—put out an APB for the local—saying she is armed, dangerous, and being sought in connection with a homicide. Do you think you can handle that, Sheriff?"

Without waiting for a response, he added, "Now put Sayed on the line!"

Hart's tone changed abruptly to one of calm control. "Sayed, I've got you on speaker."

"Yes, Commander."

"We are in the process of shutting down the airports. The President has been briefed by the DDO. I will be giving the president a more detailed briefing within the hour."

"Yes, Sir."

"Are you able to identify the jihadists?"

"I spent two months in a training camp with one of the men, so I know him well. His name is Tariq Abu al Khayr."

"What can you tell me about him?"

"He is tall, almost two meters, and lean. There's nothing too distinguishing about him other than a thin scar on his forehead. He's quite dangerous, Commander. To use one of your expressions, he has drunk the Kool-Aid. This man will stop at nothing to complete his mission."

"And his target?"

"He was sent to Chicago's O'Hare Airport."

"Who else should we be looking for, Sayed?" Hart's tone was urgent.

"Another man, Ahmed al-Shishani, was sent to Atlanta. He appeared to be one of al-Bakr's trusted guards, so he, too, will be highly competent. I only heard the third man's name once. I believe it was Kameel al-Din. His target is LAX."

"And what of your target, Sayed?"

"You should assume that Babur Qaisrani, the husband of the woman who had me locked up, took over my responsibility for attacking DFW."

"We'll have Headquarters run the names, try to pull images, and then have you confirm their identities." Hart gestured to James, who would be the point person in coordinating with the Agency. "The Qaisranis are already on the radar screen."

Taking a deep breath before continuing, Hart asked: "Who else was present at the meeting in Columbia?"

"Al Hameed and Valikhanov. Al Hameed seemed to be in charge. There were two other men, though they seemed to be less important. They were technicians brought in to prepare the weapons. I did not hear their names mentioned."

"Where did Al Hameed and Valikhanov go after leaving the Qaisranis' home?" Hart's words came out fast. He was eager to find the perpetrators before they vanished the way Bin Laden had following the 9/11 attacks.

"I don't know for certain, but I believe they were going to Chicago. They may be on their way out of the country."

Hart felt a huge sinking feeling in his chest, almost as though he was drowning. A memory flooded back from SEAL training. He had been grabbed from behind and was being yanked underwater by a 250-pound instructor hell-bent on seeing Hart wash out.

He was once again drowning. But he couldn't break free of this reality.

"Thank you, Sayed," Hart's normally confident tone was now reserved . . . almost resigned.

Sayed hesitantly offered: "There may still be hope, Commander."

"Sayed, I'm all about hope, but I'm not seeing a way out of this one. Not yet, anyway."

"Perhaps I can provide one."

"I'm listening," Hart said, though he wasn't naïve enough to expect a resurrection.

"The factory has manufactured fifty million doses of vaccine. None of the existing U.S. stockpile will be effective due to the genetic manipulations of the hemorrhagic virus. However, this vaccine is effective if given in sufficient time."

"What do you mean, sufficient time?"

"The vaccine was only tested on people who had been immunized prior to exposure, so I don't have a clear answer for you. However, I did find a note from Valikhanov to Al Hameed. Valikhanov was concerned that post-exposure vaccination might limit the effects of the virus, and thus stop Armageddon."

Hart's hope started to awaken. "And were you able to find Al Hameed's response?"

"Yes, it was clearly scrawled in large letters across the top of the paper."

"And what did it say?"

"It reminded Valikhanov that Al Hameed had been chosen by Allah to unleash Armageddon, and that nothing on earth could stop him."

"Commander," Liz interjected, "there's considerable evidence that suggests post-exposure inoculation may effectively confer some level of immunity against certain bio-agents if begun before the victim becomes highly symptomatic."

Sayed added, "And that may pose our greatest dilemma."

"How?" Hart demanded.

"Because the genetic modifications made by Valikhanov shorten the incubation period to just days. It won't be long before people begin dying in large numbers, I'm afraid."

Hart looked to Liz for confirmation. She nodded and added, "Absolutely plausible. I'm guessing that we have, at the very most, seventy-two hours. And perhaps less than thirty-six."

"Not bad intel for a guy who was supposed to be cooking drugs for a pharma plant in Faisalabad," Hart said.

Sayed appreciated the brief moment of levity and affirmation in the midst of the unfolding calamity.

"Sayed, we'll see you shortly," Hart said, terminating the call and turning towards the team.

"Tom, what do you think? Do we have a hope or a prayer of getting people vaccinated in time?" Hart asked the Colonel.

Shaking his head, Scanlon admitted, "There are going to be mass casualties. We need to accept that as fact and plan accordingly. Therefore, our hope is not to avert a catastrophe, but to limit its scope—to stop Armageddon."

CHAPTER FORTY-TWO

At 38,000 feet en route to Columbia, Missouri

Hart commanded everyone's attention as he stood at the front of the plane, jabbing his finger in the air and shouting, "Ready to lead, ready to follow, never quit!" It was a rallying cry to the troops, a promise he was both making and extracting from his team.

"Got it?" The question emanated from deep within his gut.

"Yes, Sir!" The response was shouted back by the team in unison.

"We have three immediate objectives," Hart said in a more tempered tone.

"First, I will run point with DoD regarding the primary imperative of locating and liberating the vaccine. That assumes, of course, that we can get to the factory before it disappears. Omar, you will be working with me. Obviously, this will require presidential approval, which I trust will be forthcoming. Bear in mind, we will be invading a sovereign nation.

"Second, Liz and Tom, you have dual roles. You need to determine the most efficient method of distributing the vaccine to the four principal points of contact, as well as to wherever we have redirected the four planes. Once the vaccine is delivered, we'll need a protocol for inoculating people on the ground. Start with the first responders, medical personnel, and others in harm's way before inoculating the public."

"Commander, isn't that the responsibility of DHS?" Wilkins asked.

"Yes, Liz. So what you and Tom are doing is jump-starting their response in an effort to shorten the time needed to react. Plan to do a hand-off to DHS. Secretary Blevins has been briefed."

"Got it," she responded. "And our second assignment, Commander?"

"You will work with James, Seth, and Andrew on containment strategies."

The three men had been sitting at the rear of the plane. They appeared unfazed by the disturbing conversation that had been unfolding.

As Seth began to speak, Liz wondered if anything cogent would come out of his mouth. She had always been contemptuous of field operatives—particularly para-military ones. Hart was the lone exception.

"Commander, I've been on a secured communications uplink while you've been on the phone. DHS and TSA are moving to secure the airports. Apparently they are having a tough time keeping the people in the terminals calm and compliant," Seth said.

"What's the cover story?" Hart asked.

"Passengers have only been told that the airports are on lock-down, and no one gets in or out. There are already reports of people having to be subdued. If we're not careful, we are going to have full-fledged riots on our hands. DHS is coordinating with the Governors' offices to mobilize the National Guard. We need able, armed men guarding every point of ingress and egress from these facilities. Right now, it's primarily TSA."

"What about the flights that Sayed mentioned?" Hart asked, addressing the stone that had yet to be overturned.

Seth responded, "FAA is working on a list of all flights that either departed or arrived at each of the four airports between 6 AM Central Time and when they were shut down at approximately 8:55 AM Central. As you can imagine, dozens of flights are impacted. Flights departing Atlanta are going to be the toughest challenge, since air traffic there continued unabated until almost 10 AM Eastern.

"We are already holding a substantial number of flights on tarmacs across the nation. So it's not just the people in the terminals who are growing edgy. The crews are beginning to report problems with passengers who are demanding to know why they are aren't either proceeding to a gate or departing."

"Has there been any progress in identifying which planes were targeted by the jihadists?" Hart asked.

"The Agency scoured surveillance footage in Chicago and got a lucky hit. They've got a facial ID on Tariq Abu al Khayr. Unfortunately, his flight was already in the air and headed to Boston. It will be held on the tarmac until agents in protective suits can board it. I think we can be confident that al-Shishani's Atlanta flight departed as well. Since it is unlikely that any jihadists tried to board Sayed's flight out of DFW, that leaves LAX, and I believe we thwarted that one. I'm assuming that Imad al-Din is holed up somewhere in the terminal."

"Good work," the commander praised Seth, causing Liz to wonder if her judgment of the man had been unduly harsh.

"What do you think, Tom? Any ideas about how to handle the passengers on these planes?" Hart asked.

Scanlon, deep in thought, responded, "Actually, yes, but it's not going to be easy. First, we need to triage the planes, differentiating between the two that may actively harbor a terrorist and the hundreds of flights in which the passengers may have been exposed to the virus while in one of the terminals prior to boarding. Of course, the ban on flights landing at the four airports must hold."

"If possible, we should also triage the passengers based upon the time of their departures. Anyone who departed before 6:30 AM Central probably avoided exposure."

"Continue," Hart told Scanlon.

"We may have to intern these people for an extended period of time. The more isolated the containment area, the less we risk exposure to a broader population.

"As for al Khayr or al-Shishani, once we identify both of their flights, we need to safely remove them from the planes and incarcerate them in isolation units. It sounds like we have one down and one to go."

"Incarcerate? Some of us might prefer to put a 9 mm hollow-point bullet through the center of their foreheads," said Hart.

Noting a scowl from Liz, Hart asked, "What's the matter, Liz? Don't you have the stomach for it?"

"You know that's not fair, John. I would just like to believe that there is still some rule of law amidst this chaos."

"These men know nothing of law . . . or compassion . . . or basic human decency. All they wish to do is bring an end to our way of life. Don't kid yourself; resolution of this crisis won't come through diplomatic conversations, only from the barrel of a gun or the impact of a Hellfire missile."

Liz was suddenly privy to that part of Hart that he had been careful to conceal during the six months of their budding relationship. The unfolding catastrophe was providing her with a window into his world. His shadow side, the trained assassin, was every bit as much a part of John Hart as his medical pedigree. And though repulsed by the image of a bullet careening through a man's skull, she was grateful that Hart possessed absolute resolve to bring an end to the terror.

"Gentlemen, I appreciate your passion, but we need to move beyond Hooah, right now," Scanlon suggested. "As for the planes that may be contaminated or may harbor infected passengers, I would suggest they be transported to Dugway.

"John and Liz, you both have spent enough time there to know that they can control access, provide medical assistance as needed, and maintain control." Scanlon awaited their acknowledgment.

Dugway Proving Ground had been established in 1942 to serve as a vital part of the Army's chemical and biological warfare infrastructure. Located in northwest Utah, the 800,000-acre tract of land had continued to function as the priority site for testing of chemical and biological defensive systems. Due to the sensitive and dangerous nature of its work, the Army had made sure that there was nothing within thirty miles of the base, aside from the IHG Army Hotels Desert Lodge and rattlesnakes.

Scanlon completed his thought. "My suggestion, then, is that we have these planes refuel and begin an orderly procession to Dugway."

"And what do we tell passengers sitting on the tarmac in Peoria or Pittsburgh as to why they are now headed to Utah?" Hart wanted to know.

"We tell them the truth, or at least a partial truth: That a number of airports are under attack by terrorists, and they are being transported to a military base where their safety can be guaranteed. We also tell them that their families will be notified following their processing at the base," Scanlon advised.

"And how do we stop every passenger who is carrying a cell phone from calling CNN with a breaking story?"

"The White House has to get ahead of this one with the media. They need to move now to control the release of any information until an effective crisis communications strategy can be developed."

"You are assuming it's not too late for that," Liz broke in.

As if on cue, Hart reached up and turned on the television mounted adjacent to the exit sign at the front of the cabin and pre-set to CNN. Wolf Blitzer's head soon filled the screen. Beneath him, large red letters proclaimed: BREAKING NEWS—U.S. Airports in Chaos.

"Looks like we're a bit late," Liz frowned.

Ignoring the media issue for the moment, Hart responded to Scanlon. "Tom, I agree with your plan in principle. Dugway is a great suggestion, but I'm struggling with the cover story. It's too inflammatory. People aren't ready to hear that we are under siege by terrorists. Let's confer with DHS and FASA, but I would suggest informing passengers that they may have been exposed to SARS. There is a precedent for quarantine in such situations. Plus, the only manipulation of the truth is the specific nature of the virus."

"So a small lie is less consequential than a big lie?" Scanlon asked.

"Come on, Tom. Don't bust my balls. I'm not trying to be paternalistic here, just trying to find the smartest way forward. We need to keep people from panicking."

"I'm sorry. You're right."

Hart was already on to the next problem, and Liz sensed a course-correction about to emerge.

"We don't have time to inspect what's left of the safe house in Columbia. James and Andrew, I want you to accompany Sheriff Tilson to the site and supervise the initial forensics, but don't get bogged down. I will have a plane standing by for you in four hours. You can rejoin the team in DC at approximately 1700 hours," Hart instructed.

"Let's bring Sayed on board. Liz and Tom, learn everything you can from him. Then make a decision as to your final recommendations for the planes and passengers. I will communicate with DoD and the White House. They have decisions to make, and those decisions can't wait until we arrive."

CHAPTER FORTY-THREE

Chicago O'Hare Airport

AFTER 2½ HOURS PARKED ON A TAXI RAMP far from the terminal at O'Hare, Gene English was coming unhinged. Just as his flight was about to take off, the flight crew had been instructed to leave the active runway and park on a side ramp. It wasn't just English's flight. Planes were backing up as far as he could see.

Seated in first class, two rows back from the cockpit door, English grew more agitated with each Bloody Mary he downed. After three, the flight attendant politely cut him off.

"What do you mean, I can't have another drink?" he argued.

"I'm sorry, Sir, but three is the limit."

"I've been sitting on this God damn flight for hours. There is no limit!" he demanded.

She feigned a smile, then walked back to speak to a passenger in Row Five.

The only communication coming from the cockpit had been a brief announcement by the captain that they had been instructed to leave their take-off slot and await further instructions.

A minute later, as the flight attendant was returning to the front galley, an enraged English reached up and grabbed her arm.

"Sir, take your hands off me now!"

English relinquished his grip, but not his anger: "I want to speak to the captain! I want to know why the hell we've been sitting here for hours without any clue as to when or whether this flight will depart."

He stood, pushed her to the side, and headed for the cabin door.

The man in Row Five, to whom the flight attendant had been speaking, sprang from his seat and moved to intercept English.

"Is there a problem, Sir?" At 6'4", he towered over the short, balding man.

"This doesn't concern you," English said contemptuously, as if itching for a fight.

The man reached into his blazer and pulled out his credentials. Thrusting his federal marshal's badge under the the man's nose, he said, "I believe it does. Turn around and place your hands behind your head."

"Go to hell," English snapped.

In seconds, English was cuffed and summarily shoved down into his seat.

"Not another word, Mr. English," the marshal said, after inspecting the man's boarding pass. "You are already facing federal charges. Don't make the situation any worse for yourself."

As he returned to his seat, the marshal could feel the tension in the cabin. English wasn't the only one who was reaching his limit. He could only hope that the plane would take off before another incident occurred.

The captain called into the tower, "Ground Control, United 2967."

"United 2967, go ahead."

"We've got a problem on-board. Request permission to return to gate."

"What is the nature of the problem, 2967?"

"A passenger assaulted a crew member. The passenger has been subdued but request permission to return to gate."

"Permission denied, 2967. Sorry, Captain, but you've got to ride this one out. Wish we had more to tell you. Ground Control out."

CHAPTER FORTY-FOUR

At 38,000 feet en route to Columbia, MO

AN HOUR OF FLIGHT TIME still separated Hart from his destination in mid-Missouri. It was enough time for an extended call to Aaron Littleson, the National Security Advisor.

"Littleson," came a terse response after a single ring.

"Aaron, it's John Hart."

"I'll call you back in two minutes," Littleson said, hanging up. As he ushered a small group of startled colleagues from his office in the West Wing of the White House, he said, "I'm sorry, but we'll have to reconvene later."

Almost closing the door on their heels, Littleson picked up the phone as he rounded the corner of his desk and redialed Hart.

"John, what the hell is happening? I know what Deputy Director Kahn told the president, but there's got to be more that you can tell me."

"Yes, Sir. We have additional details now." Hart gave Littleson a high level overview of what was unfolding. He explained the urgency of containing the virus, along with any passengers who may have been exposed to it. He described the hellish situation that would unfold as people inevitably became symptomatic. He closed by providing the single ray of hope that lay with vaccines residing in a factory thousands of miles away.

When he finished, there was a long and agonized silence.

"Aaron, the genie is definitely out of the bottle," Hart finally said. "Our objective now is to secure the vaccine that was manufactured at the same factory responsible for the bio-weapon. Liz Wilkins tells me we have a very short window in which to try to inoculate those who may have been exposed. We don't know if it will help, but we know they will die without it. Meanwhile, we have to do everything in our power to keep the virus from spreading."

"Surely there are counter-measures, John. My God, what have you folks been working on all of these years, if it's not for such an eventuality?"

Hart allowed the snipe to pass without comment, understanding that it was Littleson's fear and frustration spilling out.

"Sorry," Littleson offered, the hostility gone from his voice. "Tell me exactly what you are recommending."

"I'm recommending that you get General Anderson on the line with us, and the three of us outline a high-level plan that can be presented to the president for consideration. The DDO has instructed me to brief him within the hour."

"The president is expecting that briefing in thirty minutes, Commander. He's asked that I sit in on it. Let me try to reach General Anderson and see if we can get him on a conference call."

"Thank you. I'll wait to hear from you."

General Mike Anderson, Chairman of the Joint Chiefs of Staff, was among the best military strategists Hart had encountered in his long career. Anderson was alarmingly calm even in the face of overwhelming odds. Troops under his command during the Vietnam War had attested to his steel will when confronted by vast numbers of enemy troops. Those who didn't know him well assumed that Anderson chronically underreacted. Nothing could be further from the truth. He simply had a remarkable nervous system that appeared to be impervious to fear and anxiety. As such, he never allowed threats to overwhelm his logic and clear-headedness. Hart chalked it up to Anderson's Kansas roots. People on the plains are used to adversity.

A short time later, Hart's cell phone vibrated. Aaron Littleson was back on the phone.

"John, I've got General Anderson with me on the line. The White House is arranging a briefing with the president in twenty-five minutes."

"Good morning, General."

"It doesn't sound like a good morning to me, John, but I appreciate the fact that you are on the front line for this one."

"Thank you, General. As Mr. Littleson has undoubtedly advised you, we have a bio-event taking place at four of our busiest airports. We believe it involves the release of a hemorrhagic form of smallpox that is highly virulent and almost categorically lethal. Liz Wilkins and Tom Scanlon are working on confirmation of the agent. Meanwhile, initial containment strategies are being put in place. The airports have been sealed since before 9 AM Central."

Hart paused to give Anderson a moment to absorb the enormity of the news, but the general's response was swift. "Beyond assisting with containment, how can DoD help?"

"We have credible intelligence suggesting that there may be fifty million doses of a vaccine specific to this bio-agent residing in a manufacturing plant in Faisalabad."

"What makes you believe that it is sitting in some factory or warehouse? Why would UIS fail to deliver the vaccine to its intended recipients prior to the attack?"

"From what I have been told, UIS did not want to risk detection of their plan by beginning mass inoculations prior to the attack. Apparently they believed the virus would not endanger those people whom they wished to protect during the early stages of infection. Rather, it would take weeks, if not months, for the virus to cross international borders and imperil their own people," Hart responded. "So they did not feel any urgency regarding rapid immunization. If we're correct, and the vaccine is still warehoused at the facility in Faisalabad, it may be our only chance to turn the tide before it becomes a pandemic. The vaccine may confer some degree of post-exposure immunity if it is administered within a short window of time."

"How short a window?" the general demanded.

"Forty-eight hours or less."

"So what you are saying is that people must be vaccinated by Friday morning or we risk a high level of fatalities, correct?"

"Yes, Sir. That's our best guess at the moment."

This time there was a long pause as General Anderson began to calculate the logistics required to invade a sovereign nation, secure one of its commercial airports, commandeer the factory, procure the vaccine, and then extract all military forces—ideally without the loss of American life. It seemed impossible, particularly with a forty-eight-hour fuse.

National Security Advisor Littleson took advantage of the moment of silence. "Commander Hart, you understand that we will be recommending that the president sanction an act of war against Pakistan. He will be doing so without congressional approval."

"No, Sir, I don't see that way," Hart quickly replied. "That act of war was committed by the Pakistanis when ISI allowed the United Islamic State to build a bio-warfare facility under their protection. What we saw today was their first real volley—and it caught us completely unprepared."

The general asserted, "Aaron, I agree with Commander Hart. I can have a plan in motion within the hour. Depending upon the proximity of our closest assets, it could require up to twenty-four hours to execute. By the time the vaccine reaches our shores, under the best of circumstances, you are going to have a very short window in which to administer the vaccinations."

"We'll take what we can get with gratitude, General."

Littleson instructed, "Gentlemen, you have twenty minutes to prepare your comments for the president. Commander, you will speak to your level of confidence in the purported bio-attacks, as well as the potential benefit of the vaccine. General, you will outline the specific course of action recommended in response to those attacks."

As the line went dead, Hart began mentally rehearsing answers to the questions he would inevitably be asked. There were multiple points of vulnerability in his assessment, including Sayed's reliability and his limited knowledge of the attacks, the effectiveness of the bio-dispersal process in the airports and onboard the planes, as well as the ability of the virus to spread without burning itself out.

The fate of millions of Americans rested on what would play out over the next half-hour.

CHAPTER FORTY-FIVE

The White House
38,000 feet over Indiana

THE TWENTY MINUTES VANISHED in the blink of an eye as Hart's laptop beeped and alerted him to a secure email. Embedded within it was a sign-on link for the conference. After completing a retinal scan via the laptop's camera port, he was cleared. An image of the situation room popped up on his screen.

Every chair was filled by a top ranking official. There were two small rectangles on the right side of his screen— one showing Hart as seen by the meeting participants, and the other displaying an image of General Anderson.

The president entered the room and called the meeting to order. He then explained the nature of the emergency briefing. "I received a call earlier this morning from the DDO. Mr. Kahn advised me that we are now facing the type of event that has been long anticipated but which we prayed would never occur. Beginning at 6 AM Central time, four terrorists dispersed biological agents in our four busiest airports. A number of planes may also harbor the infectious agent. I have authorized Commander John Hart, who has the lead on this operation, to interface with DHS and DoD. The Commander was given one hour to develop a more comprehensive briefing."

Turning to Hart, the president said, "Commander, I believe the hour is up, and we are eager to hear what you else you have learned."

"Mr. President, we are still piecing together all of the details, but we believe that a high-ranking former scientist from VECTOR named Beibut Valikhanov was recruited by UIS to develop a biological agent for deployment against soft targets within our nation. The purported virus has an anticipated mortality rate in excess of ninety percent and a level of infectivity similar to SARS, measles, or other highly virulent agents."

The president interrupted, directing his comment to the National Security Advisor. "Aaron, I was led to believe that only the Russians possessed that type of doomsday virus, and it was safely housed in VECTOR. Are we discussing a Russian attack?"

Answering for Littleson, Hart said, "If I may, Gentlemen, apparently when Valikhanov defected to UIS, he took viral samples with him, as well as the Russians' digital library of information on genetic manipulation of pathogens. The terrorists we have identified so far are all jihadists associated with UIS."

"A viral sample is hardly sufficient means to launch Armageddon," the president said. "So explain to me how UIS managed to attack four airports."

"Yes, Sir. Mr. President, UIS built a bio-weapons factory in Faisalabad, Pakistan, with the purpose of manufacturing this particular bio-agent. They also created a novel vaccine that may offer some level of immunity—even when administered post-exposure."

"How in hell do you build a bio-warfare factory in the middle of a large city in Pakistan without anyone's knowledge?" the president demanded, his anger palpable.

"You don't, Sir. We assume, based upon our intelligence, that ISI is complicit, and therefore the government of Pakistan is complicit," Hart said, teeing up the opportunity for the general to discuss military intervention.

The Secretary of Defense was next to respond. "What are your sources of intelligence, Commander?"

"Sir, NGA was the first to observe the factory under construction. Based upon visual observations from a Global Hawk, coupled with satellite mass spectrographic analysis of the effluent gases produced by the factory, the NGA analysts concluded with a high degree of reliability that the facility had been designed to produce bio-agents."

"Let me get this straight, Commander," the president responded. "I trust all of this discussion is leading towards military involvement that will potentially include some type of retaliatory action against a key ally in the region, Pakistan. And you are basing the call for such action upon pictures from space?"

"No, Sir, we were able to place an agent in the plant for an extended period of time. His exemplary performance at the facility led to his recruitment as one of the jihadists involved in the attack. We don't have time to go into all of the details, but he escaped with the intention of foiling the plot. Unfortunately, he was too late."

"Commander, I need a confidence assessment from you regarding the validity of this agent's intelligence, and I trust it will be accurate."

"My confidence level, Mr. President, approaches one hundred percent."

Hart watched as the participants around the table fell back into their chairs. Expressions varied from shock to outrage to outright fear.

"General, what are you proposing?"

"Sir, our primary objective is the rapid extraction of the vaccine from the factory. Our primary concern is interference from the Pakistanis, who will decry that we have invaded their territory and order an immediate retaliatory strike against our aircraft and ground forces."

"Go on," the president prompted.

"The extraction process is relatively straightforward, albeit not without risks. We have two C-130 transports ready to depart Bagram Airfield in Afghanistan. They will carry the requisite forces and equipment to commandeer control of the airport in Faisalabad, then execute the primary objective of overtaking the factory and extracting the vaccine."

Clearing his throat, the general continued: "I am coordinating with General Phillips at USSOCOM and General Ward at the 455th Expeditionary Wing in Bagram. As of now, the plan is to have SEAL Team Five secure the airport and provide perimeter protection, while an ARSOF CBRN unit manages site exploitation and collection at the factory. We believe most of the required assets are within eight hours of the proposed theater of operations."

"And how do you plan to get the Pakistanis to authorize the landing of American military aircraft in Faisalabad?" the president asked.

"Sir, we think they will be caught off guard. By the time they realize what's happening, we will have neutralized their ability to respond."

"And how will we do that, General?"

"Sir, we will communicate our desire for cooperation directly to President Mughabi via one of the three drones we plan to have circling above the Pakistani presidential compound. They can be on-station within seven hours."

"Continue, General."

"It is our belief that one Hellfire missile exploding proximate to the president's residence will communicate the seriousness of the situation and ensure that there will be no deployment of Pakistani forces for sufficient time to allow the extraction."

President Jonathan Conner sat on the edge of his chair, elbows leaning into the table, as he envisioned the scenario the general was playing out.

Anderson continued: "Four F-22 Raptors armed with a combination of air-to-air and air-to-ground munitions will be positioned minutes away from Islamabad. Their primary targets, if needed, will be the presidential compound, Parliament, and the headquarters of ISI. Two of the fighters can break away, as required, to provide support in Faisalabad. At Mach 2, they can be there in less than ten minutes."

The general paused before continuing, "Mr. President, there is something we need you to do."

"Yes, General?"

"If you would place a call to President Mughabi moments after the missile launch and inform the president that the next missile will go through his bedroom window, we believe he will honor your demand for full cooperation."

A wave of nervous laughter swept through the room.

The president took a moment to absorb the full magnitude of the general's recommendations before responding. "I understand that you only had a few minutes to assemble the plan, Mike. That's a hell of a lot to accomplish in a short time," the president said.

"Thank you, Sir. I have one final recommendation, Mr. President."

"Go on, Mike."

"I'd prefer not to leave this factory operational. I suggest that one of our B-2s pay it a short visit once our assets are safely outside of Pakistani airspace."

"And so you are recommending . . ."

"A surgical strike in which we deposit a single, thermobaric bomb over the factory. Nothing will remain."

"And collateral damage?" the president inquired.

"Unavoidable, but since it is in a principally industrial area, the losses will be minimal."

"Thank you, Gentlemen." The president then turned to the assembled team and asked for comments. The silence of the room remained unbroken until the Secretary of State, Roger Collins, raised a red flag.

"Mr. President, Pakistan may choose to retaliate indirectly by launching a nuclear attack against India."

Jonathan Conner took his elbows off the table and leaned back in his chair. He momentarily covered his eyes as he processed the complexity of the decision.

Then, sitting erect, eyes wide open, he said: "Agreed that is a possibility. I will communicate to President Mughabi that we are prepared to unleash our full arsenal upon his country if there is any type of attempted retribution. That cannot be an empty threat, General. I suggest you get on the line to the folks at Whiteman."

Almost as an after-thought, the president added, "I will also need to communicate, in confidence, with the Indian Prime Minister moments before the drone strike."

"Mr. President," the Secretary of Defense cautioned, "that may cause India to launch a preemptive strike. They've been looking for an excuse to bomb the Pakistanis for years."

"You have a point, Charley," Anderson conceded. "The first person to learn of our plan will be President Mughabi, presumably as he's blown out of his bed."

"Gentlemen, unless there are further objections, I would like to proceed with the plan as outlined. I will expect a status update in four hours."

Hart jumped in before the meeting could be adjourned. "Sir, there are two more items, if I may."

"Of course, Commander."

"CNN is already leading with a story about chaos at our airports. Right now, the story is pretty thin on details. Before more damage can be done, we need a complete press black-out for at least twenty-four hours. We have thousands of people being held either in terminals or on planes. I'm sure they've been on their cell phones now for some time. We have a lot to deal with relative to containment, and we'd prefer not to add mass hysteria to the list."

"You said two items, Commander."

"We will, of course, need to have the full assets of DHS, CDC, and potentially DoD working collaboratively with us on identification, containment, triage, and treatment."

"Phil," the President gestured with an upraised chin to his press secretary. "Get on it immediately. Use the War Powers Act to communicate the severity of punishment that will befall anyone who violates the blackout."

He then turned to Blevins and said, "Joe, please continue to ensure that Commander Hart's team has the full support of DHS, CDC, and TSA . . . and anyone else they need."

As people began packing up their briefing documents, Aaron Littleson's voice could be heard breaking through the side-conversations that had begun in earnest.

"Sir, if I may, there is yet one more issue."

Stepping back from the doorway, the president said, "What is it, Aaron?"

"You need to talk to the people, Mr. President. You need to let the public know what is happening so they can take the necessary precautions to avoid exposure, where possible. If the attack was as vicious as described, it won't be long before cases of hemorrhagic smallpox emerge in cities and suburbs across the nation."

The president turned his attention to his press secretary, who said, "Mr. Littleson is correct, Sir. With your permission, I will start working on your presidential address immediately. I suggest we plan it for Thanksgiving night. Maybe that will satisfy the media. Perhaps we can end the blackout at that point and provide a full disclosure of the events in progress."

The president simply nodded in agreement. Hart disconnected the video uplink, and the conference call was over.

Minutes later, the wheels of Commander Hart's plane touched down at Columbia Regional Airport.

CHAPTER FORTY-SIX

Columbia Regional Airport

COLUMBIA REGIONAL AIRPORT WAS LOCATED halfway between Columbia and Jefferson City, the Missouri state capital. Though occasional corporate jets ferried highly paid executives and their lobbyists to the capital, a Gulfstream was a rare sight. And the last thing Hart needed was unwanted attention. With the help of ground control, the plane was directed to a quiet part of the tarmac not far from the private aviation terminal.

As they taxied to a stop, the doors opened on a waiting black Suburban. Three men emerged, one of them extremely disheveled. Hart instantly recognized the man—it was Sayed. He assumed the other two men were the local FBI field agent and Sheriff Bill Tilson.

Bounding down the short set of stairs, Hart strode immediately up to Sayed and embraced him—literally lifting him off his feet before returning him to the tarmac.

"Thank God you're alive! We'll talk on the plane," he said, gesturing for Sayed to board immediately.

Seth remained on the plane, while James and Andrew had trailed a few steps behind Hart. The commander quickly introduced them to the FBI agent, intentionally failing to acknowledge Tilson. He reminded everyone of their mission and timeline and then wished them luck. A plane would be standing by to return James and Andrew to Langley in four hours.

Before reboarding, Hart approached Tilson and put his arm around the man's shoulder.

"Let's take a short walk," he said, more as an order than a request.

Tilson was shaking visibly.

"Sheriff, I've dealt with some ignorant sons of bitches in my lifetime, but you take the cake!"

There was no response.

"So I am arranging something special for you—a ring-side seat to watch a live video-feed from one of the four airports that has been attacked by terrorists . . . an attack that Sayed was hoping to thwart."

"Why?" Tilson asked.

"Because I think you need to see up close and personal just what your ignorance cost in human lives. You'll get to watch as people die from the nastiest fucking virus the world has ever seen."

Hart dropped his arm from Tilson's shoulder and walked away, leaving a stunned Bill Tilson to ponder what he had done.

Leaping up the airstairs two steps at time, Hart entered the plane's fuselage and took a seat in an aft-facing chair. Liz and Tom were seated in two of the four chairs in the forward grouping. Sayed moved from the rear of the fuselage to take a seat across from Hart. After introductions, Hart began to brief the three of them on what had transpired during the White House video conference.

"Sayed, based upon what you have shared with us, Mr. Littleson, General Anderson, and I have briefed the president and his advisors. We've recommended a military incursion into Pakistan with the intent of liberating the vaccine and transporting it to the U.S. for immediate distribution to the four initial sites of potential exposure. The president made his decision based upon my statement that our confidence level in your intel approaches one hundred percent."

"Commander, you can eliminate the word approaches. The attack is underway. We both know that. Can I speak to the magnitude of its results? No. Am I convinced the vaccine is our only chance? Yes."

"I have many more questions, Sayed, but first I need Tom and Liz to bring me up to speed on their pressing issues."

While Hart had been absorbed in his video-conference, Wilkins and Scanlon had been formulating the initial high-level response to the event itself.

"Tom and I are recommending the implementation of a four-phase protocol that resulted from work done between Livermore and the CDC. We know you are quite familiar with it, Commander, so I will make my comments brief."

"We've got a couple of hours before we touch down in DC, Liz, so take your time," Hart said, admiring Liz's professionalism and intelligence during this overwhelmingly difficult time.

"Thank you, Sir," she said, with the first smile he had seen from her in a very long time.

"Thank *you*, Ma'am," he returned the smile, hoping to continue the thaw between them.

"Our first imperative is to construct an operational center that will serve as a nexus for all information related to the event and its management. As the primary communications hub, it will require an interdisciplinary, inter-agency staff with well-defined roles."

Hart agreed. "I'll need your initial staffing recommendations before we land."

"Understood." Liz continued, "The first responders currently in position are a security force cobbled together from TSA, local and state law enforcement, and a growing contingent of National Guard troops. Their focus is on containment. These are not health care professionals. We need to bolster security, but also add a cadre of bio-warfare professionals who can collect air samples, test particulate matter that has settled on surfaces, and ensure that registration of all affected passengers proceeds smoothly."

Liz passed the baton to Scanlon to continue the discussion.

"The third phase will involve transforming our analytic findings into a cogent threat assessment. That assessment will have four principal elements: first, the probable outcome for people exposed within the terminals; second, the projected outcome for passengers on any of the planes targeted for aerosol dispersion of the bio-agent; third, the probability of infection outside of the contained facilities among the general population; and finally, the rapidity with which that infection may spread. Of course, the most critical element will then be our planned interventions."

"Do you have any guesstimates on the number of people infected?" Hart asked.

"It's a complex calculation that depends on the concentration of the virus within the dispersed aerosol, airflow within the terminal, even the relative humidity within each airport. But if the virus has truly been engineered for optimal infectivity, it's going to be a living hell in those terminals."

"How soon will we know?"

Scanlon replied, "We can have teams on-site within hours to take measurements. Of course, we'll know definitively when the infection begins to emerge—possibly within thirty-six to forty-eight hours.

"Which brings me to our fourth phase—decontamination and remediation. We will need to ensure that there is no surviving bio-agent capable of creating active infection, as well as have an effective method for triaging people within the facilities. Finally, we have to have a method for dealing with mass casualties. That means the removal and destruction of potentially thousands of bodies."

"What needs to happen next?" Hart asked abruptly.

"We need an emergency state of quarantine declared for the four airports. Right now, we are incarcerating passengers without the legal right to do so. We need to ensure that any terrorists who remain on planes are detected and dealt with, and we need to get the remaining planes, where there is a threat of bio-exposure, en route to Dugway. Once there, the passengers will be under the same emergency quarantine. And because the infection will cross multiple state lines and jurisdictions, we need to empower the command center to create ring quarantines as potential sites of infection emerge."

"I will communicate that to DHS and ask the Director to have his designee communicate with the two of you as rapidly as possible."

Hart turned his attention to Sayed. "What is the probability we will find the vaccine intact at the factory?"

"Before I was sent to the training camp, I was asked to help coordinate the distribution of the vaccine to what Al Hameed and Valikhanov called 'the Chosen Ones.' Though the details were never spoken of in my presence, I believe the process was to begin following the attacks."

"You understand, Sayed, that we are risking a war with Pakistan, a nuclear armed nation, over your belief. I pray that you are right."

"I overheard a comment, Commander, that I believe will give you solace. It was something that Al Hameed said to Valikhanov when he assumed no one was listening: 'It will be weeks, if not months, before our people are threatened by the hand of God . . . so we must not allow impatience to trump surprise in delivering salvation from the ravages of the virus.'"

"I'm surprised that he would run that risk. After all, one infected passenger landing in a Muslim country and thousands, if not millions, of his unvaccinated followers would die."

"Commander, I'm not speaking to Al Hameed's judgment, just his actions."

Hart stood to conclude the meeting. "Thank you, Sayed."

Before moving to the front of the plane, he spoke to James. "We need to try to identify people who exited the terminals after 6 AM and contain them."

"Sir, that's going to be nearly impossible."

"I know. So I suggest you get on it immediately."

Hart sequestered himself close to the cockpit and called Secretary Blevins. He walked him through the most critical details of Liz and Tom's plan, emphasizing the speed with which orders of quarantine would have to go into effect.

"I'll need to coordinate with the AG and the White House. That's a presidential decision. Once we get the nod, CDC, FEMA, and DoD can be mobilized," Blevins advised.

"The president has promised his full support, Sir, so there should not be any hold-ups."

"I'll move on it immediately, Commander. Teresa Levine will be appropriately empowered and will serve as my designee on all matters. She will meet Tom and Liz at the Metro entrance to the Pentagon. We have you scheduled for wheels down at 2:15 PM Eastern. Tell your colleagues they will be joining a meeting in progress."

"Will do. Thank you, Mr. Secretary. Let's pray we get through this one."

CHAPTER FORTY-SEVEN

The Pentagon

MOMENTS AFTER RETURNING FROM MISSOURI, Wilkins and Scanlon were on the way to the Pentagon. When they arrived at the Metro entrance, they were greeted by Teresa Levine.

Unusually tall, Teresa had striking features muted by a thick mane of curly brown hair that enveloped her head and draped halfway down her back. Wide eyebrows framed bright brown eyes. Her lips glistened a pearlescent shade of ruby red. Her figure was close to perfect—far too beautiful to be a GS employee, Scanlon thought. She should be gracing the cover of magazines or parading down a runway, not dealing with the after-shock of a terrorist attack.

As if reading her colleague's mind, Liz playfully chided him: "Oh Tom, it's hardly the time!"

Teresa gripped Scanlon's hand firmly to communicate that she was all business. She repeated the gesture with Liz.

"I assume that Commander Hart informed you we would be joining a meeting in progress?"

"Yes, he did," they responded in unison.

"Good, let's walk. The meeting room is ten minutes away."

Liz was in heels, and the pace Levine set was just short of a sprint. But she wasn't about to be shown up by Levine and soon matched her stride for stride.

Without slowing down, Levine continued to speak, "Scott Rowland, the Assistant Secretary for DHS, and Carl Chandler, his counterpart at DoD, will be running the show. Hopefully there won't be any unpleasant surprises relative to plans that are being put in motion. They've pretty much followed the guidelines you transmitted, but don't expect to receive the credit."

Scanlon and Wilkins smiled. They appreciated Levine's candor.

Over the next thirty minutes, Scott Rowland and Carl Chandler would be like runners in a two-man relay, dexterously passing the baton back and forth as they described their agencies' coordinated efforts to address the attack.

The first order of business focused on containment and security. Thus far, primary responsibility had fallen on TSA, which was supplemented by local and state law enforcement.

"DoD is moving to federalize the NG as soon as we have presidential approval. The Guard will then be supplemented by our military. We're expecting clearance for troop deployment from the AG's office at any moment."

Chandler passed the baton to Rowland.

"While Mr. Chandler addresses issues related to security and containment, my team will focus on the critical medical and infrastructure issues created by the attacks. An incident command center is being established outside of the hot zone at each of the four locations and at Dugway. It will be staffed by a combination of federal, state, and local authorities. DHS will serve as the lead agency until DoD assumes command once the NG is federalized. Mr. Chandler and I are in the process of identifying dual-status commanders for the four sites."

Liz and Tom exchanged glances, appreciative that their directions were being followed almost verbatim.

As Rowland wrapped up, he addressed the room: "It's not a pretty scenario, Ladies and Gentlemen. What I've outlined are our objectives for the next seventy-two hours. Soon, I'm afraid we may be talking about the need for mortuary affairs and other services unless we can identify effective counter-measures.

"There is, however, some good news," he added. "The FBI has identified two of the terrorists who managed to board flights. Tariq Abu al Khayr was on board a flight from Chicago to Boston. The second man, Ahmed al-Shishani, was on a Delta flight from Atlanta to San Francisco.

"Those men were extracted from the planes by agents wearing bio-protective gear. They were subdued and taken into custody. The terrorists will be on board a G-5 shortly, headed for Langley. A special team will accompany them for a mid-air debriefing, though I'm not sure what more they can reveal at this point in time.

"The other two men are presumed to still be in the terminals. We hope to have located them, via facial recognition, within hours."

Scott Rowland then turned to Wilkins and Scanlon. Levine whispered into Liz's ear, "It's show time!"

CHAPTER FORTY-EIGHT

The Pentagon

ALL EYES WERE ON WILKINS AND SCANLON as Scott Rowland introduced them.

"I believe everyone here knows Dr. Wilkins and Colonel Scanlon. They have been on the front lines of this event and jump-started many of the initiatives that we are now expanding upon. Dr. Wilkins, Colonel Scanlon, please feel free to share whatever details you deem appropriate."

"Thank you, Mr. Rowland," said Wilkins. "Though we are awaiting CDC confirmation, it is our belief that a highly virulent and lethal form of hemorrhagic smallpox was disseminated across the terminals of the four airports in question, as well as within a small number of commercial planes. This virus has purportedly been genetically modified to incubate on a greatly accelerated timeframe. That means we are dealing with a very short window of opportunity relative to interventions. Since we may lack any effective counter-measure, this point may be academic."

A man in his mid-fifties, sitting in a row behind the table, raised his hand. Liz did not know him.

"Yes, Sir."

"So, are you suggesting that we must sit and watch as people die a horrific death, and then begin the body count, Dr. Wilkins?"

Addressing her response to the broader audience, Wilkins' inflection changed, "There is a ray of hope, though it's a small one. Apparently this factory manufactured more than just the bio-agent. The perpetrators were tasked with developing a proprietary vaccine against the genetically modified pathogen. They believed the virus would initiate a pandemic Armageddon, and the survivors would be those who had been selected for vaccination—the so-called 'Chosen Ones.'"

Now it was Commissioner Kay Summers from the FDA who took aim.

"Drs. Wilkins and Scanlon, I am going to ignore the fact that you are bypassing the FDA on issues related to administering an unproven vaccine to human subjects. But I must ask: It appears that the horse has left the barn, so what is the point in discussing vaccines? I don't understand how the vaccine will benefit people who have already been exposed and presumably have the virus cascading through their bodies."

Liz responded, "We believe that there may be a small window during which post-exposure inoculation will confer sufficient immunity to allow some patients to survive the onslaught of the virus. And, of course, we anticipate hot-spots breaking out as a result of exposed individuals leaving the terminals prior to containment. We will need rapid ring-quarantine and inoculation strategies for the broader population."

After conferring with his aide, Chandler announced, "From what I understand, military assets are in the process of being deployed and will be on station in Pakistan by early morning."

"Good. Then we should focus our immediate attention on mass immunization within the terminals, as well as at Dugway," Liz suggested. "We will need a combined medical force able to operate in a hot-zone, as well as security for those medical personnel. Having the registration process in place will be essential. A rapid assessment of the civilian medical capacity within the affected areas will also be critical."

Scanlon added a cautionary note, "And let's not forget that there are still two unidentified terrorists presumably in the terminals. They need to be identified quickly."

"How do you suggest we do that, Mr. Scanlon?" The question came from Brookings Archer, a representative from the office of the Chairman of the Joint Chiefs of Staff.

"Mr. Archer, we start by having everyone roll up their sleeves at the time of registration. The smallpox inoculation they received will serve as sufficient indictment of their complicity for now," Scanlon explained.

Secretary Rowland said, "I believe we have a clear under-standing of what needs to occur over the next forty-eight hours. I am establishing a formal command center here to coordinate with the five incident command centers at the airports and Dugway.

"Tom and Liz, before we adjourn, I'd like to hear your thoughts on how we can best utilize your skills at this precarious moment in our nation's history. Of course, we include Commander Hart and your other colleagues in our invitation."

Liz spoke. "Secretary Rowland, I will serve as your point person with the CDC. Job One is verification of the pathogen that I discussed earlier. Once that is completed, we will begin disease surveillance, triage, and treatment to the degree it is available."

"How long will it take to test the vaccine once it arrives in Atlanta . . . assuming it does arrive?" Rowland wanted to know.

"We won't be testing it, Sir. There's no time. We will, of course, monitor for serious adverse reactions, which we anticipate occurring in a small percentage of those inoculated."

Kay Summers felt compelled to go on the record one final time, asking, "Do you really believe that's the right way to proceed, Dr. Wilkins?"

"No, Madame Commissioner, I know it is not the right way to proceed, but it is the only way under the circumstances."

"And when people become symptomatic?" Rowland asked.

"Our job is to ensure that the on-site teams are vigilant. Upon the first evidence of infection, people need to be moved into a higher level of isolation. We're talking about airline terminals, not ICUs, so we will do our best."

Chandler shifted the focus to Scanlon. "Colonel, who will be monitoring the general population for potential outbreaks?"

"Dr. Wilkins and I will run interference between CDC and state and local health departments. We will be data-mining selective databases to look for clues of aberrant outbreaks of disease. As you know, we monitor the consumption of OTC drugs bought in retail settings. We have enough trending data to know what is normal and what may signal an outbreak. We will also rely on human intelligence, including such sources as school nurses, who are often the first to recognize an evolving problem."

"You have each just described jobs that will require a legion of people working 120 hours per week to accomplish. I know you are good, but I trust you are also human," Chandler responded.

"Mr. Chandler, Dr. Wilkins and I are supported by an extensive team. We have formulated an incident response chain of command for those individuals and functions for which we are responsible. Our job is to summarize that information for this group. Liz and I don't expect to get much sleep, but trust that we will get the job done."

Mr. Rowland stood to convey the significance of what he was about to say and to prepare for adjournment.

"Ladies and Gentlemen, the president will address the nation tomorrow evening. While it is clearly in the best interests of our country and countrymen, his public address will create profound issues. Hospitals should be prepared for an onslaught of not only potential victims, but also the worried well. I'm afraid that we will quickly outstrip our civilian health care capacity if things unfold as anticipated."

Turning his attention back to Wilkins and Scanlon, Rowland added: "They're going to need our help. As we move towards ring-quarantine strategies, we are going to have a tough time getting supplies through to these facilities."

"Agreed, Mr. Secretary. We will be coordinating with the American Hospital Association, the Joint Commission, and a host of other organizations to see what can be done to improve the situation," Scanlon explained.

"Well, good luck to us all." With that, Rowland concluded the meeting.

CHAPTER FORTY-NINE

Knob Knoster, Missouri
Islamabad, Pakistan

Not many people claim to be from Knob Noster, Missouri. A quiet, agricultural community situated between Columbia and Kansas City, it's not the kind of town that generates a lot of attention. But it does have one thing to boast about—Whiteman Air Force Base.

For many years, Whiteman was home to the only remaining nuclear missile silo housed on a U.S. military base. Though decommissioned long ago, in its prime, the command center had controlled ten ICBMs that stood ready for launch upon presidential order. That site had been active from 1964 to 1993. But it was not the ghost of a nuclear past that made Whiteman intriguing. It was the aircraft flown by its 509th Bomb Wing.

The B-2 Stealth bomber was striking in appearance. The flat, triangular-shaped craft looked far more like a flying wing than a traditional aircraft. Many people thought it resembled a bat. It was equally striking in performance— able to deliver thermonuclear bombs to the other side of the world while avoiding the threat of detection by radar.

Thanks to the ceaseless efforts of Missouri Congressman Ike Skelton, the B-2 had found a home in Knob Noster. And though it had attracted many gawks in the early days, by now its take-offs and landings had become routine.

Such was the case on a perfect November day, when two B-2s departed at 4 PM for a seventeen-hour flight to Pakistan. They would refuel mid-air, after ten hours of flight, then slowly circle their targets in Faisalabad and Islamabad at approximately 9 AM Central Time—7 PM Pakistan Time—on Thursday. The B-2s represented the second phase of the U.S. operation. The first phase, the ground operation to procure the vaccine, would not wait for the B-2s to be on station. It had to move forward immediately.

Far closer to the intended target, a small team of combined CIA and DoD assets sat amid the glow of computer screens in a trailer stationed at one end of Bagram Air Base. Their hands on joysticks, they were not playing video games. Rather, they were moving precision assets—Predator drones armed with AGM-114 Hellfire missiles—to a position within easy striking distance of Islamabad.

The 104-pound AGM-114 had a range of 8,000 meters, and thanks to laser guidance, could strike with pinpoint accuracy. It had proven itself time and time again, neutralizing such high profile targets as Anwar al Awlaki in 2011 and Abu Yahya al-Libi in 2012.

The third leg of air support involved Raptor pilots Bill Christiansen, Mark Wilson, Glen Thomas, and Terry Sinclair, men who had logged thousands of hours in the air and were among the most experienced combat fighters in the Air Force.

Their job, for the moment, was to wait patiently until all the other critical assets were in motion and closing on their targets. Unlike the lumbering C-130 Hercules that had departed an hour ago, their F-22s would streak undetected across Pakistani airspace at just below supersonic speeds—putting them on target in minutes.

At 4 PM Eastern on Wednesday—1 AM Thursday in Pakistan—the White House placed a call to President Mughabi. Ninety seconds later, Presidents Mughabi and Jonathan Conner were connected.

"President Mughabi, I'm sorry to disturb you so late, but we have a situation," the president explained.

"I trust it is a matter of great urgency or else it would have waited until at least sunrise, Mr. President."

"You are correct. "

"What is it, Mr. President, that is so pressing?"

"A bioterrorist event was launched at 6 AM Central Time on Wednesday at four of our nation's busiest airports. Thousands of people are feared to be infected, the majority of whom are expected to die."

"Is this true, Mr. President? How could such a thing occur?"

"We have a high confidence level that the perpetrators and the bio-agent originated in your country, President Mughabi."

"That is not possible, Mr. President. And of course, you recognize that."

"There's no time for rhetoric or denial, Mr. Mughabi. I need you to listen very closely to what I am about to say. Before I do so, however, I suggest you conference in General Malik."

Superficial congeniality gave way to open hostility as Mughabi responded to President Conner: "I'm in command, not General Malik."

"I'm sorry, Mr. President, but we both know who runs your country." Conner waited as his stinging remark sank in. "Now please get General Malik on the line."

For a moment, it was unclear whether Mughabi had put President Conner on hold or had hung up. Two minutes passed slowly until the line came back to life. "President Conner, you have both of us on the line as requested."

"Thank you, President Mughabi. General Malik, I was explaining that we have a situation. I trust the president told you of its nature."

"Yes," came the terse response.

"Gentlemen, the only hope we have of stopping the spread of this virus may reside in fifty million doses of vaccine purportedly stored at the same factory that engineered the bio-weapon."

Malik interjected, "And where do you believe this factory to exist?"

"Well, General, since it was constructed under the nose of ISI, I think you know the answer to that question."

There was a quick and sharp exchange between Mughabi and Malik. A translator at the White House whispered to the president that Mr. Mughabi appeared to be completely unaware of ISI's complicity in the event.

"We don't have time for bickering," the president said firmly. "We have military assets being deployed as I speak with the mission of securing this vaccine and safely transporting it to the U.S. Those assets will be crossing into your airspace momentarily. We have other assets already in place."

"You've violated our airspace?" Mughabi demanded incredulously.

"From what I understand, President Mughabi, millions of Americans are about to lose their lives because Islamic extremists were allowed to operate unhindered in your country and develop a weapon of mass destruction with the tacit approval of the Pakistani government."

General Malik angrily shouted, "President Conner, you are committing an act of war against the sovereign nation of Pakistan!"

As he spoke, the U.S. President gave a nod to General Anderson, who spoke a simple command into a headset: "Permission to engage."

A Hellfire missile tore loose of its moorings and rocketed at 450 meters per second towards a target just outside of the kill zone of Aiwan e-Sadr, President Mughabi's residence. Less than a second later, a second drone unleashed a missile proximate to General Malik's residence, carefully avoiding a small hospital located fifty meters east of the ISI compound.

Images of both targets were projected from the drones onto a large screen at the far end of the situation room, and an audio feed from the drone pilots could be clearly heard.

In near unison, the pilots counted, "Contact in 5, 4, 3, 2, 1."

The screen momentarily went white as the missiles struck their targets. Though they were not visible, both Mughabi and Malik had been hurled into the air by the powerful blasts.

President Jonathan Conner pulled the phone away from his ear as the blasts reverberated through the receiver. He prayed that the drone pilots had been precise in their strikes and had inflicted structural damage to nearby facilities without killing the two Pakistani leaders.

A moment later, the two most powerful men in Pakistan were on the line ranting about the fury they were about to unfurl on America and its allies.

The president's tone grew stern and unforgiving. "Those missiles were warnings. The next ones go through your windows."

The ranting stopped.

"I suggest you listen to every word I am about to say," the president advised. "You will do nothing to interfere with our operation. A B-2 bomber will soon be on station above Islamabad. It carries a single B61-Model 12 nuclear warhead. The yield has been adjusted to 150 kilotons. Upon my order, you, your government, and your families will be incinerated in a blast ten times more powerful than Hiroshima. Our generals estimate that more than a million of your citizens will instantly perish in Islamabad and Rawalpind."

The president paused. "President Mughabi, you understand the accuracy of this weapon. You were among the first to cry out in protest when we tested a dummy payload in the Nevada desert. As you will recall, it landed within sixty feet of its target. So, you are sitting sixty feet away from incineration. Think carefully about what I have said, then wait until we inform you that all United States assets are safely in international airspace before you lift a finger."

"I know you, President Conner. You are not the kind of man who would kill a million people with the push of a button. You are a good, Christian man. One with morals and a conscience," Mughabi said.

"Yesterday, I might have agreed with you. Today, the fate of my nation is all that occupies my mind. I suggest you not test me, President Mughabi.

"One final detail. Don't even think about scrambling your F-16s. They would be little match for our Raptors. Of course, you would never know the outcome of an air battle because the nuke would have already turned you into ash. I have been told that the temperature in your palace will reach 10,000 degrees Celsius."

On that note, the president abruptly disconnected the line. An instant later, the telecommunications network in Pakistan, including all satellite communication, went dark—brought down by an elite team of hackers at NSA.

President Mughabi and General Malik frantically tried calling for help, but the lines were dead. They picked up emergency SAT phones, but they, too, were of no value.

As a final insurance measure, NSA hackers had shut down the entire electrical grid, blacking out Islamabad, along with dozens of military and intelligence sites across the country. Pakistan, a country with a sophisticated electronic and communications infrastructure, had been thrust back in time to the Stone Age. And there was not a damn thing the Pakistani leaders could do about it, except sit in the darkness and wait.

CHAPTER FIFTY

Faisalabad, Pakistan

AIR TRAFFIC CONTROLLERS AT FAISALABAD AIRPORT were confused. Two U.S. C-130 pilots were requesting permission to land on Runway 2E. Unable to reach the military by phone, they assumed it was some type of joint military exercise of which they had not been informed. They granted clearance.

A Pakistan Air Force pilot was enjoying a cup of tea with the controllers as the odd situation unfolded.

"I wasn't told about this," the pilot sounded alarmed as he informed his compatriots. Setting down his cup, he slipped quickly out of the room and descended four flights of stairs to the base of the tower. He crouched low, then began moving quickly towards an outlying runway where a single F-16 was parked.

Moments later, a SEAL team crashed through the door of the tower control room and quickly subdued the staff. Snipers armed with M107A1 Barrett .50 caliber rifles and night-vision scopes established a secure perimeter around the airport. Anyone within 2,000 meters would be within the effective kill zone for this weapon.

With immediate threats mitigated, the Special Forces team rapidly off-loaded equipment for the 12-minute drive to the factory.

They crossed Faisalabad without incident, although the handful of locals they passed in the street gave startled looks at the sight of an American military force traversing their city. As the first Humvee pulled up to the factory, it was met by a single security guard holding an AK-47. Before he could raise his rifle, a quick head shot from a suppressed MP5 snapped his neck backwards and dropped him to the ground. The gate was thrown open, and the entire extraction force moved quickly to the front of the factory.

With half a dozen special operatives covering his back, a ranger ran up to the factory's front door. He took a fist-size piece of what looked like modeling clay and shaped it around the lock. After inserting a small detonator, he ran back to his group. Everyone ducked close to the earth as he shouted, "Fire in the hole!" and pressed a small, red button. The C-4 blew the steel door off its hinges—catapulting it deep into the recesses of the factory.

Their presence no longer a secret, the troops rushed in and began searching for the vaccine.

Lieutenant Eric Logan, team commander, pulled a small electronic device no larger than a cell phone from his pocket. It contained a schematic of the interior of the warehouse and the purported location of the vaccine. Surrounded by escorts, he led the unit deep into the factory until they reached a freight elevator.

"The vaccine should be two levels below us in a refrigerated storage area!" Logan shouted.

While half the team remained behind to stand guard, Logan and five heavily armed men entered the elevator and descended the twenty feet separating them from America's only hope for survival.

The lift jolted as it struck the sub-basement floor. The men found themselves with one more threshold to cross—a wide, steel door, which opened onto several thousand square feet of refrigerated space. It was unlocked. They threw it open and proceeded cautiously.

The room was empty. Completely empty. No vaccine, no empty pallets . . . nothing.

Logan got on the SAT phone to USCCOM.

The voice of General Mark Allen answered, "Yes, Commander."

"General, we are at the target, Sir, but the cargo is not here as indicated."

Allen was painfully slow to respond, seared by the implications of what he had just heard. Perhaps Hart had been too cavalier in his assessment of Sayed's reliability, he thought.

"Commander, I want you to take that place apart until you find it . . . and I pray you do find it. Allen out."

Ascending the lift, Logan addressed the entire team: "It's not there, so we've got to find it. Let's get going. Now! Zimmer, Nichols, Casper—find the loading docks; Hammer, Cross, Perry—take the lift down one level and see what you can locate. The rest of you follow me. And, for God's sake, don't touch anything!"

Just then, a burst of automatic weapons fire hit two of the men in the chest. Blood oozed from holes in their Kevlar vests, which had slowed the velocity, but not stopped the bullets from an AK.

As the group of heavily armed soldiers dropped to the ground, one lobbed a grenade in the direction of the fire. Two men cried out seconds before their bodies were catapulted into the air by the explosion.

The immediate threat neutralized, the men resumed their search. This time, they moved methodically, clearing areas before proceeding.

Less than five minutes passed before Zimmer was on the comm: "Commander, we've found it!"

On the loading dock, there were pallets stacked floor to ceiling, full of vaccine awaiting shipment. In all, Logan counted forty pallets.

Relieved, he placed a second call to General Allen.

"Thank God!" Allen responded. "Now get it loaded and get the hell out of there!"

USCOM relayed the information to the Agency that the material was being secured for transportation. They anticipated being on board the C-130s and ready to depart in approximately ninety minutes.

As the cargo was secured, the SEAL team and the Special Forces unit reboarded the C130s. Two of the Raptors were redeployed from Islamabad to provide close air support. After waiting to ensure that all traces of the U.S. forces had departed Faisalabad, a lone F-16, parked on a distant runway, fired up its engines.

With the C-130s safely en route to Bagram, the second phase began. Lt. Colonel Mike Murphy received orders to guide his B-2 into position over the factory in Faisalabad. It carried a laser-guided, 2,000-pound thermobaric bomb. He knew the devastation would be immense. His father, also an Air Force pilot, had shared with him stories of the unimaginable devastation wrought by the first thermobaric bombs deployed by his unit in Vietnam.

At a predetermined altitude, a small explosive within the bomb would disperse its contents, creating a cloud of fuel that, when combined with the air, would set up a massive explosive charge. Once the cloud had completely enveloped the factory, a second charge would ignite it. The resulting blast wave would destroy the structure and every living organism within it.

After releasing the bomb, Colonel Murphy jerked the plane's yoke up and to the right. Even at altitude, he needed to be clear of the blast-wave.

When the bomb exploded, the night sky lit up with the brilliance of sun-drenched day. As the immense fireball eventually subsided, nothing remained of the factory. In fact, nothing within a quarter mile remained standing. A trench measuring the length and width of two football fields now replaced the factory. Cameras mounted on each wingtip recorded the images and digitally relayed them to the Pentagon.

Meanwhile, Bill Hendricks' nuclear-laden B-2 was flying undetected over Islamabad. With its weapons system armed, it would remain on station until he received further instructions from the president.

With less than a hundred miles separating him from the border, one of the C-130 pilots received an electronic warning of a plane closing fast. The F-16, which had departed Faisalabad, was sixty miles out. That meant it could achieve missile lock on the C-130 in thirty miles, unleashing its deadly AMRAAM air-to-air missiles. Laden with several tons of vaccine and moving at a mere

370 knots, the plane would be a sitting duck. Traveling at Mach IV, the missile would reach its target in less than thirty seconds.

Chris Anthony, piloting Raptor Alpha 4, radioed Bagram: "Bagram, this is Alpha 4. It appears that we have unwelcome company approaching at a distance of sixty miles. Unknown aircraft appears to be closing at 950 mph, and systems indicate it is an F-16. Request permission to engage."

"Roger, Alpha 4. We're tracking it," came the response from Bagram. "Permission to engage."

Anthony broke sharply from formation, turning his fighter directly into the path of the oncoming F-16.

"I have him on screen," Anthony reported. "Awaiting missile lock."

An instant later, Anthony again spoke: "Missile locked on; missile away."

"Impact in 4, 3, 2, 1," he counted.

As he was counting, an alarm fired off in the cockpit of the C-130. The F-16 had a radar lock on the plane and was preparing to fire. The C-130 pilot shoved the yoke forward, forcing the lumbering plane to lunge steeply downward and momentarily breaking the radar lock. It was the precious extra second they needed to survive.

Anthony's excited voice broke through on the radio: "Direct hit! Direct hit!" he shouted as the F-16 vanished from the screens.

"Grateful you took the shot when you did!" came the response from the C-130 pilot.

"You can buy me a cold one once we're down," Anthony joked as he brought the F-22 side by side with the cockpit of the C-130—close enough to return a salute from its pilot. Then speaking into the mike, "Bagram control, threat neutralized. Requesting priority landing instructions."

CHAPTER FIFTY-ONE

Chicago O'Hare to Karachi, Pakistan

Early Tuesday morning, after each of the jihadists was safely en route to his target, Al Hameed and Valikhanov had departed Pierpont, Missouri, for Chicago O'Hare. At precisely 8 PM, they boarded Pakistani International Airlines Flight 200 for the thirteen-hour trip to Abu Dhabi. Upon arrival, they disembarked and proceeded to the gate for their final flight to Karachi. Video cameras in the terminal tracked their movements. It would take only a few hours for the video feed to be processed for facial recognition and the men identified.

Close to twenty-four hours elapsed before the wheels of the Airbus 320 squealed as it touched down at Jinnah International Airport. The methodically planned attacks were now over. Jubilant in their success and grateful to be home on Islamic soil, the only thing left to do was await confirmation of the emerging Armageddon.

The moment he and Beibut entered the terminal, Al Hameed recognized Omar Qazan, the ISI operative who had been instrumental in providing safe refuge for

Beibut, who was waiting to greet them. After exchanging cursory pleasantries, little more was said as Qazan drove Al Hameed and Valikhanov to a safe house on the northern edge of the city.

Thanks to a paucity of traffic, the trip took only thirty minutes. Throughout the drive, Qazan carefully monitored his rearview mirror to ensure that no one was following them.

Trailing silently behind the car at an altitude just over 4,500 feet was a small drone. Its images were being relayed in real time to CIA Headquarters. Beyond the drone operator, only three people would be privy to the images: the Director of the CIA, the National Security Advisor, and the president. Not even Hart would know of Al Hameed's detection until President Conner decided how and when to take action.

Al Hameed and Valikhanov were exhausted. Neither had slept much in the past two days. Moments after entering the safe house, they retired to bed and did not reappear until mid-morning.

Entering the kitchen, Al Hameed turned to Qazan, who was leaning against the counter, a cigarette drooping from his mouth, and asked, "What news do you have from America?"

"We know that the four targeted airports have been shut down. So has all air traffic flying to or departing from those locations."

"Is that all?" Al Hameed asked impatiently.

Valikhanov intervened, "You must give this a few days. Our attack was not one of bullets and bombs, but of a silent blanket of death that will soon cover America. Be patient, Ahmed."

But Al Hameed was in no mood to be patient. He glared at both men before responding. "Tell me when you've learned something of value. I want to know that we have pierced the heart of the Great Satan, not merely caused chaos at their airports!"

Qazan turned on the tap and ran water over the hot tip of his cigarette before tossing the butt into the trash. Turning to Al Hameed, he said, "We've been instructed to take you to al-Bakr. We will leave in a few days. Until then, I hope you will accept our hospitality."

At five o'clock the next morning, Qazan urgently summoned Al Hameed and Valikhanov to the study, where a computer screen displayed a broadcast from CNN International. The American President was preparing to deliver an address.

They listened with glee as President Conner described the after-effects of a horrific attack on the four busiest airports in America. It was what they had prayed to Allah to hear—the beginning of the end for an imperialistic regime and its allies.

But then the president said something for which they were unprepared. Their smiles faded as Conner revealed that the Americans not only knew of the vaccine, but were in the process of acquiring it.

As the broadcast ended, Qazan's cell phone began to vibrate. He picked it up, turning his back on the group, and spoke softly into the receiver. There was a very long pause before he spoke again—appearing to acknowledge what he had just been told. Returning the phone to his pocket, he slowly turned towards Al Hameed.

"There has been an attack on our country. Apparently the communications and power grid were effectively shut down for hours while we slept. There are few details. What we do know is that the Americans have stolen all of the vaccine."

"And the factory?" Beibut asked urgently.

"There is no factory. Now there is only a crater," Qazan responded.

"You fool!" Al Hameed screamed at Qazan. "How could your military have allowed this to happen?"

But there would be no answer. Certainly none that would satisfy Al Hameed.

Turning to Valikhanov, he asked, "What does this mean, Beibut? Our years of planning and work will have been for nothing?"

"No, there will be massive deaths," Valikhanov responded, though his deflated tone spoke volumes.

"We were not called upon to create massive deaths, but Armageddon! Death on a scale never before witnessed. Will that happen?" Al Hameed was almost pleading.

"It depends upon how rapidly the Americans transport the vaccine and how well they contain the pandemic," Valikhanov explained.

Pacing back and forth, Al Hameed was out of control. He suddenly lurched forward, and gripping the edge of the kitchen table, threw it high into the air. Its contents shattered as they fell to the floor.

"It was Sayed," Al Hameed seethed. "No one else could have known about the vaccine, let alone where it was stored. He's a dead man. I will tear every piece of flesh from his body if it is the last thing I do on this earth!"

He stormed out of the room.

CHAPTER FIFTY-TWO

Atlanta Hartsfield International Airport

Lieutenant Tim Morrison of the Georgia National Guard had been on station outside of Atlanta Hartsfield's Terminal B for hours. Fatigue, exacerbated by stress, was beginning to set in. Morrison was as patriotic as the next man, but he never expected to be guarding fellow Americans barricaded within a U.S. airport, and certainly not with a mandate to shoot to kill anyone trying to escape. All Morrison and his fellow Guardsmen had been told was "a situation was unfolding." He couldn't fathom what kind of situation would justify the use of lethal force.

He let his hands drop to his sides, no longer atop the M2 .50 caliber, jeep-mounted machine gun. Would he use it if he had to, Morrison wondered, mowing down people as they tried to flee from the chaos? He tried taking a deep breath, but the air was slow to come, choked off by anxiety.

Guard Commander Colonel Jack Martelli stood less than fifty paces to Morrison's right. He was close enough for Morrison to see the phone in his hand. Morrison prayed the Colonel was receiving word of reinforcements . . . maybe even an order to stand down.

Tension inside the terminals was at a boiling point. Imprisoned passengers watched as military and medical personnel, clothed in full-body protective suits and respirators, entered and exited the facilities. Thousands of cots were being brought in, and makeshift hospitals were under construction. It was clear nobody was going anywhere soon. Out of sight, morgues capable of burning bodies on-site would soon be in place.

Lieutenant Morrison watched as Colonel Martelli ended his call and then signaled to a captain to join him. Orders had come through from Washington. The president was federalizing the Guard. This allowed the troops on the ground to be reinforced by Army and Marine units stationed nearby. An incident command structure, the skeleton of which had been in place since the first troops arrived, would be fully operational within hours. Morrison's immediate reaction was relief, but it was quickly tempered by the realization that something very serious must have occurred to catalyze such a deployment.

Within the hour, the personnel required to staff the registration process were in place. The ticket counters provided a perfect venue for people to queue up. However, the lines that quickly formed seemed without end. Each passenger's pertinent information was recorded, and a digital photograph was taken. Men were asked to roll up their sleeves so their arms could be inspected for signs of a recent vaccination. Once the three-minute process was completed, detainees were issued an ID card, as well as a surgical mask to limit further exposure. They were sternly warned not to attempt to leave the facility.

The same scene was unfolding in the three other airports. Reports of civilians being shot at the Chicago airport were beginning to filter down to the rank and file of the Guardsmen. It was just the beginning of the unrest.

Sam Hardesty was a veteran and a no-bullshit kind of guy. After surviving three tours of duty in Iraq and Afghanistan, he had returned to the states and had gone to work for his father's construction company in Durham, North Carolina. It was a tough business that required a firm temperament—one that could weather the cycles of feast or famine that followed swings in the economy. Hardesty was accustomed to leading men who could be impulsive and sometimes expressed their feelings with their fists.

Sam was in Atlanta for work. He'd been visiting a job site in Buckhead, about twenty miles from the airport. It was a bread-and-butter project, a 40,000-square-foot medical office building. Fortunately, his crew on the project did not require too much supervision. He didn't mind traveling. It came with the job. But he hated the crowds during the holidays.

He had arrived at Atlanta's Hartsfield International Airport at 7:45 AM for a 9 AM flight. Eager to see his family, he was first in line when they called the A boarding group. Before she began accepting boarding passes, however, the ticket agent picked up the microphone.

"If you are traveling on Flight 1806 to Raleigh-Durham, I am sorry, but your flight has been cancelled. We ask that you stay in the gate area, and we will provide you with more information as soon as it becomes available."

"Oh, shit." The words slipped inadvertently out of Sam's mouth. The last thing he wanted was to miss Thanksgiving dinner with his wife, Andrea, and their three children. He hurried up to the desk where the agent stood, microphone still in hand.

"When is the next flight you can get me on?" he asked, radiating impatience.

Without even looking at her computer screen, the agent said, "I'm sorry, Sir, but it appears that all flights have been cancelled."

"What are you talking about? It's a perfectly clear day! Why in God's name would the airport be shut down?"

"I'm sorry, Sir," the woman replied, "I can't answer that. You will simply have to wait."

Sam gave the woman a look of disgust as he pushed away from the counter. To hell with it, he thought, it was only a six-hour drive. So he headed towards the main terminal's baggage claim area where the rental car counters were located.

When he arrived at Hertz, there were no reservation agents in sight, only a sign indicating that they were out of cars. He walked a few yards to Budget. No one there. Avis the same thing. What the hell is going on, he wondered, before deciding to bypass the counters and go to where the cars were housed.

As he approached the nearest terminal exit, a National Guardsman stepped forward, blocking his path.

"I need you to return to the terminal, Sir."

Sam started to weave to the soldier's right, causing him to raise his rifle and adopt a combat stance.

"I'm not going to ask you again, Sir," the command had become a threat.

"Listen, buddy, I did multiple tours in Iraq and Afghanistan—3rd Ranger Battalion. Just tell me what the hell is going on."

"We have strict orders, Sir. No one is to leave the terminal."

"Why? That doesn't make any sense, unless you're looking for someone in the terminal, and I don't see any kind of operation underway."

"I'm sorry, Sir, that's all I know."

With no option other than a direct confrontation of the well-armed soldier, Sam turned and headed back to the terminal. He rode the escalator up to the main floor and planted himself in the food court before calling his wife.

"Hi, Sweetheart, can't wait to see ya! The girls are so excited," Andrea said as she picked up her cell phone.

"Hi, Darling. Well, I'm hoping to see you and the girls, too, but right now I'm stuck in Atlanta. I don't know what's going on here, but they've shut the airport down, and nobody is being allowed to leave."

"Oh, baby, I'm so sorry. Don't worry about us, we're fine. I'm just sorry for you. I know you're ready to be home."

As a former Army wife, Andrea had gotten used to disappointments. There were furloughs that had been canceled . . . delayed flights home . . . and a deployment that stretched months longer than anticipated. She took it all in stride, loving to have her man at her side, yet fully capable of enjoying her time alone with the girls.

"Honey, don't worry about what you can't change. I'll say a prayer that you get back on a flight soon. The girls and I will be happy to see you whenever you get home."

"Thanks, Darling. I'll call you when there's more to tell." As he hung up the phone, Sam again assessed his options. It appeared that his only choice for now was to sit tight and hope the internment ended quickly.

The day passed interminably slowly. With every hour, Sam grew angrier. Andrea could hear it in his voice each time her husband called with an update. Still clinging to the hope that he would get out before evening, Sam approached the boiling point when he was issued a cot that night.

After lying on his cot ruminating for a couple of hours, Sam took two Benadryl capsules out of his dop kit and slugged them down with a gulp of tepid coffee. He finally fell asleep around 3 AM and remained asleep until shortly after 6 AM The drug still active in his system, Sam awoke groggy and momentarily confused. He reached for his wife, thinking he was home in bed, until the reality of his situation flashed back with a vengeance.

Propping himself up, he surveyed the area. There were now numerous guardsmen throughout the terminal, as well as medical personnel, TSA, and local law enforcement. They were easy to spot. Each person was wearing a full protective suit similar to the MOPP IV chem/bio suits he had been issued in Iraq. He didn't know what was happening, but he did know that he had to escape this craziness.

A few yards away, three Marines, who were clearly on leave for the holiday, lay adjacent to one another on cots. Sam heaved himself upright, walked over, and struck up a quick conversation.

"Where you guys headed?"

"Chicago, Sir," one of the men responded.

"Toledo, Sir."

The third man, who was older, looked at Sam closely before responding, "I don't think I'm headed anywhere in the near future, Sir. How about you?"

"I think we're all in the same boat," Sam suggested.

"I've got a wife and a new daughter waiting for me at home," one of the Marines said. "I can't wait to see them. When do you think we'll get out of here, Sir?"

"I don't know, but I've got a wife and three daughters waiting for me, and I'm getting awfully tired of sitting on my butt waiting for something to happen. It makes me feel like I'm back in the service, if you know what I mean."

The three men nodded their heads and laughed.

"How about if we find a way out of here?"

"Do you think that's wise, Sir?" the oldest Marine asked cautiously.

Noting the man's stripes, Sam responded, "Sergeant, I want to see my family on Thanksgiving, not be holed up in some damn airport."

"What are you suggesting?" the man asked.

"I'm suggesting that we find an exit with the fewest number of Guardsmen and extricate ourselves."

"And if the exit is guarded?" the man asked. "Are you suggesting that we overpower military personnel securing this terminal?"

"Look, I'm not suggesting that anyone gets hurt. I think the four of us can get the hell out of here without too much of a scuffle, unless that's too tough a mission for this former Army Ranger to ask of you Marines?"

Within minutes, the men were descending the escalators to baggage claim, where they walked across the terminal until they found an exit guarded by a single man. The group approached him, smiling as though they simply wanted to ask a question. As he took his hand off the trigger grip of the weapon, Sam lunged forward, striking the man hard across the jaw with his elbow. The Guardsman dropped to the floor.

"Let's go!" Sam shouted, and the four men burst through the exit. Eyeing a parked rental car shuttle no more than a block away, Sam motioned to his team before breaking into a sprint towards the vehicle.

The order to *stop and drop* came almost instantly. It was piercingly loud and crystal clear, but the men kept going. A second later, a shot rang out, followed by a repetition of the order. The men knew it was a warning shot and, for the briefest of moments, it served its purpose. But then Sam, followed by the three Marines, were up and running again.

Four shots rang out in rapid succession. Each man was struck a single time in the head by bullets from Army snipers. They fell to the sidewalk, their legs simply folding under them, a few scant yards from the vehicle they had hoped to commandeer. Sam's uprising had lasted only seconds. It achieved nothing more than a quick death for three servicemen and one veteran.

In those few seconds, Andrea was transformed from a devoted wife to a widow. She had always braced herself for the possibility of losing Sam while on deployment. It came with the turf of being a military spouse, and it was reinforced as many of her husband's colleagues lost their lives in combat or returned home maimed by an IED. Nothing, however, could truly prepare Andrea for the news that her husband had been killed by U.S. forces.

Word of the incident spread quickly and catalyzed a debate at the highest levels of government regarding whether additional information should be provided to airport detainees ahead of the Presidential address. After some heated exchanges, it was finally agreed that no information would be released until the president spoke.

The planes were a different story. People could not continue to sit on the tarmac indefinitely. There was the very real possibility of a riot on board if no action or explanations were forthcoming. So a cover story needed to be put in place—one that would appear credible to the passengers and buy some time.

Delta pilot Benjamin Goldstein picked up the intercom and keyed the mike. In thirty years of flying, he had never seen a prepared statement from the FAA remotely resembling what he was about to read to his passengers and crew. Before speaking, he took a quick glance at his co-pilot and shook his head, mouthing the word *bullshit*.

"Ladies and Gentlemen, this is Captain Goldstein. I know how tired you must be of sitting on the tarmac waiting for take-off. I am sorry for the extraordinary inconvenience. We've been under strict orders to hold the flight due to concerns that you may have been exposed to the SARS virus. As you may know, this respiratory virus is highly contagious, and people presumed to have been exposed must be quarantined until it is determined that there is no threat." The captain paused.

"You may have noticed a fuel truck off the left wing. I have received orders from the FAA to transport you to a new destination in Utah. We are setting a new heading for Dugway Proving Ground, where we will be met by medical personnel. I'm sure there is little reason for concern, but

I understand how terribly disruptive this may be for you. Please give the flight attendants your full cooperation. We will be departing in five minutes."

An elderly woman turned towards the young mother seated next to her. "Honey, what did the pilot say—something about SARS? Do you know what that is and where exactly they are taking us?"

Caroline Beck thought about her own mother and how frightening it would be for her to be in such a situation. She reached over and took the woman's hand. "I'm sure everything will be fine. I don't really know much about SARS, and I'm afraid that I've never heard of Dugway, but I trust that they are doing what is in our best interests. You will be back with your family soon."

The woman nodded, grateful for the small gesture of compassion, then closed her eyes and lay back in her seat.

The announcement had rendered most of the passengers numb and silent, as they struggled to comprehend what they had just heard. The same scenario was playing out on countless airplanes destined for quarantine at Dugway. A few pilots reported incidents shortly after the announcements—all were quickly contained. Within the hour, every plane in question was airborne and proceeding to a remote landing strip in Utah.

As Captain Goldstein's flight neared the Army installation, he once again picked up the mike and read from a script. "This is your captain. We have begun our initial descent into Dugway. Please listen carefully. Once you disembark from the aircraft, you will be loaded onto buses for transportation to a centralized facility for processing. You will then be sent on to a medical facility for a short initial examination. You will not need your luggage. Everything you need in terms of clothing, medications, or personal items will be provided. You will also be required to relinquish your cell phones."

Even through the thick cockpit door, Goldstein could hear the collective groan of his passengers. He knew cell phones had come to represent people's lifeline to the world, and it was about to be severed. The instruction to relinquish their luggage only added to the angst.

He continued. "When you register, the names of your relatives and their contact information will be requested. They will be informed of your situation." Goldstein wondered if this information was truthful, and whether their families would, indeed, have any inkling as to the fate of their loved ones.

"Do not be alarmed when you see personnel in bio-hazard suits or wearing full-face respirators. This is just a precaution. Finally, please do not attempt to step out of line or run away. The federal government takes these matters quite seriously and will be completely intolerant of non-compliance."

Taking his thumb off the mike key, he turned again to co-pilot Steve Hensen and said quite forcefully—"BULL-SHIT!" Then he added, "Albeit Mach Frei (Work sets you free)." It was a slogan emblazoned over the entrance to Auschwitz in an attempt to deceive incoming Jewish prisoners as to their fate.

Dugway's most important attribute was its isolation, far removed from any trace of civilian population. The military base encompassed more than 1,250 square miles. The site consisted of high desert scrub abutting mountains and mesas. It was a perfect location for the Army's principal facility for testing chemical and biological agents.

Before the first planes landed, work was already underway to accommodate an unprecedented number of civilians. Thousands of cots, tents, food and water rations, and medical supplies were being flown and trucked in from the military bases in adjoining states.

Dugway's 1,700 staff members, who were fatigued from two weeks of hosting their annual S/K Challenge, in which defense contractors from around the world came to test the effectiveness of their latest chemical and biological systems, had to buck up and move quickly. Fatigue was irrelevant. There was an enormous amount of work to do.

When the planes landed, the passengers, perhaps still in shock, readily complied with the crew's instructions to deplane, as their luggage remained entombed in overhead bins or stowed in the bowels of the plane. Captain Goldstein watched as they shuffled off his plane and were herded towards the processing area.

When the last passenger was out the door, he growled at Hensen: "I don't know what the fuck is up, but it sure as hell isn't SARS! Not with this level of intervention."

"Agreed, Ben. Years ago, when I was stationed at Nellis, we didn't even like to fly over Dugway. We were afraid that some of their bugs might reach up into the stratosphere," Hensen said wryly.

"No shit, Steve. Let's hope we're not about to become victims of the Andromeda Strain."

Stepping out of the cockpit, he motioned for Hensen to join him. "Well, they're expecting us, too. We'd better get in there."

CHAPTER FIFTY-THREE

The White House

AT 6 PM CENTRAL TIME ON THANKSGIVING, television monitors in the nation's four busiest airports suddenly came to life. Medical and security personnel interrupted their routines as all passengers' eyes turned towards the nearest screen. The overhead paging systems amplified the audio of the presidential address. He was standing in the press room, which was filled with journalists.

"My fellow Americans, I come to you on this day of Thanksgiving—a day when we celebrate the grace that has been bestowed upon this wonderful and bountiful country of ours—with a heavy heart. Our nation faces what historians will someday label *the darkest chapter in American history.* They will speak of a time when all citizens faced a threat of unparalleled magnitude. One that could destroy the very fabric of our nation.

"Yesterday, an attack was launched against our four busiest airports—Atlanta, Chicago, Los Angeles, and Dallas. The terrorists also attacked passengers who were on board flights, creating a uniquely difficult challenge for us to manage.

"It was a bloodless attack. There were no bombs or automatic rifle fire. In fact, it was something far more devastating. A group of jihadists aligned with the United Islamic State unleashed a biological weapon that exposed thousands of unsuspecting travelers to a dangerous virus. Symptoms of that disease are just beginning to appear in a small number of exposed passengers, but we assume that these numbers will grow substantially in the coming days.

"This disease is a particularly virulent form of smallpox. For those of you wondering how a disease that was purportedly eradicated from the face of the earth in the 1970s could be used as a biological weapon, the answer is complex. For now, suffice it to say that UIS scientists were able to obtain laboratory samples of a genetically engineered form of the disease by stealing it from a laboratory in Russia.

"There are no effective treatments for this form of smallpox within our medical arsenal. We are holding out hope that a newly developed vaccine may provide a level of post-exposure immunity. If this is true, the vaccine may help reduce suffering and spare lives. But we cannot count on it.

"The passengers who were within the terminals at the time of the attack, as well as several thousand people who boarded aircraft after being in the terminals, are being held in isolation. It is imperative that they not spread the disease outside of the terminals. It is not our intent to restrict the movement of these passengers any longer than absolutely necessary, but we must protect the broader population.

"My address is being simulcast within the four terminals attacked yesterday. It is my fervent hope that the passengers in those terminals will muster the bravery required to remain calm and honor the quarantine that has been imposed on those facilities. To do otherwise is to risk igniting a pandemic that could claim the lives of millions. For those of you in Chicago O'Hare, Atlanta's Hartsfield, LAX, and DFW, I realize the sacrifice that I am asking of you. I ask that you put the safety of your fellow Americans ahead of your personal needs. And I ask that your families support you in the turbulent hours ahead."

The president continued, "Even with these efforts, there will be outbreaks in communities across the nation. It is therefore imperative that you do everything in your power to minimize unnecessary exposure to the virus. It is also vitally important for you to be familiar with the symptoms, a list of which will follow on your screens following my comments. If you or someone you love becomes symptomatic, we have a process in place for you to notify authorities and receive help.

"For those of you who possess a strong faith, this would be a good time to pray for our nation and its people. We will emerge from this national tragedy stronger, more united, and resolute in our conviction to wipe the threat of jihadism forever from our world. Those who have perpetrated this unthinkable act will be brought to justice.

"Thank you, and may God heal our country!"

The president ended his address to a hushed audience. Even the most ardent of journalists appeared momentarily speechless. There would be no questions.

Finally people understood why they had been interned for so long without explanation. But the relief that came with learning the truth was short-lived as the ramifications of the president's words struck home. Each person hearing the announcement might die a hideous death, and each infected person had the ability to infect countless others. That was the truth and the reason for their confinement. Finally, there was the president's plea to act with bravery and integrity: to allow the walls to stand, and the people to stay put. When the president's address was finished, the monitors shut down and the terminals became unearthly quiet. It was difficult to predict what might follow.

CHAPTER FIFTY-FOUR

Chicago O'Hare to Prairie Village, Kansas

TOMMY AND MEGHAN JOHANNSEN had chosen to remain in Chicago's northern suburbs following graduation from college in 2012. The handsome couple had met their junior year at North Park University. Tommy was a third generation North Parker from Prairie Village, Kansas. Meghan was the first member of her family to attend the school. They had married in 2013, and Meghan had given birth to their first child, Noah, in 2014.

The couple shared many things in common beyond being alums with similar faith backgrounds. Most important was their love of family. Having spent last year's holiday season with Meghan's folks, they were looking forward to spending Thanksgiving in suburban Kansas City with Tommy's parents. Like most young couples, they were somewhat cash-strapped and had planned to drive. But then a check arrived from Tommy's mother, Anne, two weeks before Thanksgiving. It was more than enough to cover their airfare.

"Don't tell your father," the note said. "I just didn't want you to have to make the long drive with Noah. This way you'll be nice and fresh when you arrive."

Grateful to be spared long hours on crowded highways, they had booked an early morning flight for Wednesday from O'Hare to Kansas City International. It would be a short hour-and-fifteen-minute hop across Illinois and Missouri.

Although they had set an alarm for 4:45 AM, Tommy and Meghan didn't need it. Noah was already up and unusually fussy that morning. It took Meghan thirty minutes longer than anticipated to soothe him enough to allow her to finish getting dressed and gather the things she needed for the baby. They arrived at O'Hare a few minutes after 6 AM.

By that time, Tommy knew making their flight would be tight. But somehow, even with the baby in tow, they managed to check in, clear security, and reach their gate just as the final call was being announced. A gate agent helped them down the air-bridge before closing the door on the plane.

"I didn't think we were going to make it!" Tommy said to his wife with a smile of relief as they climbed into their seats.

"Me neither. Sorry, Honey, I didn't expect Noah to wake up on the wrong side of the crib this morning," she said, cradling her baby in one arm.

Tommy reached for Meghan's free hand and kissed it gently. "Just let me know when you want me to hold him." He smiled before turning his attention to the pocket of the seat back in search of something to read.

The flight to Kansas City was remarkably smooth. Noah barely stirred until they were on final descent into the airport. Then, almost on cue with the flight attendant's announcement to bring all seat backs to their full and upright position, he let out a raspy cry.

"It's his ears," Meghan said, as she rocked him gently. "He'll be fine."

Fifteen minutes later, Tommy, Meghan, and Noah were being welcomed with hugs by David and Anne Johannsen.

"Oh, what's wrong?" Anne asked in a lilting voice as she looked into the moist eyes of her still unsettled grandson.

"He's fine, Mom. Just not thrilled with the changes in cabin pressure," Meghan said to her mother-in-law.

"Well, we'll get him home and he can take a little nap. In fact, all three of you can probably use a rest. I'm sure it was an early morning for you."

"Our little wake-up clock here got us up at 4:30," Meghan said. "I think a nap is a great idea."

The day seemed to fly by in an instant. Once Noah had finished his nap, the family had taken a long walk along the tree-lined streets of Prairie Village. Massive oaks and maples, most of which had been saplings in the 1950s, when the neighborhood had been developed, towered above the houses, forming a canopy over the streets. It wasn't the stark, flat, tornado-scathed Kansas portrayed in *The Wizard of Oz*. Rather, it was a picturesque community and an ideal place to raise a family.

For dinner, Dave fired up the Weber and grilled steaks along with some asparagus. A short round of Boggle followed; then everyone was off to bed.

On Thanksgiving morning, Tommy and Meghan awoke to the smell of frying bacon. The Johannsens had a clear tradition that began with a bountiful breakfast, for there would no lunch. Instead they would be serving others at the downtown rescue mission.

"Darling, would you mind asking your parents for a couple of aspirin," Meghan said to her husband as she got ready for breakfast, "I'm not feeling so good."

"Are you okay?" Tommy said, looking concerned.

"I guess. I've got a headache. I hope I'm not coming down with something."

"Maybe you should stay home and take it easy," Tommy suggested, but her look told him that was not going to happen.

As they walked downstairs and into the kitchen, they found the buffet covered with cheese scrambled eggs, smoked salmon, bacon, and hearty bread. Anne motioned for Tommy and Meghan to take a plate from the stack of china at one end.

"Wow! That's quite some breakfast!" Tommy said.

"We've got work to do, and it's a lot easier when you're not hungry," Dave advised.

"So, I assume we're scheduled for a shift at the Rescue Mission?" Tommy asked.

"We're on from 12 to 3," his father responded. "Hope that's okay with you, Meghan," he added.

"Don't worry, Honey, I'll help with the baby," Anne said quickly.

"Meghan's got a headache," Scott said as his wife shook her head, not wanting him to mention something so insignificant.

"Are you sure you don't want to rest, Darling?" Anne asked. "Maybe it would be best if you stayed home with Noah and took it easy."

"Tommy said the same thing. Thanks, but I'll be fine," Meghan patted her mother-in-law's hand.

The four adults and Noah lounged leisurely for much of the morning before piling into the minivan for the thirty-minute drive downtown. It would be a privilege to spend several hours helping others before enjoying a quiet Thanksgiving dinner together at home.

Though the economy had rebounded nicely since nearly going off the tracks in 2008, the after-effects of the Great Recession were still visible in Kansas City. The Rescue Mission anticipated serving more than a thousand meals this Thanksgiving, and based upon the crowd at noon, that estimate appeared to be conservative.

After donning aprons, the four assumed their positions in the food line. Meghan was the first to greet the Mission's guests, speaking warmly to each person before handing them a plate and offering fruit salad. Baby Noah slept close-by in his baby-seat, oblivious to all the commotion.

Tommy was next, serving the turkey and dressing, followed by Dave, who ladled out mashed potatoes and rich gravy.

Anne was at the end of the line and responsible for desserts. She smiled lovingly as she placed a piece of pie on the tray of a woman who, though probably close to her age, looked decades older. This is my sister in Christ, she thought, as she looked upon this soul whose life was so radically different than her own. "But by the grace of

God," she said to herself, and prayed the woman would find joy in today's meal.

It was a rewarding but heartbreaking three hours as a constant parade of homeless people passed through the line. Some of them looked as though, with a hot shower and some fresh clothes, they would be indistinguishable from their neighbors in Prairie Village, while others were disheveled and appeared to be lost in their own world.

Grateful for the opportunity to serve, Dave, Anne, Tommy, and Meghan were nonetheless ready for a break. After saying their goodbyes to the other volunteers and staff, they headed back to a very different world.

When they arrived home, Tommy knew that Meghan was ill, and it was more than just a headache.

Turning towards her in-laws, Meghan said, "Would you all excuse me? I think I need to go to bed. Maybe a few hours' sleep will help me feel better."

"Of course, take care of yourself," came the responses in unison from Dave and Anne. Tommy took his wife's arm and walked with her to the bedroom. She seemed weak as she attempted to negotiate the stairs.

"Tell me what's going on, Honey."

"I'm just tired, Tommy. Can you watch the baby for me and feed him in about an hour? There's a bottle of breast milk in the refrigerator. Your mom can show you where we put it."

Meghan rolled onto the bed, her eyes closed. Tommy started to help her undress, but she stopped him.

"It's okay, Darling."

"Of course," he said, gently kissing her forehead.

"Go down and enjoy your parents. I'll be fine. I'll come down in a couple of hours." Meghan opened her eyes for moment and forced a smile.

"Okay, babe, but I'll look in on you in a while," Tommy promised as he moved towards the door.

Each time he checked on her, Meghan was hard asleep. In fact, she slept through the night, missing dinner completely. Tommy didn't have the heart to awaken her and hoped she would feel better in the morning. About 7 PM, he fed Noah and put him down for the night.

The next morning, Meghan was not better. She was far worse. Her slight headache was now a relentless pounding in her skull, and every part of her body ached with growing intensity. It looked like the flu, except for her eyes. They were intensely bloodshot, unlike anything he had ever seen.

"We need to get you to a doctor," Tommy advised, but Meghan did not want to move.

"I'm fine, Darling. Maybe just a touch of the flu." She reached up slowly and patted his shoulder. "I knew I should have gotten the shot this year. I guess I'm paying the price now." She did her best to smile. "I just don't want you or Noah to catch it."

"I need to let Mom and Dad know what's going on. I'll be right back. Can I bring you anything, Darling?"

"No, Tommy, but don't upset your parents. I don't want them worrying about me."

"Where's our sweet Meghan?" his mother asked as Tommy entered the kitchen.

"She's not feeling well, Mom. I think she may have the flu."

"Oh, no, I'm so sorry," Anne responded. "Do you think she should see a doctor?"

"Yes, but she doesn't want to. If you could help me with Noah, I'll keep an eye on Meghan. If she gets any worse, I'll insist she go."

Over the next few hours, Meghan declined precipitously. When Dave and Anne went up to check on her, they were shocked by her listlessness.

"Tommy, you need to take her in now!" Anne insisted. "Dave, bring the car around. We'll take you both to the ER at St. Margaret's. I'm sure doctors' offices are closed today."

Meghan moaned as Tommy lifted her carefully out of the bed. Still wearing her clothes from the previous day, she drooped in his arms as he carried her down to the car. Dave opened the rear door for him. St. Margaret's was a fifteen-minute drive on streets rendered quiet by the holiday weekend.

Arriving at the ER, they were surprised to see a line forming at the door. But what was more disturbing was the sight of two nurses in full protective suits, triaging patients as they entered.

As they approached the nurses, Tommy asked, "What's going on? Why are you both dressed like that, and why are there so many people here?"

"Didn't you see the president's address?" one of the nurses asked, as if puzzled by Tommy's questions.

"What address . . . what are you talking about?" Dave interjected.

"Last night, on television."

"No, we missed it. And what does that have to do with anything?" Dave asked.

"The president said there had been a biological attack against the United States. It involved a very dangerous virus," the nurse responded as she began assessing Meghan on the spot. She took her temperature with a remote infrared scanner, then looked at the whites of her eyes and the inside of her mouth and lips.

"Where was this attack?" Tommy's tone was urgent.

"At four airports . . . Dallas . . . Los Angeles . . . Atlanta . . . and Chicago."

"Oh, my God," was all Tommy could say, stunned. He looked pleadingly towards his parents, and then to Meghan. He wondered if she was taking it all in.

Though she remained silent, tears were brimming in Meghan's eyes.

The nurse put a mask over Meghan's mouth and nose and handed masks to the family. "Take her in and go immediately to the left. A nurse will meet you there," the triage nurse instructed Tommy. He nodded.

Turning to his parents, she advised, "You've been exposed to a highly contagious virus. I'm afraid you are going to have to stay at the hospital."

Anne reacted viscerally. "But we don't have what we need for the baby! Please, let us go home. We'll come back as soon as we have gathered a few things."

"I can't let you do that. Anyone who comes into contact with you will be at risk of infection."

There was a long pause. The nurse sighed, then yielded to the pleading look in Anne's eyes. "Okay. Straight home, straight back. No stopping."

"Agreed." Anne managed a weak smile.

Pulling Tommy down to her face with the little strength she could muster, Meghan said, "Darling, whatever happens, take care of Noah. I love you more than you could ever imagine. Always remember that!" Tears streamed freely from her eyes.

"Nothing bad is going to happen to you!" Tommy said with conviction, trying to reassure himself as much as his wife. "I won't let it!"

Within hours of Meghan's admission to an isolation unit, Tommy began to exhibit many of the same symptoms that had struck his wife the previous day. It was the beginning of his rapid descent.

Dave and Anne had stayed just long enough to gather the supplies they would need to care for Noah before returning to the hospital. Meghan and Tommy were now both in isolation rooms. Tommy's parents were horrified to discover that Meghan, unable to breathe on her own, was on a respirator. As they stared through a sealed window, a public health worker approached them. She introduced herself and asked if they were the parents and in-laws of Tommy and Meghan Johannsen.

That began an extensive interview in which they were asked to recount every detail of Tommy, Meghan, and Noah's movements since arriving in Kansas City. They were also asked to reconstruct as much as they knew about their children's day of travel. The woman was particularly interested in the exact time of their flight and when they had arrived at O'Hare. She also asked them to write down the names and contact information for everyone Meghan and Tommy had come in contact with since arriving at the airport.

Anne rolled her eyes in disbelief. "You've got to be kidding! My family spent Thanksgiving serving hundreds of people at the Rescue Mission. We don't have any idea who they were, just that they were people in need."

"Would you excuse me?" the woman said, without betraying any emotion. Anne and Dave nodded.

Walking to the quietest corner she could find, far from the earshot of patients' families, the woman called her director at the Health Department.

"We have a problem," she said as soon as he answered the phone. "I have two patients at St. Margaret's that appear to be victims of the attack on O'Hare. They flew in the day before Thanksgiving on a 7 AM flight."

"They are contained, right?" the Director responded.

"Yes, but they spent a good portion of Thanksgiving day serving meals at the Rescue Mission downtown. By the parents' estimation, they fed several hundred people, if not more. The wife was symptomatic at the time."

There was a very good chance that Meghan had unknowingly infected dozens upon dozens of people. Each one of them was now a ticking time bomb. The problem was finding people without addresses whose homes consisted of cardboard boxes.

When the public health worker returned, she expressed her sorrow for what the family was going through, and then explained that they would not be allowed to leave the hospital. The Johannsens and St. Margaret's Hospital were under quarantine.

Over the next forty-eight hours, Dave and Anne would maintain a vigil at the hospital, doing their best to meet the needs of their tiny grandson, while his parents lay dying on beds just on the other side of a glass wall.

The only time they left the nursing unit was to go to a small sanctuary to pray for their children. The six pews spanning the width of the sanctuary were full. It was a respite for the many grief-stricken families locked within the hospital. Men and women prostrated themselves below a crucifix, some crying out to Jesus to save their loved ones.

Towards the end of the second day, Anne and Dave began to feel feverish.

As things unfolded at St. Margaret's, a virtual army of health department workers, aided by CDC staff, began canvassing the homeless communities proximate to the rescue shelter. They found far more sick people than they had anticipated. If there was good news amidst the devastation, it was that these people, who had no real means of transportation, had not traveled far.

On the Monday following Thanksgiving, Meghan stopped breathing. Her internal organs had failed hours before, and attending physicians knew it was beyond their power to intervene. Tommy mercifully never learned of his beloved wife's death. He was comatose at the time and succumbed to the virus thirty-six hours later. Anne, Dave, and baby Noah would all become tragic statistics amidst the growing number of fatalities resulting from the horrific attack.

Similar scenarios were playing out in numerous communities, large and small, across the nation. Each town or city faced the same urgent need—to extinguish the spreading fire of this infection before it became uncontrollable.

CHAPTER FIFTY-FIVE

DFW International Airport

TWENTY-FOUR HOURS AFTER THE VACCINE had been recovered from the factory in Faisalabad, it was finally reaching the hands of hundreds of medical and military personnel at the inoculation sites located within the airport terminals, incident command centers, and Dugway. The initial recipients were the first-responders—military and NG troops, local and state police, and fire, public service, and medical personnel. Smaller inoculation sites were also established within the major hospitals in Chicago, Atlanta, Dallas, and Los Angeles in anticipation of the need to inoculate large segments of the population. Unfortunately, it would be several days before ancillary sites were established in hot zones such as Kansas City. Days too late for Tommy and Meghan, and mere hours too late for Dave, Anne, and Noah.

Inoculation of the detainees was next, via a process that mirrored registration. At the airports, the hundreds of ticket counters soon housed teams of nurses, med-techs, EMTs, and doctors, all of whom were capable of administering the vaccine. Their shifts were short due to the disabling heat inside the full-body suits and respirators. Despite this fact, within thirteen hours, 47,000 people had been immunized—including all individuals contained within the four airports and at Dugway.

As people progressed through the vaccination process at LAX, one of the passengers claimed to have lost the identification card issued to him during the registration process at the airport terminals. Three Guardsmen were quietly summoned to surround the man, and he was asked to roll up his sleeve. Complying with the order, the man revealed an oozing, circular sore high on his arm. Photos were snapped and forwarded to the Agency for analysis. In minutes, the man was positively identified as Kameel Imad al-Din.

The only jihadist not accounted for was Babur Qaisrani, who had driven through the night and crossed the Canadian border shortly before dawn. He was only minutes away from being reunited with Sarah.

Despite the relative speed with which the vaccine had been administered, it was not soon enough for some passengers in the terminal, who were already beginning to exhibit symptoms of an overwhelming infection. Passengers such as Mary Ellen McGuire.

The retired school teacher and grandmother of seven adoring grandchildren was returning home to Tulsa after visiting her eldest daughter in Dallas. Though Helen McGuire had insisted on waiting until her mother's flight departed, Mary Ellen had been equally insistent on sending her on her way. That was before she learned that her flight was canceled. No explanation had been given.

Initially more annoyed than panicked, she reassured herself that it would surely prove to be only a minor inconvenience. So she headed for Starbucks, ordered a double mocha Frappuccino, and took a seat in the food court. She sat there from 6:45 AM until close to 8 AM, when she learned that no one was allowed to enter or exit the terminal with the exception of military personnel clad in protective suits. That's when the alarm bells sounded for Mary Ellen McGuire.

She immediately telephoned Helen.

"Darling, I don't mean to frighten you or Charlie, but there's something strange going on here."

"What do you mean by *strange*, mother?"

"No one is being allowed to leave the terminal, and I can see army troops with jeeps and machine guns through the window."

There was a long pause as Helen tried to rein in her emotions. "We'll be right there, Mother. We'll call you when we're close."

"I appreciate the thought, Helen, but the only people coming into this terminal are wearing body suits and breathing masks. It looks like something out of a science fiction movie."

"We're still coming down, Mother!"

With that she hung up the phone, grabbed her husband, and made a bee-line for the car. Forty minutes later, they were in a sea of traffic being held at bay on the fringes of DFW. A National Guard sergeant approached the car and motioned for Charlie to roll down his window.

"I'm sorry, Sir, but this is as far as you go. You need to turn your car around and leave this area."

"I don't understand, Officer. We're just trying to pick up my mother-in-law at the airport."

Helen burst in to tears, screaming, "Why can't we get her? Why are you stopping us? My God, she's eighty years old, alone and scared. Let us help her!"

"I'm afraid you can't help her, Ma'am. Now, turn the car around and leave the area." His tone went from empathetic to forceful.

With his wife sobbing on his shoulder, Charlie thought about speeding past the officer and barricades. But he knew he wouldn't make it far. So he reluctantly did as instructed.

Trying to compose herself, Helen called her mother. "I'm sorry, Mom, but they wouldn't let Charlie and me through. You're going to have to sit it out. Please call us, tell us you are alright! We love you . . ."

Charlie took the phone as Helen broke down in tears. "Mary Ellen, I'm sorry we can't do more. We'll give you a call in a few hours to check on you."

"Go home, Charlie. Take care of my Helen and my wonderful grandchildren, and don't worry a thing about me."

Despite Mary Ellen's attempts to sound convincing and unafraid, Charlie knew that something was desperately wrong.

About 11 PM, Mary Ellen was issued a military cot. A woman who identified herself as a National Guard nurse tried to comfort her. Speaking through her face mask, she suggested that a good night's sleep was what Mary Ellen most needed, and things would look brighter in the morning.

But they weren't any brighter when the sun came up. It had been a sleepless night for McGuire. After tossing and turning for hours, she tried to rise from the cot but was forced back down by a splitting headache. Soon, severe back and abdominal pain followed.

Mary Ellen tried to call her family, but it was impossible to get a cell signal. She didn't know that all cell phone communications emanating from the terminal had been shut down under government order.

Her daughter and son-in-law had tried to call her dozens of times, obsessively dialing her cell phone in the erroneous belief that a call might get through. All they received was a rapid busy tone. When they called the Verizon operator, they were told that system issues were preventing calls from going through. There was no way to reach their loved one, at least not for now.

Flagged by a roving nurse on the look-out for patients who appeared symptomatic, McGuire was one of hundreds being triaged to the medical units established within each facility. Without explanation, her temperature had been taken. Then a mask had been placed over her mouth. Once in the medical unit, she was observed, but no interventions were given other than for pain relief. There was nothing that could be done beyond trying to comfort her.

In the hours that followed, the pain got far worse, and the medicine given to Mary Ellen barely touched it. Soon, other symptoms began to emerge, including the appearance of red and purplish spots.

It was a warning that the disease was about to enter a devastating phase, and death would ensue within days. Frightened and failing to understand what was happening to her body, Mary Ellen began to pray her rosary.

Within a few hours, the once vibrant grandmother was fading in and out of consciousness. Nurses assessed her every hour, noting everything from the bloodstained whites of her eyes to the dark patches forming under her skin. When a thin trickle of blood could be seen streaming from her ears, the nurses and doctors knew that death was at hand.

Mary Ellen did not live to see the morning sun. Her family would not learn of her death for days—not until after their own lives were also threatened by an emerging pandemic ushered in by a handful of heartless and hateful men.

CHAPTER FIFTY-SIX

Dugway Proving Ground, Utah

THANKSGIVING SAW A NON-STOP PROCESSION of airplanes landing at the normally quiet Dugway Proving Ground. The first flight to land was a military transport laden with vaccine. Following close on its tail were the dozens of commercial flights that been redirected from across the nation.

As the gantry door swung open on each flight, passengers stepped into a frighteningly unfamiliar and dystopian world. They were engulfed by army personnel in protective gear, who shepherded them towards a fleet of buses parked at one end of the runway. Once fully loaded, each bus headed to a makeshift processing area. Here the passengers' identification was logged, along with data pertaining to their flight and the amount of time they had spent in one of the four terminals.

Individual passengers were then triaged into one of three groups based upon their likelihood of having been subjected to the virus. Alpha Group was deemed to have the lowest probability of infection, followed by Bravo Group and Charlie Group. Each group was physically segregated into tent camps with enough separation to prevent the likely spread of infection. Each tent camp contained a mobile hospital unit staffed with physicians, nurse practitioners, nurses, and para-professionals flown in on an emergency basis from the region. After being triaged, all passengers underwent a basic medical examination. Since only a short time had passed since the terrorist incidents, it was assumed that most passengers would be asymptomatic.

Late the next day, the vaccination process began. Passengers reassembled at the mobile hospital units, where they were told to roll up their sleeves for an immunization. Each patient received multiple small needle jabs that pushed the vaccine under their skin in a circular pattern. Before returning to their bunks, they were given a flyer that described the warning signs of an adverse reaction to the vaccine.

Predictably, virtually everyone demanded to know the answer to one question: "Why are we being vaccinated?" Thus far, all they had been told was that they had been exposed to a dangerous virus. Some people, old enough to remember the days of smallpox vaccinations, thought they were receiving a similar immunization.

A man in his mid-sixties was among the first to speak up. "It appears that you are vaccinating us against smallpox. Is that correct?"

The male nurse simply said, "No," without offering any further explanation.

"Young man, I am a physician. If not smallpox, then what?"

Finishing up the inoculation, the nurse said, "I'm sorry, but I am not at liberty to discuss the matter. The president will be addressing the nation shortly, and you will have a chance to hear his comments."

That night, monitors were brought in and distributed across the vast expanse of tents crisscrossing the high Utah desert. At 5 PM Mountain Time, a recorded version of the president's address began to play. Just as each airport had remained as silent as a shrine, so, too, did Dugway as passengers learned they had been exposed to a deadly variant of smallpox. Passengers prayed the president was being truthful about the glimmer of hope represented by the vaccine they had just received. For those exposed, it was the only possible reprieve from death.

Once vaccinated, each member of Charlie Group was checked for vital signs every four hours. Bravo Group was assessed every eight hours, and Alpha Group was monitored twice each day. If any passenger showed evidence of a potential infection—a temperature greater than 99.2—he or she was immediately moved to an isolation unit. Here, too, three orders of acuity were used to separate the sickest patients from those with minimal symptoms.

Over the next five days, hundreds of passengers from Charlie Group fell ill. A far smaller number of passengers in Bravo Group evidenced symptoms, and members of the Alpha Group appeared disease-free. For the vast majority of those stricken, the virus appeared not to be life-threatening. Doctors wondered if the vaccine had done its job or if this was a false calm before the pathogen sprang to life and overwhelmed patients' systems.

CHAPTER FIFTY-SEVEN

Across the Nation

THE AIR IN THE TERMINALS WAS HEAVY with the smell of death. It was impossible to escape the stench, despite efforts to rapidly dispose of bodies. Blood and bodily wastes covered the floors. It was an unimaginable scene of horror and human suffering.

Thanks to a video-feed from inside the makeshift hospitals, Commander Hart had delivered on his promise to provide Sheriff Tilson with a ringside seat to the emerging catastrophe. Tilson watched as people writhed in agony— their organs slowly liquefying, while blood emerged from every orifice of their bodies. Many patients showed massive dark patches under the skin where capillaries had simply burst. It was a level of carnage that was almost unfathomable . . . a death that one would not wish upon their most mortal enemy. After eight devastating hours, Hart sent Tilson on his way.

Over the next seventy-two hours, nine thousand travelers became symptomatic. Of those stricken, seventy percent benefited to varying degrees from the vaccine. The remaining thirty percent developed full-fledged hemorrhagic smallpox, which proved almost universally fatal. In the end, 2,756 people died in the first wave of the outbreak.

Within days, new hot spots began to emerge in various communities proximate to the airports. Seven people were sick in Skokie, twelve more were identified between Elmhurst and Aurora, and that was only in suburban Chicago. Around LAX, Westwood, Malibu, and Pasadena all had active cases. In Texas, Arlington, Irving, and University City reported cases. But it was not just the four metropolitan areas adjacent to the airports that showed signs of infectivity. Hart knew it would not be long before the pandemic went global.

Calls were pouring in to the CDC from large and small communities across the country. From Portland, Maine, to Portland, Oregon, no community seemed out of the reach of the virus. Each case could be connected back to exposure at one of the airports. These were the people who had somehow slipped through the cracks before containment strategies were rigidly in place—the walking time bombs, armed with fuses of unknown lengths and ready to detonate.

Although hundreds of public health officials were now working in tandem with local law enforcement and the military to ensure rapid containment, it was not enough. More workers needed to be summoned. When governmental resources were exhausted, the incident commanders turned to academia and local health care communities to mine their resources. Many civilians were asked to take on great personal risk for the greater good of the nation, although not before receiving an immunization.

The majority of Americans meanwhile hunkered down in their homes—hoping and praying that their food, water, and other essential supplies would last until the outbreak ended. Many were also well-armed and stood ready to kill anyone who tried to disturb their refuge.

Fortunately, the airport terminals had remained relatively quiet, showing few signs of violence. People had risen to the president's challenge, putting the well-being of others ahead of their self-interests. The level of self-sacrifice was hard to fathom. Here, the attack had brought out the best in people.

Even so, unless the Herculean effort to contain the pandemic was maintained, it would be virtually impossible to extinguish. But for now, the ring quarantine strategies were holding, and everyone held their breath and prayed that the good luck would continue.

CHAPTER FIFTY-EIGHT

Matheson Island, Manitoba, Canada

DESPITE BEING A LAST-MINUTE REPLACEMENT, Babur had performed flawlessly. And, thanks to Allah, he had avoided internment in the terminal. Now, all that separated him from his beloved Sarah was the long, snaking driveway to their Canadian home.

Sarah Qaisrani thrust out her arms in an exuberant welcome to Babur. He acknowledged her with a loving smile, but gestured with an oustretched arm for her to wait before embracing him. Walking over to the stone fire-pit surrounded by a few old metal chairs, Babur stripped down to the bone and threw his clothes on top of a thick pile of ash. It was thirty degrees out, but he did not want his tainted clothes to contaminate the home.

He walked naked over to a shed and grabbed a can of gasoline. After dousing the clothes, he returned the can to the shed. A single match turned the fire-pit into an inferno, with flames licking the branches of overhanging trees. Babur threw a few pieces of wood onto the fire, then turned to Sarah.

"Let me wash carefully and dress, and then I will give you the proper welcome from a husband who has desperately missed his wife."

"Take your time, my darling. You deserve some comfort after what you've been through. Al-Bakr and Al Hameed will sing your praises!"

"It is only Allah whom I wish to serve. If he views me as his devoted servant, then I have done my job."

With that he walked past his wife and straight into the shower.

Babur emerged ten minutes later, wrapped in a heavy robe to fend off the chilly air. Lunch awaited him on the table where Sarah was already seated.

Sarah appeared overjoyed at the sight of Babur and could not wait to hear all the details. As Babur started to recount the odyssey, a buzzer on the stove sounded.

"That's your biscuits, Babur. I'll only be a minute," Sarah said as she turned towards the oven.

"Here you go," her right hand guiding a small plate laden with two steaming biscuits towards Babur's placemat, while her left hand rested lightly on his shoulder.

Babur felt a brief but sharp prick on his neck close to her hand. He winced with pain.

"What was that!" he asked in surprise, the sharp twinge now replaced by a slow dull burning.

"I don't know, dear. Perhaps something stung you! Why don't I look?"

"As I suspected, Darling, you have a large red spot on your neck." She pretended to pick up a dead insect and carry it to the trash. "Another bee, Babur. You make it through

Armageddon, only to return home and be stung. Where's the justice in that?" she joked.

Babur smiled, then started to speak, but he was having trouble forming his words. A look of confusion crossed his face, a look that Sarah recognized with indifference.

He began to panic. "Call someone, Sarah . . . you need to call for help!" He struggled to get out the words.

"It won't do any good, Babur," Sarah stared at him unflinchingly.

He was rapidly losing control of his muscles. He slid down from the chair and rolled onto the floor. Sarah looked down upon him, still unmoved.

A miniscule but lethal dose of succinylcholine chloride, a paralytic agent used to keep patients immobile during surgery, was circulating through his bloodstream. He tried to stand, but his legs gave way, and he again collapsed onto the floor.

His breath became labored as the drug began shutting down the muscles responsible for respiration. Though he was trapped in an immovable body, his eyes communicated the depth of his fear.

Sarah stood up, not with the intent of coming to Babur's aid, but to leisurely assume a position on the loveseat, from which she could watch in comfort as Babur died. For several minutes, he lay motionless but alive, watching his wife draw deeply on a cigarette, then exhale in a flourish of smoke. It was a forbidden behavior and something Babur had never seen her do before. But she was not yet done with him.

Brandishing the pencil-thin syringe with which she had administered the toxin, she smiled at Babur contemptuously.

"You poor fool," she said spitefully, wanting to ensure he heard and processed every word before departing this world. "You thought I was in love with you! All the while I was bored out of my mind living in that piss-ant town of ours."

She added, "My only relief came when we had visitors, and only then when I shared our bed with them. You were too caught up in your precious academia to even notice.

"Oh, Babur, I know I shouldn't talk that way. Allah wouldn't approve! Well, my dear husband, after I dispose of your body—don't worry, I will wait for you to die first— there will be many men invited into my bed."

The muscles of his body fully frozen, Babur could only listen. How could he have been so blind, so trusting? He fleetingly recognized the folly of his marriage before he was mercifully snuffed out by the drug's final effect: asphyxia.

"Now what am I going to do with you?" Sarah asked lyrically of the body lying in front of her. Letting out a small sigh before her next performance began, she picked up the phone and called 911.

"911 operator, with whom am I speaking?"

A now hysterical woman said, "My name is Rachel Carson . . . Rachel Carson Patel. I think my husband, Avram, is having a heart attack . . . he's not breathing."

"What is your address?" the operator asked calmly.

Through wailing sobs, Sarah choked out the address.

"Does your husband have a pulse?" The questions were coming rapidly now.

"No! No, I need help or he is going to die!"

"Ma'am, do you know how to perform CPR?" the operator asked.

"Yes," Sarah struggled to regain her composure.

"You need to begin it now," the operator instructed. "I've dispatched EMTs, but it will be some time before they reach you."

"Okay, but . . ."

"Just do your best, Ma'am. I'll stay on the line until the EMTs arrive."

It took nearly twenty minutes for the EMTs to reach their remote home. Although he didn't need a stethoscope to confirm Babur's death, the lead EMT listened for heart sounds. Of course, there were none. They attempted CPR, more as an effort to console the grieving wife than with any hope of resurrection. After ten futile minutes, they offered Rachel their condolences and loaded Babur onto the ambulance.

"Where are you taking him?" she asked, her lower lip trembling.

"We are taking him to the hospital, Ma'am. The RCMP will contact you shortly."

It would be another hour before a Mountie appeared on her porch. Cowering as she opened the door, Rachel said, "I don't understand how this could have happened," and then broke down completely. She would have fallen to her knees had the Mountie not caught her.

After helping Rachel into the house and getting her situated comfortably on the loveseat, he inquired, "I know this is not a good time to ask, but I need to know if you wish to have a post-mortem examination performed on your husband's body. When someone your husband's age dies unexpectedly, it's standard procedure."

As though shocked, Rachel said, "But that would be a desecration of his body! We are Hindus. We do not believe in such things."

"I understand, and I did not mean to offend you. I see no reason why we would need to proceed. I am very sorry for your loss, Mrs. Patel. I will check on you in a few days and see how you are getting along. You will, of course, need to make arrangements."

"Of course," she said, in her most subdued voice.

CHAPTER FIFTY-NINE

The White House
A Safe House near Karachi

IT WAS SUNDAY NIGHT IN THE NATION'S CAPITAL. Hart was shown into the situation room of the White House, which was beginning to feel like a second home. As had become customary, he walked to the one open chair placed directly to the right of President Conner. The president smiled and welcomed him.

The senior leadership of the United States was contained in that room—every Cabinet member and every senior representative of Congress—and all of their eyes were directed at a single image projected onto a far wall. There were no obvious landmarks, just a night-vision image, apparently from a drone feed, of two men leaving a house in a suburban area. They had just opened the doors of an SUV and climbed in when Hart realized he was watching Al Hameed and Valikhanov.

His heart began pounding in his chest as adrenaline coursed through his veins. The men who had rained down such destruction upon the United States appeared to be squarely in their cross-hairs.

As they sat, the president informed Hart that Al Hameed and Valikhanov had arrived in Pakistan earlier that week. Despite innumerable ceiling-mounted cameras in the international terminal of Chicago O'Hare, the two men had managed to board their flight to Karachi, via Abu Dhabi, undetected. However, upon arrival, they had been picked up on surveillance and were observed being met by an ISI team and taken to a house on the outskirts of the city.

"Why wasn't I told, Sir?" a clearly perturbed Hart asked the president.

"Because I knew you would want to retaliate immediately, Commander."

"But we've not intervened! We have a positive ID, a drone in position, and yet we're doing nothing more than surveillance?" Hart asked, dumbfounded.

"Patience, Commander. We wish to cut off the head of the serpent."

"There are three heads to this hydra, Mr. President. I'd be satisfied with chopping off two of them right now." But his words fell on deaf ears.

Little was said over the next forty minutes, until the tail lights of the SUV signaled it was slowing down. Soon it turned onto a smaller road that led to a walled house. The drone dropped just enough in altitude to provide a surprisingly sharp image of Al Hameed and Valikhanov as they exited the vehicle and began moving towards the walled enclosure.

A small man with distinctive round glasses could be seen emerging from a gate. He walked briskly up to greet the men. The three-headed hydra was now full exposed, and Hart was itching to decapitate it.

"We have a positive identification, Mr. President," came word from the Chairman of the Joint Chiefs.

President Conner simply nodded his head.

The trail of the missile was far brighter than any comet as it streaked through the night sky. When its warhead exploded, the image momentarily whited out.

It took time for the fire to subside sufficiently for the group to see that nothing, not even a cockroach burrowed deep within the walls of al-Bakr's refuge, could have survived. Even so, the drone made several low altitude passes over the site. Lying in a clump, a few yards from the vehicle, were what appeared to be the incinerated remains of two people. The SUV was now nothing more than a charred chassis.

Hart couldn't help himself. To hell with decorum. He leaped to his feet, pumped his fist, and shouted, "Yes!"

Under his breath, he prayed that these assholes had caught a glimpse of the missile streaking towards them moments before they were obliterated—just enough time to experience the kind of absolute terror that they had inflicted upon others.

The room exploded in applause as everyone leaped to their feet. Aaron Littleson turned to Hart. "You wanted to send them straight to hell, John. Mission accomplished!"

The only one not standing was the president.

"Bring it around again," the president ordered as the drone completed its first loop. "I want to see the charred remains of that little son of a bitch," he said.

But nothing resembling human remains was visible except the two jihadists.

"God damn it, Charlie, find me something, for God's sake . . . even if it's just a pair of round glasses."

CHAPTER SIXTY

Washington, DC

MACALLAN 15 WAS THE ONLY MEDICINE that would dull the ache in Hart's soul. Though he'd been jubilant the day before, the news he had received that morning had hit him hard.

He picked up the once-full bottle of single malt Scotch and assessed its contents. It looked about half empty. Sprawled across the couch of his Georgetown apartment, he wondered what really separated his barbarous actions from those of the men he wished to kill.

A light knock on the door broke his self-absorption. It was 11 PM, too late for visitors—particularly for a man with few friends.

Picking up his Sig Sauer, he lifted the safety with his thumb, then glided silently towards the door. Before he could ask, his visitor announced herself.

"John, it's Liz."

Restoring the safety, he lowered the gun and opened the door. He motioned her in without a word.

"I've been calling you for hours," she said.

"I didn't feel like talking to anyone."

Picking up the bottle of Macallan, she looked at him: "I imagine this was full when you started?"

"Yep."

"What the hell is wrong with you?"

Hart didn't respond.

"My God, John, this is a momentous day! We got Al Hameed! We got Valikhanov! And, most importantly, we got al-Bakr! Why aren't you dancing in the street?"

"We *think* we got al-Bakr . . . time will tell. Cockroaches are known to survive nuclear blasts. All we hit him with was a missile packed with eighteen pounds of high explosives."

"You know that no one could have survived that blast."

"That's where you're wrong, Liz. I don't know that. And the niggling belief that he's still alive is making me crazy."

"Is that what this little episode is about? Drowning your sorrows in a bottle of booze? That's hard for me to buy. You've always told me that you just have to tough it out and keep moving . . . no matter what you are handed in the mission."

There was a long pause as Hart stared into the golden liquid swirling in the bottom of his glass before speaking. "Bill Tilson killed himself this morning."

"What!"

"His wife and kids heard the shot . . . a single shot, coming from the basement of their home. His wife rushed downstairs and found him. He had a half-dollar-sized hole in his right temple."

"Oh, my God, I am so sorry," Liz said, as she pictured Tilson being forced to watch the horror unfolding in the airports.

Hart studied Liz closely. "Can you imagine what it must have been like for his family . . . ? Daddy lying in a pool of blood with half his head shot away, and Mommy screaming?

"What do you think that did to an innocent little girl's mind? Do you think she will ever lose the horror of that moment—magically erase it from her head? I don't. I think it's seared into her soul and will forever change her life."

"Why did he . . ."

Hart cut her off before she could complete the thought.

"Why do you think, Liz? Because some bastard forced him to look death in the face—countless deaths that could have been prevented, but he was too fucking ignorant and prejudiced to listen to someone he saw as inferior. God damn him and what he has done to his family and to this nation."

But there was far more sorrow than condemnation in Hart's words. It was easier to curse Tilson than himself, though not without the aid of Macallan.

"There was a note," Hart continued, his voice now subdued. "Tilson apologized for what he had unwittingly done to contribute to the pandemic. And he apologized to his family for all the anguish he had brought upon them. And then he begged for forgiveness."

"Oh, John, I didn't know."

"Why did you come by, Liz?"

"Because I was worried about you . . . something you have a hell of a time accepting."

Hart turned towards Liz, and slowly put his arm around her. After a moment, he buried his face in her chest. "I shouldn't have been so damn hard on him, Liz. I told him he was responsible for the deaths of millions. I planted the seed in that small, narrow mind of his without giving a thought to how it might grow."

"John, his death is not your fault. He couldn't live with what he had done."

"But I'm the one who shined the flashlight on it, who brought it out of the darkness and thrust it in his face."

"We are dealing with death on a scale that none of us has witnessed before. It does things to us. Sometimes it brings out the best in us, when we are scurrying to save lives. And sometimes, it brings out those parts of us for which we feel no pride. John, for God's sake, let yourself be human for a change. Accept what has happened, make amends with your God, and move on. You have to."

As he lifted his head, Liz saw a tear forming in his left eye. He gave her the hint of smile and quietly said, "Okay, Commander, but I think it's going to be a while before I'm leading the calvary again.

"I am going to have to do something for Tilson's family when the time is right. I don't think they will accept anything from me. I may need your help establishing a fund for his wife and kids."

"Giving money to appease your soul?"

"No, giving them a chance to have a life after losing their source of income. Showing them the mercy I was incapable of showing Tilson."

"John, I will support whatever you want to do."

Cradling her face in his hands, he leaned in and kissed her on the lips. It was a gentle kiss, then another, and then it was Liz's hands that were pulling them closer together.

He needed to let go . . . to let the intense rush that came with touching her body wash over him and remove the pain.

"I think I need just one thing," as he scooped her up in his arms and carried her to the bedroom, laying her on the bed.

"Are you up for this, Cowboy?"

"I don't know, Liz. But right now, I want to turn off the horror we've witnessed . . . all of it. I need the world to be no bigger than this bedroom. I need to feel, if even for an hour, that there is good in the world. I need to have you back."

CHAPTER SIXTY-ONE

Washington, DC

HART HAD BEEN UP FOR MORE THAN AN HOUR when Liz finally joined him in the kitchen. She was wearing one of his checked flannel shirts, which barely covered her thighs. Hart greeted her with a hug; her bare bottom felt warm and inviting to his hand.

Playfully pushing him away, she said, "It's good to feel your arms around me again."

"In my mind, they've been there all along. I haven't been able to get you out of my head."

"Really?" Liz said tauntingly. "Then why haven't we slept together for months?"

"You're asking me? Last thing I remember, I was being shown the door, but not before you told me you couldn't live with a man whose life was enshrouded in secrets. Or am I just imagining that?"

"No, that's exactly what I said, and I meant it."

"So what's changed?"

"My naïve and safe little world."

"You, naïve? Liz, you were the CDC's poster-child when they needed someone to proselytize about the dangers of bioterrorism. That doesn't quite jive with naiveté."

"John, it's one thing to intellectualize evil and quite another to experience it. I understand now why we need people who spend time in the shadows, who aren't afraid of what lurks there."

"Liz, even if we get through this, there will be more incidents in the future. We can never banish evil any more than we can change human nature."

"Why would you want to hitch yourself to someone like me, Liz? You're a doctor. You've pledged an oath to heal people. I'm a killer. I've pledged an oath to destroy those who might otherwise destroy us. We've proven we can co-exist on the battlefield, but how do we coexist in a home . . . beyond the bedroom?"

"I never said it would be easy, John. I just know, in my heart, that there's no one else for me but you. And I'm willing to bet there's no one better for you than me."

Hart laughed, "I like your confidence, Commander."

"I don't need to be in charge, John. An equal partnership is just fine with me."

CHAPTER SIXTY-TWO

The White House

Two weeks had elapsed since the attacks had thrown the nation into chaos. There were prayers that the virus would burn itself out within the terminals and at Dugway, but the number of active cases was still expanding.

Expanding too were the hot spots erupting in all fifty states, as well as in more than a dozen foreign countries. Each day, at noon Eastern, the president held a status update involving the CDC, DHS, and the White House. Identical electronic maps populated by a common data source provided a graphic representation of the spreading pandemic.

Minute dots of white light appeared, each representing ten cases. When the number of cases in a community reached fifty, the lights turned yellow, signaling a significant emerging threat. When the rate of new cases exceeded the ability of health department workers to administer ring vaccinations, the lights appeared red.

On this particular day, President Conner was disheartened by the rapidity with which the virus was spreading.

"Dr. Wilkins, does the CDC have new projections on the anticipated number of cases, as well as mortalities, based upon current incidence rates?" the president asked, without taking his eyes from the maps.

"Sir, I realize there appears to be a preponderance of red lights illustrating uncontained outbreaks, but we remain optimistic. I can go through the numbers in detail with you, if you'd like," Liz responded.

"That won't be necessary quite yet, Doctor. But tell me, how can you look at this map and be optimistic? I don't mean that harshly, Dr. Wilkins, just honestly."

"No offense taken, Sir. Let me cite a few examples of what we are seeing on the ground. As you can see from the map, Richmond is illuminated in red. There were, as of this morning, 116 reported cases of smallpox, up from eighteen a week ago . . ."

"You are making my point for me," the president interjected.

"What the map fails to depict is the efficacy rate of the vaccine. In Richmond, as in virtually every other town and city thus far inoculated, the vaccine has reduced mortality from greater than ninety percent to less than five percent. We know we can bring the number down to one or two percent if we can reach people within twenty-four hours of initial exposure. That, Sir, is what makes me optimistic," Liz concluded.

Turning to address the man to his left, the president said, "What about you, Commander? Do you agree with Dr. Wilkins' assessment? Or are you less optimistic?"

John gave the question thought before answering it. He needed to be honest, but he also had no interest in undermining Liz's authority. "Mr. President, I believe that there is good evidence to support Dr. Wilkins' optimism.

Yet I was trained never to let my guard down. Therefore, I remain cautiously optimistic."

"That's a nice hedge, Commander. You should have been a politician," Jonathan Conner noted. "Colonel Scanlon, I'd like to hear your opinion."

Scanlon stood to address the president, but Conner motioned him back into his seat. "Relax, Tom. We're going to be doing this every day until this fire is under control."

"Thank you, Sir. I think Dr. Wilkins and Commander Hart have presented an accurate representation of our domestic situation. The airports and Dugway have experienced a devastating level of lives lost. Thank God, the virus has largely burned out at those locations. Within a few weeks, we believe the remaining passengers will no longer represent a threat to society."

"I sense hesitation, Tom. What are you not saying?" the president asked.

"The virus jumped our borders early in the game. There will be enough vaccine, for a short time, to share with Mexico and Canada, as well as with our key allies in Europe. But those supplies will likely be exhausted with the next wave or two of illness. Furthermore, the ability to handle mass inoculations is not nearly as robust in some of the countries that are projected to be hardest hit."

"What are you advising, Colonel?"

"Dr. Wilkins and I are collaborating with Syntec and other pharmaceutical manufacturers. They are in the process of replicating the vaccine with the goal of having several hundred million doses available in the coming weeks and months. It won't be soon enough for many, but it's the best we can do."

"What about Russia? This damned thing started in their lab. Don't they have the vaccine?" Conner asked of Wilkins, Hart, and Scanlon.

Hart eyed his colleagues, who gestured for him to respond. "Mr. President, the Russians had not perfected the vaccine. It caused an abnormally high percentage of adverse effects—effects that could be just as fatal as the disease. We are in communication with leadership at VECTOR. They want this genie back in the bottle as much as you and I, and they want to see UIS exterminated. This may be the first time we've shared an aligned interest with the Russians since the end of World War II."

Now addressing the larger group, the president asked: "So what more can we be doing to minimize the catastrophic effects of the virus—or are we truly doing everything within our power?"

Wilkins rose. "Sir, I believe we are doing everything within our power, and we will see the situation improve week by week. The one thing that might help is for you to reach out and give Americans a reason to hope. I don't want to appear too impetuous in making that recommendation, Sir, but the people trust you and they need to hear that the sword of Damocles no longer hangs so threateningly over their heads."

"Agreed, Dr. Wilkins. I will get the press secretary working on it. Anyone else?" When there was no response, the president adjourned the meeting.

An hour later, Hart called Wilkins' cell. "Nice job, Sweetheart."

"Thanks . . . I don't want to sound naïve, hoping for the best while everyone else is awaiting the worst."

"Don't worry, you made a hell of a case for feeling hopeful despite what's happening around us," Hart responded. "Do you still have to fly down to Atlanta today?"

"Yes, but how about if I come home on Friday? We'll have a full weekend together."

"Can't wait."

CHAPTER SIXTY-THREE

The White House

THE SIX MONTHS FOLLOWING THE CATACLYSMIC EVENT had transformed a seemingly invincible nation into a country deep in mourning and crying out for retribution. Had it not been for the tireless cheerleading of President Conner, offering hope when things seemed hopeless, the country might have crumbled. But it hadn't crumbled. The indomitable American spirit had won out, despite overwhelming odds against it.

The specter of Armageddon was lifting as the virus burned out across the nation. In total, it had claimed more than 85,000 lives—an enormous number, but one that paled by comparison to what might have occurred without rapid intervention.

The pandemic produced more than death and destruction. It galvanized once bitter enemies into a unified force calling for the wholesale destruction of UIS and other radical Islamic terrorist organizations. The previously rancorous relationship with Putin was replaced by a new era of cooperation with Moscow, as Russia became the first non-NATO country to join in the fight to eliminate radical Islamic terrorism. Between the Taliban and violent Chechen extremists, the Russians had had plenty of experience dealing with Islamist jihadists, and they were smart enough to know that they might be the next target.

What emerged was a world-wide joint task force with a single objective—to destroy the last remaining vestiges of UIS and its aligned organizations. They were to be hunted down across continents and vast oceans. The so-called Chosen Ones topped the list. Intelligence sources had found Valikhanov's copy of the playbook in the subterranean room at his house in Faisalabad describing all of the planned points of vaccine distribution, as well as the recipients. It was detailed with Nazi-like precision. After all, they were ushering in a new world order, and records had to be impeccable.

Thanks to Hart and others, the true Chosen Ones were not the radical Islamists—rather, they were the innocent men, women, and children whose lives were saved following an unconscionable act of terror.

The task force agreed that UIS's unprecedented act of barbarity sanctioned the use of any tools within the allies' arsenal. Clearly, the moral constraints on collateral damage still had to be considered, but eliminating the scourge of Radical Islam took priority over all else.

The Pakistani government also had hell to pay for their complicity in the act, although the United States government would take time to determine the right punishment to fit the crime.

EPILOGUE

CIA Headquarters
The White House
November 23

IT WAS THE FRIDAY AFTER THANKSGIVING, and John Hart sat quietly in his office at the CIA contemplating the devastating attack that had unfolded one year ago. He replayed the first meeting with Sue Goodman in which she and Liz shared their concerns regarding a pharmaceutical factory under construction in Faisalabad. He remembered his sense of urgency to place an operative on the factory floor to gather intelligence.

But their efforts to foil the evolving plot had taken too long. Tens of thousands of lives could have been saved if they had just bombed the hell out of that factory. Would that have been wrong? he wondered.

Such ruminations accomplished little, he realized. He had to keep moving forward, towards the light, as he had done every day since the attacks.

A quick rap on the door broke his concentration.

"I'm sorry for interrupting you, Commander, but the DDO is requesting your presence at an urgent meeting."

Before the man could complete his message, Hart was out of his chair and striding towards the north staircase. He ran up two flights of stairs to where the DDO and Carl Smith, a senior analyst, were awaiting him.

"Grab a seat, Commander, we're going to be here a while," Kahn instructed.

"Yes, Sir," Hart responded. "If I may ask, what is this about?"

"It's about failing to take out the son-of-a-bitch responsible for the bio-attack."

"We had a confirmed kill on Valikhanov and Al Hameed," Hart countered.

"But not on al-Bakr. I don't need to tell you that . . . you were in the room. Conner wanted irrefutable proof of his termination."

"Yes, Sir. I recall him directing the drone pilot to do a fly-by looking for evidence of a third body, which never materialized. Based upon where the missile struck, it's possible al-Bakr's body was simply torn to shreds."

"Without evidence to the contrary, President Conner remains convinced that al-Bakr managed to survive. He is betting dollars to donuts on it."

"What makes him think so?"

"We have heard rumblings that he may be directing a new attack, Commander."

"Another bio-event?"

"No. A nuclear event."

The cycle was beginning anew. Even as the pandemic was finally burning out, another threat was being birthed. Hart thought despairingly that every seeming triumph over evil was but a momentary victory. Darkness could be forced to recede, but it was never fully dispelled.

"That's a bit of a leap, isn't it, Sir? Where would he get the bomb?"

"I think you can answer that better than I, Commander."

"He might start with his Pakistani friends . . . one of a handful of senior officers responsible for safeguarding their nuclear arsenal."

"Agreed."

"Are we aware of an intended target, Mr. Kahn?"

"Only that it may be a major city on the East Coast. Right now, we are dealing in conjecture . . . hunches, not hard data. But if our hunch proves true, it could be the nightmare we've long sought to avoid. That's why you're running point on this one, Commander. The pandemic killed thousands. Multiply that tenfold for a nuke. But it's more than just lives that are at stake. It's the very spirit of our country. You've got to get ahead of this one.

"I'll be praying like hell that you do."